WHISKEY

DARK WATERS
BOOK 2

J.L. DRAKE

CAST OF CHARACTERS

- **Daniel:** Cole's father, first generation Blackstone. Married to **Sue,** Cole's mother.
- **Edison:** Cole's grandfather. Married to **Meg,** Cole's grandmother.
- **Abigail/Abby:** Mark's adopted mother, Cole's childhood nanny, house aide. Sister to **June.**
- **Dr. Roberts:** House psychologist. Dating Abigail.
- **Frank:** Blackstone contact for the Army. First generation Blackstone member.
- **Zack:** First generation Blackstone member.

FAMILIES

- **Cole:** Owner of the Shadows safe house. Leader of the Blackstone special ops team. Married to **Savannah**. They have two kids, **Olivia** and **Easton**.
- **John:** Blackstone member. Married to **Sloane.**
- **Mike:** Blackstone member. Married to **Catalina.** Daughter **Gabriella.**
- **Keith:** Member of Blackstone. Married to **Lexi.** They have two kids, **Brandon and Reagan.**
- **Mark:** Blackstone member. Married to **Mia.** They have a set of twins, **Liam** and **Ethan,** and a daughter **Tabby.**
- **Paul:** Blackstone member. Deceased.
- **Dell:** North Rock member. Dusk Safehouse in North Carolina.

- **Davie:** North Rock member. Dusk Safehouse in North Carolina.
- **Steve Chamness:** North Rock member. Dusk Safehouse in North Carolina.
- **Denton Barlow:** The American. Deceased.

ANIMALS

- **Goats:** Friendly reminders of home.
- **Chickens:** Annoying and always in the way.
- **Scoot:** A-hole house cat.
- **Butters:** Mark and Mia's Husky.
- **Tripper:** John and Sloane's German shepherd.

*To all of you who needed to go "home" again.
This is for us.*

NOTE FROM THE AUTHOR

Since Savannah and Cole's story was released years ago, I've heard from so many of you asking endless questions about Shadows and how it all started. Your request for more has been heard. After the Blackstone Series was finished, it was obvious that the story needed to be expanded because it just wasn't enough to satisfy your appetite. I'm certainly not one to argue that. After all, I could write these characters until the end of time. My imagination missed them, too, and is always eager to conjure up more adventures for my full list of Blackstone characters.

So, here I am, back with an exciting new series, and let me tell you, this is-going-to-blow-your-mind!

Let me explain a few things, before you dive into the story.

I decided to start this series a little differently. So, just how did the Shadows Safehouse come to be? Exactly who started it and why? I thought a lot about how to tell the whole story to give you all the answers you'd asked for. I considered doing a short novella with sprinkled treats and surprises throughout in a way that answered the questions. But after some thought, I wondered if it might be better to write the full story. I'd start you off in present day, then draw you back to the very beginning. Then I could move you forward to drop you back off into the present again. That way, you could hit the ground running for book two, Whiskey.

So, that's what I did.

Don't worry, this isn't a book that flips you back and forth through memories. It's a smooth transition of present, past, and present again.

I consider this to be a "bridge book" to bring you forward to the new Dark Water series. Dark Water delves into a whole new team with brand new characters I want you to meet.

In the present, I set the scene of what's to come in Whiskey. Though it will be a brand-new story, you will also be living with the Blackstone Team, old friends who have moved on to Dusk, and of course everyone else you've met along the way…and maybe, just maybe, a few other characters will pop up.

Remember to watch for the little things, I never put something on the page without a reason. I hope in writing this book I will satisfy your curiosity, but I also want you to come along with me back home again. I know I've missed everyone. I hope you enjoy the ride.

ONE

Location: Afghanistan
Coordinates: Classified

TY

"Move, move, move," I screamed at Moore as I knocked Brown in the head to wake him from a dead sleep. Fire licked the side wall and traveled up to the roof like a lit matchstick. "Grab your shit, Hill!" I dove outside and drew my gun into position to scan the perimeter. I rested my cheek on the butt of the stock of my M4 and tuned out the crackle of flames as they consumed the hut. I closed my eyes for a second and took a deep breath to focus.

My sixth sense had never let me down before, and it had surfaced just in time. I rolled quickly to one side and *zip! zip!* I sent two bullets to my eleven and heard a groan. I sent another three to my twelve and caught sight of a man as he twisted and fell, blood sprayed high in the air. I felt the heat of the flames on my back and knew it was time to move.

Moore's hand landed on my shoulder as he low crawled up next to me. We moved as one away from the burning structure and out into the night. There had been a time when this terrain made it difficult to move about, but now it was second nature to us. The rocky mountainside still made us work hard as we picked our way up. Thank God for the military issued kneepads.

Zip! Zip! Zip! Bullets nipped at our heels as we scaled the side. We kept low to use whatever cover we could find.

"I thought we lost these fuckers thirteen miles ago," Brown hissed. "They're like friggin' bloodhounds!" The last word was cut off as bullet hit right above him. "I seriously hate this place. I need a desk job."

"You wouldn't last five minutes in a cubicle," Moore barked as I covered him, and he made his move. More bullets rained all around us.

"They look at us the same way we look at them." I motioned for Brown to move up behind Moore. "Kill or be killed."

Hill took Brown's place and glared at me. We'd had tension between us ever since we made the decision to stay behind and accept this volunteer mission. The rest of the troops had all been called back to the US. I knew he wanted to go back but probably felt like an ass when the rest of us voted to stay. He'd kept his mouth shut then, but now it was apparently my fault he was still here. I didn't care; he was the one who made the decision. I was glad he'd been put under Captain Flex's command. Trouble was now, ten days in, our teams were tangled up after we'd been ambushed and some of our men were switched up. Flex had two of mine, and I had three of his, and one, regretfully, was Hill. Our mission was compromised, and now both our teams were scrambling to make it back to the rendezvous point where a chopper would meet us to get us the hell out of there.

"Go," I ordered Hill, and he waited a beat and glared at me before he moved. Rivera then wiggled up into his spot and waited for his turn to head to the top. He was a good soldier, but he was tight with Hill and had a real attitude problem with my guys, so I kept an eye on him as well. I nodded at him, and he left. I was last.

I rolled on my back and arched my neck to watch Rivera's boots disappear. Then I started to shimmy upward. I kept as flat as possible. Bullets peppered around, but thankfully none hit me.

Once I reached the top, Moore slapped my shoulder, then we all froze when we heard the unmistakable whistle of a rocket launcher.

"Duck!" I shouted, and we dove for cover wherever we could as it hit the side of the cliff. It shook us like a carnival ride, dust filled our lungs, and rocks flew about without mercy.

I blinked back the grit that layered my pupils and made out an opening now exposed where a rock had been. I called out to the others. We took turns and shimmied inside the cave to seek relief. As we caught our breath, we all did a quick body check to see if we were injured. The shock of an unexpected attack sometimes left you momentarily numb to pain. Thankfully, we all seemed to be in one piece.

I cracked a glow stick, so did Brown, and we did a quick scan of our surroundings. It seemed safe enough to spend a little time there. I knew we all were in desperate need of sleep, and with the lack of camaraderie among the team, tempers were at a fever pitch.

"Hill, watch the entrance," I ordered, and he shook his head at me as he fought to catch his breath. I held up a hand. I wasn't in a mood to tolerate his pushback. "You don't want to be here, no one's stopping you." I inclined my head at the opening to the cave. He glanced at Rivera, who looked away. *Good.* Brown got down on his belly and crawled to the opening.

"That was close." Moore puffed his cheeks at me and blew out hard. The adrenaline still rushed through our veins. "I can still taste gunpowder." He flapped his arms to relieve the stress.

"Maybe if we hadn't sat like ducks on low ground, we would've been better prepared," Rivera butted in.

I tuned them out while I tried my radio. It crackled with static, and I strained to hear around it. The reception was terrible here. Two different tones could be heard, so my guess was that Captain Flex was radioing in at the same time.

"You were the one on watch," Moore shouted, and Rivera rose to match his stance. "Maybe we should be pointing fingers at you. You were probably asleep!"

"Enough." I was tired of their shit. "We'll spend a few minutes here to rest, but they aren't far behind. We need to keep moving. So shut up and take a break." I moved to the opening and relieved Brown. I needed to get away from all the friggin' bickering. I knew we should stay on the move, but we also needed clear heads, and the proof was in their tempers. We needed rest. We'd only had about three hours of solid sleep in the past ten days, and now that we'd been outed, they were gunnin' for us hard.

My team had been a well-oiled machine, but when we collided with the other team a few days back and got split up, tension built. I found a space to tuck myself into that still allowed a panoramic view of the hillside below. I needed to watch for any possible unwanted company.

Shots could still be heard, but it seemed like they were on the other side of the mountain. Where we were seemed relatively safe for the moment. I took a minute to admire the stars that shone brightly above me while I rested my body. My mind remained alert for any sound.

I'd spent just over eight years in this country, in a continuous battle with faceless men. I'd seen women and children treated like animals by their own kind. The idea of freedom was merely fiction to those who lived in this place. Hope for some kind of life might still be there, but it was buried deep with fear.

When I was ordered to return to base camp with my team, I wasn't sure what it was all about. When we were told we were going home, part of me was confused. The fight wasn't over; these people still needed our help. Then while I attempted to get my head around it, my commanding officer pulled me aside and explained that one of our officers had been taken and we needed to get him back. He had some crucial information that we couldn't let the Taliban have knowledge of. I knew they were experts at interrogation. Though it was proposed as a voluntary mission, we really didn't have a choice. I stepped up quickly. I wasn't ready to go back to the kind of normal I knew I'd face back home, anyway. Of course, my team followed my lead. Since Flex had been in the room with the rest of us at the time, he not so willingly spoke up for his team, too.

It was important for us to remember that some of the locals were willing to put themselves out there and offer us supplies and help if need be. The citizens of Afghanistan had asked for our help, and I'd done everything in my power to do what I could. That's why I struggled hard when I watched our troops being loaded onto a plane. They were about to leave a war that wasn't even close to being over.

"You good, Beckett?" Moore slumped down next to me with a sigh.

"Yeah," was all I offered. He listened to the bullets hit randomly on the back side of the hill and allowed himself to relax for a second.

"I'm nervous if Hill and Rivera meet up with Flex. I don't trust they won't mess with some Taliban and get us in trouble before the chopper arrives. They're reckless. We shouldn't separate again."

"Yeah, agreed." I closed my eyes with a nod and hated that I couldn't trust their motives.

"Listen," he cleared his throat, "I'm really worried about Brown."

"I'm watching him," I assured him, and he let it go, but I shared his concern. Brown showed some serious signs of mental wear. On a few occasions, he'd wasted ammo when he thought he saw things or reported to me on events that had happened years ago. As a captain, I was taught to watch for these signs, and I definitely saw them in Brown. But, I reasoned internally, we were only a few days away from our return to the United States. I hoped he could hold it together just a little longer.

"Remember when Brown soaked Jamie's boots in cat pee, and for the rest of the summer we called him Catpiss?" Moore chuckled.

"You can't mess with Brown." I smirked as I remembered how he was always the fun one. Practical jokes were taken to a whole new level if anyone dared to mess with him, or us too, for that matter.

"I had so much fun watching him fuck with people." He rubbed his face. "I miss that Brown."

"Yeah, me too." I nodded. I knew we were close to losing our lifelong brother mentally if we didn't get him some help soon. "We should get moving." I pulled back and struggled to my feet then called to the rest of the men.

It didn't take long to understand why the Taliban had pushed us in the direction they had. We soon found we could no longer go any higher. We were now forced to head back down; it was the only way we could go. After a long struggle through thick, low scrub brush that tripped us up and only provided about an inch of ledge for your boot to hold on to, we found ourselves at the top of a twenty-foot slope that went straight down into dark water. Dark water of the Kabul River held God only knew what.

"Shit." Moore struggled to keep his footing as he peered down. "Beckett please don't tell me we're going for another dip."

"Shh." I held up a hand and slipped my night-vision goggles on to scan around us. "We have five coming over the east ridge."

"Have we been spotted?"

"I don't think." I ducked low, careful to balance my weight on my toes, and the others followed suit. The men threaded their guns over their shoulders and started to make their way toward us. I searched for options, but the only one that would save our asses was below us. The water.

"Rope," I whispered to Brown through the radio. He made quick work of removing it from his rucksack. I did the same with the rope that I had and quickly tied a knot in the ends to make it longer then made a loop. "Moore, you're up first," I ordered, mainly because he was right beside me. He wrapped it around his waist. "We don't have much time, so this'll be fast," I warned him.

"Brown, tell me when to stop." He flipped down his night vision goggles and gave me a fist in lieu of a thumbs up. Some hand signals weren't worth using here because they meant different things. With our heels planted, we lowered him quickly, and at a signal from Brown, we stopped him right above the water. Moore lifted the loop up over his head and let it go as he slipped into the water without a sound.

We repeated the action until only I was left. Using a root that was sticking out of the ground, I made a pulley and hoped to hell it would hold my weight. I tested it, and it felt solid. At a sound above me, I froze, and I heard them walk right over my head. Dirt hit my shoulder as I flattened to the side of the rock. I prayed the guys were out of sight in the water below. I inched my blade out of its sheath and steadied my breathing. If I was going to have to kill, it was going to have to be silent. Tonight, we were the prey, and one hell of a bounty was sure to be on our heads. One wrong move and it would be over.

I heard voices, and they seemed to be arguing. I knew they were close and only needed to go a few more yards before they would get to the spot where we'd been earlier, and then they'd soon be right on me. I had a very short window to get out of there. I moved carefully and eased my weight out and over the side then rappelled quietly down the mountain, staying as close as I could to the rock face.

Just as I slid into the water, I reached up and, with Moore's nod, gave the rope a sharp tug at the same time as he threw a rock as hard as he could in the opposite direction. It hit farther up on the side of the mountain. The diversion worked, and the men fired their weapons in the direction of the sound. I prayed they didn't hear the rope as it smacked hard in the water. The last thing I needed was to have them discover the rope that would lead them right to us. It sank under the water, and I gathered it quickly to me. I held my breath and kicked toward the direction where the men hid in the wet plants that grew up from the muddy bottom. I slowly coiled up the rope as I went so none of us would get tangled in it and looped it on my belt.

I led them in a slow, measured swim away from the cliffs. I was sure the others struggled as I did as we moved through the dark, murky water. I worried that something would either grab us and pull us down or we'd hit a booby trap hidden underneath. It came with great difficulty to push the thought that both countries' waste poured into the river.

Finally, I found a ledge where I could get my feet under me. There was a spot where the brush grew out over the rocks, and we could get ourselves under it. That was where we spent the night. If it wasn't for the cover of the brush, and the dark water to conceal our whereabouts, we'd surely be dead.

Hours later, the sun lined the mountaintops, and we drank in what was waiting for us if we dared move. There must have been at a least seventy Taliban members crawling over the mountainside we'd rappelled down. They scoured the hills looking for any sign of us.

I glanced at Brown, who'd barely moved all night. His eyes were cast straight ahead, and he seemed to be in a trance.

I slipped back into my head, too. It was all we could do. That, and pray they'd move on soon.

I remembered my parents' faces when I Skyped them on the night I got word that our special "volunteer" mission was about to ship out. They'd thought I was about to return home with the rest of the US troops. They had music on and held sparklers when the call connected. I felt horrible when I shared my news with them, but I knew their life just wasn't for me anymore. Not now, anyway, maybe never. They'd respected my decision to stay and tried hard to hide their disappointment and fear.

My sister, Shelly, was the only one who allowed herself to show she was pissed. She held up her daughter who was now nearly a year old and shook her head at me with tears. She told me I'd missed so much of her life already. I promised her this would be the last mission, but I knew the truth. If I was offered another, I wouldn't hesitate to take it, and I thought she knew it, too. I was a soldier. I was meant to make a difference here. There was no end date on freedom for these people. I stayed because that was all I knew how to do. I just had to survive.

Shouts pulled me from my thoughts, and we watched as the Taliban started to cheer and hoot. They held their weapons in the air and jumped around. A few ran back up the slope.

"You think they found Flex?" Hill hissed to Rivera, who shook his head. I hoped to God they hadn't found the other team, but they'd found something, and it was time for us to move.

We were used to all types of elements as soldiers, but it didn't help that wet boots and slippery rocks made your ankles and knees ache. Mind over matter was what kept me going, but two hours in and Brown was dragging, so I drew back and checked in with him.

"How's the hip doing?" Brown had taken a pretty bad hit to the hip a few nights back when we were outed, and I noticed he now had a bad limp.

"Fine." He squeezed his eyes shut for a moment like his head was in a battle.

"Four days from now, I'll buy the first round at some dive bar with greasy burgers and fries." He nodded, and we walked a little farther in silence. His eyes twitched when I looked over at him, and I decided I should give him a little reminder of our pact we made when we joined. "Whiskey."

"Alpha," Moore huffed over his shoulder.

"Tango," Brown answered in a low voice, and I felt a little relief come over me.

"Good." I squeezed his shoulder. "Not much farther." Hill glanced back at me with a scowl. He and Brown often seemed to butt heads. I knew they'd gotten into it back in the States over some girl. Hill was used to getting the women. I never asked about it because, frankly, I didn't give a flying shit as long as they did their jobs.

A while later, something in my gut warned me, yet again, we weren't alone. I held up my hand to warn the others to get low.

My heart pounded in my chest and my fingers flexed on my weapon when I heard the pound of horse hooves.

"Dammit," Moore groaned, "there's got to be at least seven of them."

"Possibly eight, and probably more." I squinted at something slung over the back of one of the horses. In a last-ditch effort for help, I cupped my mouth and sent our signature signal through the mountains in hopes my echo would find the ears of our fellow soldiers. It was a deep wolf howl that went high at the end to ensure my team knew it wasn't an actual wolf. The idea was to stand out against nature without drawing too much attention from the enemy.

"Should we drop?" Hill hesitated, and I glared at him. He looked at me then turned away and did his annoying habit whenever he was unsure of combing his hair with his fingers. Moore called it his Kenickie move. Moore's thing was to always reference movies. I guessed everyone had something. I shrugged it off and concentrated on Hill.

"If you drop your weapon, I'll shoot you myself," I snapped. We would never surrender, especially to such animals.

The men pointed their guns at us as they approached and circled us with whistles and shouts. We moved into a circle, backs to each other, and kept our weapons held high. If this was it, we'd go out swinging.

"I will soon live like a king," the leader of the pack said in Pashtu. "Round them up and bring them back to camp," he ordered.

"We won't be going anywhere with you." I let him know I spoke Pashtu as well. They warned us not to let the enemy know if we could speak their language. That way, we could eavesdrop if captured, but today I didn't care. They wouldn't get their bounty because we'd fight to our death.

"Ah," he smiled and tilted his head at me, "you speak my tongue?" He spoke in English. "Good. You should know I always get what I want. So, do yourself a favor and get moving."

One of his men pointed a gun in my face, and I shoved it upward so hard I could hear the crack as his nose broke. He fell backward and flew over the horse's ass, tumbling to the ground. The leader shook his head and nodded at another man who went to stab me, but I stepped out of his way and grabbed his arm, twisting it at the elbow. It snapped, and he cried out as his knife fell to the ground.

"Enough!" he ordered, and they all pointed their guns at me. "Fire!" They hesitated for a split second, I was sure because of the bounty on our heads that was about to be lost, and then fate suddenly was on our side.

Bullets whipped through the air, and the men jolted in their saddles then fell to the ground near our feet. I popped two in the leader's head as he tried to ride away. I raced after the horse and grabbed the reins. We could use the horses to give our feet a break. As I circled back, I grinned at the familiar face.

"Heard your call." Captain Flex stepped out of the shrubs. He signaled for the others to join him.

"Appreciate the timing." I shook his hand.

"Finally," Hill grunted as he approached and motioned for Rivera to follow. "I couldn't do another day here." I wanted to punch his face in for his lack of respect.

Moore rolled his eyes at me, and I looked away, happy that they were leaving so I didn't have the urge to give him a black eye. I hated being down two men, but we'd be better off without those two.

"Who's that?" Dustin, one of Flex's men, pointed to the body draped over the horse I held by the bridle.

"Don't know." Hill moved forward and went to investigate. He poked the bulge with his rifle, and the body jerked. "He's alive, whoever it is."

"Untie him," Flex ordered.

"Copy that." Hill loosened the ropes around his arms and legs and let him fall to the ground with a thud. Hill pulled off the blanket he was wrapped in and roughly ripped the sack off his head. "Oh, shit, it's a kid."

The young boy, maybe nine years old, blinked at the sunlight while tears streamed down his cheeks. He sat up when he saw us and wrapped his arms around his knees for protection.

I bent down and removed his gag and inspected his cuts. He studied my clothes then looked up at me with confusion.

I handed him my water and urged him to drink some. He hesitated at first but took it and swallowed back a good amount. His wrists were bloody, and his neck was rubbed raw, which told me he likely had been on the back of that horse for quite a while.

"Hungry?" I spoke in Pashtu, and when he didn't answer, I switched to Dari. He nodded, and I handed him a protein pack.

"He's one of them, Beckett." Flex came up next to me and stuck the barrel of his gun in the kid's face. "We need to keep moving."

"He's a child." I pushed the tip of his gun away. "Just because he looks like them doesn't mean he's one of them." We learned that lesson day one of being there.

"Just shoot him and be done," Hill huffed.

"You shoot him, and you'll have me to deal with," I

grunted, and he waited a beat before he stepped back with a curse.

I looked the kid over and noticed his clothes were expensive looking and his satchel had beadwork on the side. It was unusual to see such items on a typical Afghan child.

"Wait here," I told him and pulled Moore and Brown aside. "I think this kid is someone important."

"Because of his clothes and the bag?" Moore looked at the kid. "Maybe. But shit, Beckett, that's extra baggage."

"He's a kid." My gut screamed at me to take him with us.

"He could also make us an even bigger target." Moore shrugged.

Brown rubbed the back of his head nervously. "He could be carrying drugs or maybe even be a mole. Fuck, this entire thing could have been planned for us to take him. They're most likely watching us right now." He looked wildly around.

I shook my head. This wasn't Brown's typical thought process, and even Moore gave him an odd look. He was slipping. The three of us had been ridiculously close growing up. I knew Brown better than he knew himself, and right now my brother needed to get the hell out of this place. The signs were all there in his eyes and in the constant movements he made. Yes, those tics were a dead giveaway that he needed help. I knew we had to get him home fast.

I stepped back and turned to face the others.

"Let's vote. Take the kid, or leave the kid?"

"I think I speak for my team when I say, leave 'im. We aren't going to get sucked into another of your volunteer fuck-ups." Flex looked at the guys, and they all nodded in agreement. "We aren't far from where the truck's waiting, but I'm not taking a kid."

I turned to Brown, who shrugged but hit my shoulder to indicate he'd side with me. Moore nodded to imply the same.

"We need to leave before they come." Brown looked about, worried. "We need to go," he repeated.

I turned to Moore so only he could hear. "Go with them. I need your ears. Meet me at the last check. We'll take the horses, and you go in the truck with the others. Get settled at the house but don't let your guard down. Safe place or not, keep your eyes open."

"You sure?" His face twisted as his eyes went to Brown. I knew he wasn't sure it was a wise idea to leave me with just Brown, but Brown needed one on one, and so did the kid.

"Yeah, keep Anderson and Gail close, but yeah, go." I didn't trust that the others wouldn't sell me out and trap me somewhere. I trusted Moore with my life. I knew he'd have my back, especially with the other two guys.

"Be safe." He fist-bumped me and raced to join the others. I knew they'd get to the rendezvous well before we would, but I wasn't going to leave the kid here. The horses would help as long as we could keep out of sight of the Taliban.

I crouched back down in front of the kid and rubbed my chin. I knew we didn't have a lot of time to get out of there. We were too exposed, but I needed a minute.

"Where are your parents?" He shrugged, and I could see his cheeks pink up. "Are you hurt?" He shrugged again, and I looked at his bare feet. I leaned back, untied and wiggled a boot off one of the dead men. I held it to the kid's foot, but it was way too big. I looked around and spotted a smaller size and tugged them off the guy with a hole in his chest. I handed them to the kid, and he slipped them on without hesitation.

"We need to move, okay?" I patted his head, and he nodded but looked unsure. I peeled back a small Velcro flap on my jacket and pointed to the flag on my arm. "I'm not here to hurt you." He hopped to his feet then stumbled to find his footing. He'd hung over that horse too long. I scooped him up and sat him on the back of the horse then jumped up behind him on the saddle. Brown mounted up but looked a bit awkward on the horse. I knew we'd make better time on horseback. We just needed to be extra careful. I kicked hard, and we took off toward higher ground. I checked back, and Brown seemed able to follow. I hoped he wouldn't fall off the damn thing. His face was a picture of concentration, and it almost made me laugh. I was glad I'd ridden a bit as a kid.

Location: Afghanistan
Coordinates: Classified

Ty

Warm light peeked through the sheer curtains, and a beam of sun brushed over her bare legs. Her dark hair was tousled across the pillow, and her skin nearly glowed as I gawked at her flawless body.

I ran my finger down the artwork along her spine and noted the color from the fallen feathers became faded as I stopped at her tailbone. The intricate bird on her shoulder tilted as it flew away toward the evening sun.

"Aren't you going to ask me what it means?" she mumbled from the pillow.

"No." I retracted my fingers and pulled my phone cord from the charger. She chuckled as she rolled over and let the sheet fall away to expose her bare breasts. Her pink lips parted, and when she caught me looking, her gorgeous brown eyes blinked behind long dark lashes. The thin chain she wore held a cross close to her throat, and it caught the light when she swallowed. The contrast of her skin against the crisp white sheets was beautiful, and I fought the need to reach out and touch her again. But I didn't and wouldn't.

"I wish you'd tell me about this." She reached over to run her finger up my stomach to my chest, but I snagged her fingers, giving them a kiss before I let her go.

"Hungry?" Her voice was all breathy.

"No."

"Of course not." She sighed and swept an arm to clear away her long hair. "The night's over. It's my cue to leave." I simply shrugged, and her head shot back. "Will my payment be left on the nightstand, or will you pay me over an app?" she spat, and I knew her hackles were up. I hated what she said. I didn't want her to degrade herself like that. I knew she had two degrees and worked hard in her family's business.

"Stop," I warned.

"Why?" she challenged.

"Because I said to."

"I see." She rolled her eyes. "Well, if you say so." I sent her a look, and she returned it. "The dangerous Eric Noah doesn't show feelings, huh?"

"They're pointless."

"I beg to differ."

"Then we differ."

"But you have no problem showing me how you feel at night?" She tried to make sense of a senseless situation.

"It's sex."

"Right." I could tell that hurt. "You call me Escaper, instead of my real name. Why is that?" I ignored her question as I thumbed through my emails. "Is it because I'm your escape from the world?"

"No."

Yes.

"Eric," she got up on her knees and crawled over my lap, "we've been sleeping together for over two years. You come get me, we have sex, I spend the night, then in the morning you can barely look at me. God forbid you should answer a question."

"And?" I knew how I sounded, but it had to be this way. It would always be this way.

"And I'm tired of it." She held her head high, and I could tell she was more than upset this time. "I want more."

"I can't give you more."

"Why?" Hurt raced across her face. When I still said nothing, her eyes glossed over. "You don't just have sex with me, Eric, you make love to me like I'm the only one for you. But the moment the sun comes up, I'm just one of the women out there, just a nightly hook up to… what?" Her eyes blazed. "To blur the pain of your lifestyle?" Her words cut hard, but I remained impassive, unreadable. "You don't use my name, never want to know anything about me, and I'm supposed to be okay with it?" Her soft hands pushed against my chest, and I fought the urge to flip her over and have my way with her again.

"I don't," I pulled her hands up and away from me, "expect anything from you. Just like you shouldn't expect anything from me."

"Wow." She ripped her hands from my hold, dried her tears, and got up. She began to gather her clothes and tripped over her bra in her hurry to get away from me.

Everything inside me wanted to pull her back to bed, but the truth was I wouldn't.

I'd known this day would come. I'd allowed myself to get comfortable with her, and now I needed to hurt her because of who we were. Both of us were wrapped deep in the Cartel. I worked for her cousin, and she worked for her father. Though we were of the same world, we were miles apart. If I publicly dated her, I'd have to answer to more than just her family. I'd have to answer to mine… and that just wasn't an option.

"Don't call me, Eric, because this won't happen again." She tugged her dress on and shimmied into her shoes.

Just as she reached the door, I flew off the bed and

whirled her around by her arm to look at me. Her expression carried so much hurt, but there was hope there too, and I knew it was time. I knew she was the one person who could take me down. I'd hurt many women in the past, some worse than others, but the one who stood in front of me now needed to go. I was angry at myself. I'd known better, but I'd been selfish and lazy. I'd grown comfortable with her and didn't want to look for another.

Everything was on the tip of my tongue. How I did know her real name, and I only allowed myself to use it when she was asleep. Or how I was the one who sent her those white roses on her birthday. It was me who sent the bottle of wine and candies a month after Valentine's Day, because I hated that day. I enjoyed the idea of her reaction that some unknown person thought to send her gifts. She deserved the world, but I sure as hell wasn't the one who could give her that.

"I—" I snapped my mouth shut.

Don't.

"Yeah," she sniffed, "I thought so."

I love you, Talya.

She leaned up and kissed my cheek. "I want more, Eric." Her lips brushed over my skin again.

"And I don't," I lied.

"Then this is goodbye." She ducked under my arm and slipped outside the door, leaving me to fall apart in silence.

My phone lit up on top of the white blanket, and I ran a hand through my hair as I retrieved it.

> Castillo: Pick up and transport the next payment. 1:30 p.m.

I swiped the message away and zeroed in on the time. I had just under an hour before I had to make the pickup. Beer bottles clinked outside the door, and I closed my eyes and tried not to lose my shit. I hated people in my house, but parties were a must in my world, and I planned to make my way up in it.

"Where're you off to?" someone called out, and I heard a woman laugh as a man called back.

Fuck this. I grabbed my gun, ripped open the door, and fired a couple rounds in the air.

"Get the fuck out!" I yelled and heard the ruckus as everyone scrambled to their feet.

"Alejandro," I spotted my right-hand man, "we leave in forty." I slammed the door shut and headed for the shower.

The spray from the shower beat my face, and no matter how much I pushed away the pain and tried to close the door on Talya, it was impossible. She was the only one I'd ever let inside my tightly closed heart. She'd managed to break down my walls, but only in bed. When we were alone in the dark, I would let my guard down, never with words, just with action. But the moment the sun came up and broke though that protective dark shield, I immediately pulled back and reminded her she was good for one thing. Sex. The lies I told her repeatedly burned at my soul.

I never thought we'd last this long, but shit, it hurt. I knew I couldn't allow matters of the heart to intrude on the careful life I'd built here. I pressed my hands against the shower wall and hung my head back and let the water flow into my nose and mouth until my lungs begged me to move. I gasped in a breath and felt the pain flood through me again. This had to stop; it was a maddening loop. I turned the water off and stepped out. I glanced in the mirror and slicked back my hair to try to get a good look at my face.

I swiped the fog from the mirror with the back of my hand and took in my expression. The tormented face that looked back at me gave me a reason to reach for the jar of pain killers in the cabinet. I swallowed them back with some tequila I kept next to the sink. I saw it was nearly empty as I swallowed and tried not to cough at the burn in my throat. The burn went straight down to my stomach. I tossed the bottle in the trash and headed for the closet.

"You look like shit, boss." Alejandro cringed when I finally emerged from my room. I buttoned up my shirt, rolled my sleeves, and caught the eye of one of my guys. I jabbed my thumb toward my room to let him know to get my place cleaned up. "I told you not to mix the tequila and those pills Filippo brought. That shit messes with your head." His eyes went wide. "I saw dragons last time I done that."

"Yeah." I tuned him out as we headed outside. The heat hit us both like a slap to the face. I never touched any of the product these guys pumped through my party. If I didn't keep a straight head in this business, I was as good as dead.

"Where we goin' today, boss?" He fiddled with the climate control and lowered the blast of cool air that was aimed at him.

"Pick up, drop off." I headed down the driveway and out onto the main road. "Then church."

THREE

TY

I held the kid's hand as we stepped onto United States soil. It had been a long time, and I hoped it would feel better than it did. I looked back at the chopper and wondered if I'd ever be back in the Afghan mountains again.

When we changed planes, I had to make the call to Frank about Brown. He told me we'd discuss everything once we got back. I barely had enough time to think before we were whisked back into the air.

When we landed, Moore raced by and threw me a small grin, and I tried to return it. He was glad to be home, but I knew we were both still in shock over Brown. I hated to think how our heads would deal with what happened once we finally got time alone. The thought haunted me. I kept moving, not bothering to look back at the rest. They weren't my brothers.

Frank walked out to greet us and then ushered us inside along with a few other soldiers. I knew I needed to get through this first, then I would deal with everything else. The kid deserved this moment.

"Welcome back, Captain Beckett." Frank looked down at the kid. "Seems you found someone we've been looking for."

"It seems so."

"Come, his parents are waiting through here." The doors were opened for us, and we were whisked through security and down a long hallway.

"Halim!" his mother yelled when she spotted him. He raced toward her, leapt in her arms, and burst into tears. His father hugged and kissed him as Frank glanced at me.

"You had no idea who he was?"

"No. I didn't even know his name until we were in the chopper."

"You have no idea what you just did for our country."

"I didn't do it for the country, I did it for him." I felt a weight lift off my shoulders when his father looked at me with joy and appreciation.

"I can't thank you enough." He gave me a bow, and I just nodded. I didn't want a thank you; the moment was enough for me.

His mother lowered him so his siblings could hug him with cries and happiness.

"Thank you, thank you so much." She held her hands together and cried. "You gave us back our son. Our family is one again."

The word family hit my gut, and I fought to settle my rage.

"He's a good kid," I turned to Frank, "but a kid who will need some help." I tapped my head.

"I have a therapist lined up."

"Good." I knew he'd need it. We had a lot to do before I could get out of there, so I stepped forward and sat down on the chair. "Kid," I said in Dari, "come here." He pulled out of his brother's arms and came over to me. I knelt to get on eye level with him. "You did real good out there, braver than most of the soldiers I've seen. Don't ever let anyone tell you different." He nodded. "Tyler," I pointed to myself. "That's my name, okay? If you need anything, you let that guy right there know," I moved my finger to Frank, "and I'll be there." He leaned in, and I wrapped him in a bear hug. I felt a prickle of sadness break through my shield as I held him. We had a bond, that kid and I, and one that would last a lifetime.

"I'm Halim."

"So, you do speak, and in English." I glared at the little shit for not speaking up sooner.

"I made this for you." He pulled out his pouch and tugged loose one of the leather straps with a few washers on it. He held it up for me to see. "That means *Captain*. That's you, and this is for me, *Halim*." He had pounded the letters in Dari. "And this in the middle," he turned the washer around so I could see the pounded shape of a dog, "is our *wolf*." My gaze flickered up to his. "Tall, strong, and he'll send powerful echoes to save the people he cares for."

"Wow." I couldn't believe he'd made something so meaningful at such a horrific time for him. He wrapped the leather strap around my wrist a few times and tied it at the end. "Thank you, Halim. This is very special to me." I grasped his hand and shook it.

"You won't forget me?"

"Never." I stood and ruffled his mop of hair. I said a quick goodbye, as I had a sudden need to be alone. I rounded the corner and pressed my hands into the wall. My arms vibrated at the picture of Brown's eyes as they bulged when the bullet drilled through his skull. My heart raced, and I fought to control my anger.

Hill dropped Brown's rucksack at my feet.

"You should be stripped of your rank." He spat at my boots, and I saw red just before I took a swing. Everything I'd held back came out in a flood as I snapped.

———

The clock ticked loudly on the wall as I leaned forward in the chair. I rested my forearms on my thighs, and my head was heavy and low. I looked down at my fingernails, now stained with Hill's blood, then opened and closed my fists and studied the swollen knuckles. They were as battered as Hill's face.

I was together enough now to know I'd lost it. I remembered the shouts as the men came to try to tear us apart, and it was only when I heard Halim's pleading voice that I finally stopped and allowed them to pull me off him. The boy shouldn't have seen me like that that, but I'd managed to hold it together for him until he was safe with his family. It was too much to ask of me at that point. If I hadn't let loose on Hill, I would have exploded. The tension that had filled me had finally left me now, and I felt I could breathe. It wouldn't bring Brown back; he wasn't here and never would be again. I rubbed my face to try to clear the picture of his lifeless body out of my head. I didn't give a rat's ass about Hill's condition. I hoped he was dead. I didn't care about what happened to me now. I only wished I'd fought Hill over there and not waited until I was back on US soil.

"Eight years, he was over there." I heard Frank's faint voice. "Trust me, in spite of whatever just happened out there, he's what you're looking for."

I moved my tongue around my mouth. I might face consequences for Hill, but if I was going down, I was determined to bring him with me. If he was alive. If he was, I'd do whatever it took to make sure that shit ended up behind bars, hopefully as someone's bunk bitch.

"Captain Beckett." Frank was now in the room. I prepared myself for what was about to happen. "I don't know exactly what happened between you and Hill, but I know it had to do with Brown's death. I'll need all the facts, and we'll get to that. You're lucky he's alive after the beating you gave him. I can only assume you had a reason for it, and I know it was a bad situation over there. Up to now, you've had an exemplary record, and nothing like this has ever been reported before, so I'm going to ask for your cooperation."

I looked up at him, but I couldn't think of a thing to say, so I just looked back down again.

"I want you to take an immediate psych eval." His voice was firm. He wasn't asking. I looked up again and wondered why a psych eval was being done first over what I assumed would be my arrest. I still didn't know what kind of trouble I was really in. Frank's hand fell away from the door handle, and he bent down close to me. "If you get cleared by the doc, I've an opportunity you might be interested in." He leaned in. "Your future didn't stop outside on that tarmac today. It starts now. I'm counting on you, Beckett. Now, follow me, soldier."

"Yes, sir." I got up and followed him inside the office and wondered what in the hell all that was about.

"Captain Beckett," a well-dressed doctor stood and shook my hand, "I'm Dr. Roberts. Please sit down." Frank left the room and shut the door on his way out.

"Ah, sure." I wasn't at all sure, but I wasn't going to ask any questions either. I took inventory of the room, what was on the desk, how the windows opened, noted a door that most likely led to a bathroom. I shifted and looked back over my shoulder at the door I'd entered through.

"Everything all right?" He studied my face. I knew to answer with the truth or some sugar-coated version but never to dismiss the question altogether. The moment I walked in, I was being watched right down to my hand movements and how often my eyes shifted around.

"Okay if I change the angle of my chair?" I asked.

"Of course." He waited until I was settled and seemed to understand my reason for it. I waited for the typical questions they usually asked. I could answer them in my sleep at this point in my career, but the doctor watched me instead. "Why don't you give me the Cliffs Notes on your history in the military."

"I was in JROTC in high school, went to college, headed straight to Afghanistan the moment I could, been doing special ops ever since."

"Yes, I understand you've spent eight years over there. That's a long time to be away from home. Do you miss your family?"

"Yes, I do," I answered honestly. "But I feel I fit better over there."

"Most soldiers would give a different answer to that."

"With all due respect, Dr. Roberts, I'm not like most soldiers."

"Meaning?"

"I'm the exception to the American rule. Square peg in a round hole, if you will. I'd rather be roughing it the woods or mountains, fighting to stay alive, and protecting those who can't protect themselves. I need that kind of purpose in my life. I'd shrivel up and die if I had to be stuck in some subdivision or condo driving a minivan full of kids to soccer practice." I cringed at the thought of a life like that.

"You do seem to be good with kids."

"I like kids. I just don't see myself as a father."

"Halim took a liking to you."

"He's a good kid, but I was happy to hand him off to his family."

Dr. Roberts opened an iPad and started to scribble notes over the screen with an electronic pen.

"Let's talk about this last mission a bit." I tried not to shift with discomfort. "How'd you end up with Hill and Rivera and Captain Flex with Anderson and Gail?"

"Our mission got made. When we found our mark had been killed, the Taliban were waiting for us, and we were ambushed. Everyone fled for cover, and we ended up mixing our companies."

"How did Hill and Rivera do under your command?"

I licked my dry mouth.

"They didn't agree with how I ran my team. There was a lot of disrespect." I tried to speed the story along. "Then we had an altercation with more Taliban, and we met back up with Captain Flex, and that's when we discovered the kid on the back of the horse."

"I see." He went back to writing. "What made you decide to take Halim with you when I understand everyone else was against the idea?" he asked and put down the pen. He gave me his full attention again.

"He's a child." I shrugged. "If we left him, he'd most likely be dead."

"He brought you a lot of extra attention with the Taliban. Did that cause more tension with the team?"

"Some, yes, but my gut told me to take the kid. I knew he had to be someone important, but I'd have taken him with us anyway. I made the call the way I saw it." I took a deep breath. "The kid just added some extra pressure. The men were already a problem."

"He was lucky you were the one in charge." He gave me a small smile.

"I guess, but maybe if I hadn't taken the kid, Anderson and Gail would still be here."

"You don't know that for sure, so don't carry that on your shoulders. They weren't under your command at the time." He shifted as he thought. "Let's jump forward, to Brown's death. For full disclosure, Hill had just given his version before, ah, the unfortunate incident outside." I stilled. My breath caught in my chest, and I tried to play it cool, but inside anger instantly bloomed. "Hill said that when he came up on you, Brown had a gun to the head of a little girl. He said Brown held her in his arms and screamed he was going to kill her because they'd let the

Taliban know you were all there." *The fuck?* When I didn't respond he swiped the screen.

"I see." I choked back my rage to idle. I knew I couldn't let it take over if I was to get through this.

"I take it that's not how it was from your perspective?"

"No, that's nothing like how it was."

"So, Hill didn't try to distract Brown so you could disengage him?" When my eyes widened at the blatant lie, he went on. "He said that you then ordered him to leave, he obeyed, and a moment later he heard a gunshot."

I couldn't help my reaction to the utter bullshit that was being said. My head shot back at what he said, but I played it off as just a shift in movement to relieve stress in my neck.

"Again, with all due respect, Doctor, that wasn't even close to how his death happened."

"Why don't you tell me what happened?"

I kept calm as I retold the story of my buddy's murder. I needed to show I had gained control of Brown and had never lost control of the situation. Every word twisted my insides because I knew there was a very good chance Hill could get away with this. A lot of things slipped under the radar while we were over there. We had our own law and order.

"That's very interesting, Beckett." The doc nodded slowly. "I'll be sure to pass your story of what happened along to Colonel Frank." He checked the time on his watch. "I do have one last question for you." I nodded for him to go ahead. "What now?" He cocked his head to one side as he asked.

I loathed that question.

"I'm going to try to find my way back to the only thing I know." He gave a small smile at my words, and I wondered what he was thinking.

Once outside the office, I was directed to a different room and told to wait. Before I stepped inside, I heard a voice.

"Hey, Beckett." My buddy Rowe stopped and leaned his shoulder against the wall. "Heard you punched Hill."

"Yeah." I shook off the fact that everyone knew what I'd done.

"I'm sure he deserved it."

He deserved a bullet in the head, but I'd keep that to myself for now.

"When'd you get back?" I tried to smile as I spoke but knew it probably was more of a grimace.

"A few weeks ago." Rowe followed me inside the room as the cleaners went by with their cart. "Trying to figure out what's next."

"You going to reenlist?"

"Nah," he shook his head, "I got three weeks left before I'm out."

"How's your sister?"

"How's yours?" He smirked. He loved to give me shit about the time he'd kissed my sister at a party, while I only asked because I knew his sister had been quite sick. I dropped my head and rubbed my aching skull. Rowe sensed my stress and cleared his throat.

"Look, Frank's got this lead on a town in Montana that needs some police. I guess they're short staffed, and since it's a training town for a military camp and more tourist flock there for vacation, they're looking to hire. I know it's way below what you're used to, and I don't know when your contract's up, but…" He shrugged, and the weight of us being pulled from the place we'd spent years protecting hit me once again. I could tell he was done with the military. "Jay, Spade, and Beam are all considering it."

"Yeah?" I let out a long breath. "Thanks. I'll think about it." I appreciated the information. Jay, Rowe, Spade, and I all trained together but later moved in different directions within the military. Beam came later. He was great until he took a hit to the leg a few years ago. I heard he was back, and I hoped he'd pass the physical. I wasn't ready to leave this life, but if I was about to land in shit for assaulting Hill, maybe I'd pull the cards and join them in the mountains. I did love the mountains.

"Take it easy, Beckett." He waved and left, and I sat back and tried to relax. The door was slightly ajar, and I could see a man around my age speaking to Frank and Dr. Roberts. I tuned in to them.

"There's stuff there," I read the doctor's lips, "but I feel you've got something. He kept that boy alive through countless encounters, and to top it off, they formed a bond. That's not something you can teach. You have it, or you don't. Moore…" He turned slightly, so I missed the rest of what he had said.

I went back to staring at my stained fingernails and fought but lost myself in the replay inside my head. I could still hear the sound of horse hooves as they stamped loudly, then Brown's cry, then Moore in my face telling me to leave him.

"Captain Beckett." A man's voice brought me back. He spoke loudly, as if he'd had to repeat himself. "I'm Colonel Cole Logan." I'd heard of him before, and Frank had a picture of him on his wall. I quickly stood and greeted him. "I'd like you to meet my father, General Daniel Logan."

"Sir." I nodded respectfully and saluted him.

"I'd like to speak to you about something." Cole motioned for me to sit with them. He spread a map of the route I'd taken with the kid out on the table. It was high-lighted in red. "You managed to cross one of the most dangerous areas in Afghanistan with Brown and that boy. You managed multiple encounters in a countryside heavily armed and crawling with Taliban. That whole area has been a Taliban stronghold for over a year. You did all that and managed to live."

"Not all of us did," I corrected.

"That's correct, but I'm focusing on you right now." I nodded. "Why?"

"Why?" I questioned.

"Yes."

"It's my job. It's what I'm trained to do." He watched me for a beat.

"Was there ever a time where it got so bad that you second guessed your choice of bringing the child along?"

"Never." I shook my head without a doubt. "It's simple. Black and white. He was a kid, taken from his family. He had no one and needed someone. I was that someone. I don't care if it was from here to here," I traced my finger along the red line, "or from here to here," I traced the entire map. "I knew I was meant to bring that kid home. So, I did."

Cole stood and paced the room for a moment, lost in thought. I waited for him to speak. I had only done what I had to do and wasn't sure what this was all about.

"What if I told you I could offer you an opportunity to continue the fight?"

That caught my attention. "I'd say I'm very interested in hearing how."

"I'd like to offer you a position." Cole locked eyes with me. "How would you feel about working with a senior team of special operatives? Ones who slip in and out of Mexico, snatching back kidnapped victims from the Cartel?"

"I've never heard of anything like that, but it sure sounds interesting." He had me hooked already. "Tell me more."

"The Cartel is getting stronger and bolder every day. While you've been in Afghanistan fighting the Taliban, we've been fighting a whole different war back here. We have a safehouse where we live and train. We have one established team at the house, but we desperately need a second. You'd be the leader of that team, and once you've seen how things work, and you're comfortable, you'd start the process of building it."

I nodded as he stopped for a moment to see if I was still with him. I could already feel the beginning of something resembling excitement deep in my stomach.

"We've a lot of rules," he continued, "and the place we stay is nowhere near any kind of city life, but Frank brought you to us, and since you've already got the clear from Doc Roberts, we think you're just what we're looking for."

"So, I'm not in trouble for what happened out there this morning?" I couldn't believe that would go away.

"Let me deal with that." Cole waved his hand, and I looked at both men, shocked this was even being offered to me.

"What do you say, Beckett?" General Logan drew my attention over to him. "Want to step into a whole new kind of war?"

FOUR

IVY

I taped the last box and scribbled the word *books* in black marker along the side then pushed it against the wall. I looked out the corner of the window where I'd spent the last three days worried about being watched.

My reflection in the glass couldn't hide the fact that I was on edge, sleep deprived, and frustrated with the events of the day before yesterday. I'd thrived at my job, and now things were heading south in a massive hurry.

I hated to leave my patients, let alone with no warning. I'd secretly worked all yesterday morning to clear my schedule. I'd worked damn hard to become a psychologist, and after being promoted to the position I was in with the US Army, it was like a dream come true.

"Is this the last of it, Dr. Knight?" I jumped in surprise at the sudden voice and felt my head tingle from the rush of nerves that came over me. "I'm sorry, I didn't mean to scare you." One of the younger men from the office had offered to help me with the move. I thought he was still outside, so his sudden appearance made me jump. He gave me a sympathetic smile.

"Yes, that's it. Thank you so much for your help, Lawrence." I leaned my hip into the windowsill and concentrated on my breathing, in and out. Once I was settled, I'd let myself feel disappointed. I wasn't sure how I felt about this move, but I knew I couldn't stay here. Not until…I shifted my gaze to the dent in the wall and felt my heartbeat in my throat. I pressed my hand against my chest and pushed the memory away. *Not now.*

"Well, as agreed, I'll meet the moving truck day after tomorrow and get everything to the storage unit for you. Are you sure there's nothing else I can do?"

"No. You've been such a help." I smiled at him, but as I did, I couldn't help the need to look past him over his shoulder to make sure the two officers were still posted at the door.

"Okay, well, I wish you the best, and thanks for all the stuff you gave me." He gave a wave and went out the door. I heard him speak to someone on the way out.

"Hey, you okay, kiddo?" My uncle stood in the entrance looking stylish in a snappy suit and a pair of designer sunglasses. I smiled at his name for me. I was, after all, a twenty-eight-year-old woman, but I loved when he called me that, and I was glad he was here.

"Yes," I lied and shook off all the negative thoughts. "Oh, Frank called about something. My secretary took the message. Any idea what it's about?"

"He just wanted to wish you luck and to remind you it's not permanent."

"Mm." I hoped that was true. I wasn't a huge fan of the country. Even though I was born in a rural area, my parents later moved us to the city. The idea of disappearing for a while felt like a wise idea. Plus, any extra time I could soak up with my uncle was just a bonus.

"No other news?"

"No." He shook his head, looking grim. "Not yet." I swallowed and felt the uncomfortable lump in my throat. It had lodged itself there and hadn't moved since… "Your mom called me on my way over. She's worried."

"I know." I knew my mom would call her brother when I didn't check in this morning. Which also meant I'm sure she called Frank too, and that meant my uncle would have heard it from him as well. They had a friggin' phone tree whenever it came to me. My uncle and Frank went way back, so there were never any secrets; they told each other everything.

"You should call her."

"I will."

He moved into the room, leaned on a pile of packed boxes, and crossed his long legs at the ankle. I had to shake my head at his natural good looks and easy personality. His hair had gone slightly gray at the temples, and it only added to his looks. I could tell he wanted to probe me with more questions, but I'd already cleared a psych test that morning, and it proved I could handle the storm I'd found myself in. At least I was good at selling that I was.

"Ivy, no one is going to think less of you for leaving. What happened here wasn't all right at all."

"I know," I reached for my purse and tugged it up over my shoulder. "We should probably leave, as we're going to hit traffic and our flight won't wait for us."

"Ivy." His voice held a parental tone.

"*Uncle* Reid." I barely used the word uncle anymore, only when I really wanted him to hear me. "I'm not okay, but I'm okay enough. I know what happened isn't right, so that's why I agreed to make this move. I just need to take it moment by moment, and I promise if I feel like I'm about to slip, you'll be the first to know."

He gave me a satisfied smile. "You know when we get there you can't call me Uncle Reid, right?" He switched topics, and I loved that he always knew when to back off.

"I only use Uncle Reid when I need you to hear me."

"And it works." He chuckled.

"I know it does, Dr. Roberts." I laughed as we headed for the car.

———

By the time we flew into North Dakota, we'd switched SUVs two times, and it wasn't until we crossed the Montana border that I finally stopped scanning faces. My stomach was in a knot the entire trip, and I felt a little nauseated as I got farther and farther from home. I hoped I wasn't going to be sick. I loved my life in Washington. My family was there; my friends were there. I even loved the little old man who always parked in my spot by the office every Tuesday. He drove me nuts, but he'd made me smile every time, as he'd toss his hands in the air and make his apology. Then he'd hand me a banana muffin wrapped in paper, saying his wife made them. She probably made them on Monday, because he gave me one every Tuesday. I was going to miss those muffins.

I sniffed and a whole new wave of feeling sorry for myself came over me. I shook myself out of it. I needed to try to start a whole new life, even if it was just temporary. I had to find daily things that would make me happy. I knew the most difficult part would be to familiarize myself with a whole new batch of patients.

"How upset was the Blackstone team when they were told you were switching to the new team?" I asked as we started up a winding mountain road. He glanced forward and shrugged.

"Change isn't always a bad thing."

"I beg to differ," I whispered.

"It isn't."

"It isn't when you have control over the decision, maybe, but not when someone has made the decision for you." I knew I sounded petulant, and he glanced over at me. I sighed and looked out the window then went back to the files on my lap.

"You remind me so much of your mother," he huffed.

"Yes, well, so do you."

The driver cleared his throat as he hid his amusement.

"You're not helping." Uncle Reid smacked his shoulder, and I couldn't help but notice how at ease he was with the driver. I wasn't introduced when we got into the car, as I was on the phone with a client back home who needed me. It seemed to have been forgotten after that, and now, I felt rude for not saying anything. I was about to speak up when the vehicle suddenly veered off the road and onto a rough dirt road. A couple miles later, we stopped at a checkpoint and were scanned and waved on. Farther and farther we drove into the forest. I wasn't comfortable with all these trees. It felt like we were in the middle of the wilderness. I swallowed hard and hoped I'd get used to it.

"You could have warned me heels weren't going to work here." I looked at my uncle. I thought about what I had brought with me. "Where was this conversation?"

"I guess it slipped my mind. Although I did say to bring comfortable shoes."

"Hey, Ivy," I mocked my uncle, "lose the heels and grab your wilderness boots and flannel. You're going to be living in the middle of the woods." I glared, and again the driver chuckled, only this time he didn't even try to hide it.

"What in the world are wilderness boots?" My uncle shook his head with a chuckle.

"Boots that cover your ankle and have big, thick soles with ropes for laces."

"Have I taught you nothing?"

"I'm not sure how to tell you this without breaking the bubble you're in, Doc, but have you looked in the mirror lately? You're not exactly the hauling hay and slinging cattle type."

"Says the woman in six-inch heels and a Vera Wang skirt."

"I rest my case." I chuckled as he rolled his eyes and knew I'd won the argument. My uncle was, in every sense of the word, preppy.

"Okay, look," he patted my shoulder, but humor still laced his voice, "I'll take you into town and we'll get you some new things."

"Do we airlift out? Or do I need to jump on a saddle and ride my way there?"

The driver hit his steering wheel and roared with laughter. I glared at him in the mirror.

"Lopez, you're seriously not helping." My uncle smiled.

Lopez?

I thumbed through the tabs of the files on my lap and gave a hiss when I found his and put it on top. Major Mark Lopez. Yup, he was one of my new clients, and he'd just been a witness to my freakout. Oh, and to add to it, he was Mia's husband! Frank barely spoke about his personal life, but I had met Mia once before and thought she was nice. That was just great. I glared at my uncle as I pointed to the file. He said nothing, just gave a shrug.

"Again, a little warning goes a long way." I flared my nostrils at him.

"Oh, shit," Lopez laughed, "Dr. Knight, you're going to fit in so well here."

"You sure about that?" I huffed. "Because right now I don't exactly feel like I'm in a Hallmark mov..." My words trailed off when we approached what only could be described as a massive resort. "Aaand plot twist," I whispered with my eyes wide.

"Welcome to your new home." Reid smiled at me, and we exited the car. "City girl or not, I think you'll find this place will suit you well."

Out of the corner of my eye, I saw something huge racing in my direction, and just as I was about to scream, Lopez stepped in front of the beast and caught all hundred or so pounds of it and saved my life as it flashed in front of me.

"This, Dr. Knight, is Mr. Butters." The dog licked the

length of Lopez's face, and he kissed him back. "Down, Butters. Stay now. Mind your manners," he said firmly to the giant dog who immediately stood still and wagged his tail.

"Nice to meet you, Butters." I dabbed at his floppy head in an attempt to show him I wasn't food.

"I'll give you a tour, Ivy, but we should get your stuff inside first. The weather can change in a matter of moments here." Reid grabbed my bag while I rolled my suitcase behind me, breathing in the fresh evening air. As we walked toward the house, I couldn't help but notice how grand everything looked. The door flew open, and a woman walked toward us. She was a positively stunning sight in a fabulous knee-length designer wrap dress. She smiled warmly at me.

"You must be Dr. Knight. Welcome to Shadows. I'm Savannah."

"Nice to meet you, Savannah. Please call me Ivy."

"Only if you call me Savi."

"Deal." We both smiled happily at one another as she reached for my suitcase. She chatted away to the big dog as we followed her inside. Reid gave me a knowing grin. Okay, fine, he won a few points with Savi. I really liked her already.

I was handed a glass of cabernet sauvignon once I told her I liked red, and as the others whisked my belongings away, Savi took me on a tour.

"This will be a lot, but everyone here is super friendly and will stop whatever they're doing to help you out." She beamed as she sipped her wine and moved on. "You'll get the lay of the land in no time."

"Okay." I took a sip of what proved to be a really tasty wine and followed her.

"Now, this is the living room, and it's where we often come together before and after dinner." I gasped at the spectacular view of the mountains. They were all you could see through the massive floor-to-ceiling windows. A huge stone fireplace stood in the center of the room, and exposed dark wood beams crossed above me and made the place feel even larger than it already was. Red couches had black blankets draped over the backs of them. When I looked over at Savi, she was admiring it with me. "Sometimes I like to just stop and look at where I live now. I try not to take any of it for granted."

"For the record," I felt I should say it, "Doc Roberts hasn't told me anything about this place or any of you."

"That's what makes him such a great doctor." She smiled at me. "Over time, we'll catch you up, and I'm sure you'll learn a lot from Blackstone."

"I'd rather learn about them from a friend's standpoint."

"That was a really good answer." Savi gave me an interesting look as she motioned with her head for me to follow. "Here's the dining room. As you can see, it seats a lot of people. There are always guests over, other teams, children, you name it and we feed them."

I loved the sound of that. I always enjoyed it when all

my friends would get together, and we'd host dinner parties.

"And here's the kitchen." She laughed at something. "This was the first room I was shown on my tour when I arrived, and I remember this right here was pretty amazing." She opened a door and let me peek in at the wine cellar.

"If heaven had a door." I grinned and folded my hands against my cheeks, as she laughed harder.

"Come on." She showed me where her husband's office was by the stairs which led up to where the bedrooms were and then showed me where my office was. It was right next to my uncle's, which was nice. Downstairs had a huge entertainment room, games room, other bedrooms, another kitchen, and conference rooms. Savi said over the years as more people joined the family and they had to increase some staff members, they had to build on to the property to accommodate everyone. I lost count and knew I'd be asking for help at some point. Outside was impressive too, but as Savi said, we were getting close to her kids' bedtime, so she'd show me the rest the next day.

She ended the tour at my room. I had to count how many doors down it was from the stairs. She pulled a yellow band from her pocket and wrapped it around the handle.

"This is a little trick I taught my daughter, so she'd remember which room was whose." I loved how warm and understanding she was about my being there. I had felt like an outsider being imposed on them, but I already felt welcome. "So, this is your room." She opened the door, and my mouth opened at how stunning it was. A sleigh bed was against the left wall near a big window. There was a huge fireplace of my very own with a leather chair and couch placed close enough you could enjoy its warmth. A big table sat in front of the couch, a walk-in closet was straight ahead next to the bathroom, and a TV was mounted on the wall so you could watch it from the bed. Nothing had been left out, it was wonderful.

"Don't worry, you're not kicking anyone out of this room, and each room is basically the same. Once the guys on Team Blackstone began to marry, we built them their own homes right here on the property, so the house is fairly empty up here now. The staff quarters are just past our place." My eyes grew wide. "Yeah," she laughed, "we have lots of NDAs in place now."

"That's good to know." I felt tiny in such a huge room, let alone in the house. "May I ask who is up here on this floor besides me?"

"Of course. Well, there's a new soldier arriving tomorrow, I believe. He'll be the new team's leader. Doc Roberts will be working with them. I'm sure you know that." She smiled as I nodded. "More men will arrive as he builds his team. They'll take over the rest of the rooms up here."

"I see." I couldn't help but feel nervous about that.

"Frank handpicked the new guy who's arriving tomorrow. He's a pretty big deal. I know if Frank likes him, he must be a stand-up guy. I actually had a chance to look at his file, and I'm confident he'll fit in here or he wouldn't have invited him." She must have read my nerves.

"Frank is picky, so that's good to know," I agreed.

"I'm really glad you're here, Ivy." She seemed to hesitate. "There's been a little shakeup here at the house in the last while. I think you might just be a positive distraction we all need." She drew me in for a hug, and I noticed we were the same height and build. She was warm like a sister, and she eased my nerves immediately. "I'll let you get some sleep and see you in the morning. We'll have lots of time to finish your tour and meet everyone."

"Thanks, Savi. I really appreciate you being so welcoming."

"Oh, Ivy?" She turned when she got to the door. "For the record, we know very little about you either. Well, Cole and Daniel do, but we don't. The other wives and I all have our stories, some worse than others, but nonetheless, all of us—the spouses of the team members, I mean—we're all seeking the same thing here. To be happy."

FIVE

Ivy

I spent the next day meeting everyone. The wives of the team were incredibly nice and much like Savi in the warmth of their welcome. The only one I didn't get to meet was Lexi, who apparently was away visiting someone. I caught a few looks between the girls whenever her name came up, and it wasn't hard to figure there was more to her absence than they let on. Lexi was Keith's wife. I met him and found him to be kind, but it didn't take a professional to see he was in pain. He was quiet and withdrawn even as he introduced me to his two children. His adorable boy, Brandon, who they sometimes call B, was the spitting image of his father. His full-of-life daughter, Reagan, had a good part of her father in her, but you could see what I assumed was her mother as she looked up at me. That their family hurting was clearly written on their faces no matter how much Reagan tried to smile through it. I wondered what the story was but knew it would come in time.

Mia, Frank's daughter, was married to Mark Lopez, the cute Latino who had picked us up from the airport. They had a little girl named Tabby and twin boys, Liam and Ethan. All three kids were just like their dad, comedy all the way. Mia quietly whispered in my ear, "It's nice to see you again, Ivy."

"You too." I loved that she was like her father, private with personal information.

Sloane, a stunning Hungarian and Latino woman, was John's wife. I really liked John. He had a calming nature and was obviously very much in love with Sloane. They did not have any kids, but they did seem to love sneaking the kids candy while the others weren't watching.

I loved that the kids could be wild and free here. It seemed like the type of place where people could just be themselves, especially the children. Their shrieks of laughter and constant activity made me laugh out loud.

Catalina, who was married to Mike, had an interesting large angel tattoo on her back. I could see parts of it, and Savi confided that it covered the entire length of her back. They were most definitely an interesting pair. Mike, a huge man, was a walking piece of artwork himself. He was covered from head to toe in tattoos. I couldn't wait to get to know them better. Their daughter Gabriella was a real sweetheart.

Savi's husband, Cole, was the leader of Team Blackstone. He seemed a little intense but warmed up as the day went on. Savi explained he had a lot going on and asked me to give him time and I'd see him relax. Their daughter, Olivia, was the spitting image of Savi. Savi assured me she had the mind of her father, though. Apparently, very little ever got by that little girl. Their son, Easton, was hands down a clone of Cole. All I could do was chuckle at what would come later in life for them.

I wanted to get my office set up, but also enjoyed the chance to meet everyone and establish myself. I decided to stay outside with the kids, so I gave myself permission to just enjoy it and played with them.

By the time the evening came and dinner was cleaned up, I headed outside to the patio with a glass of wine in my hand. I sat and listened to the crickets, who were in full swing.

I thought of everyone I'd met, and I put my own little spin on each one in my head from what I remembered. It was fun to think of each couple in terms of their children. After I had spent a little time that afternoon playing with them, you could really tell whose child each one was. I made a game out of it. It helped a lot to concentrate on that and not allow my head to slip back to my own problems.

"There you are." Reid slid the door closed and sat next to me. "Well, you seemed to make an impression on everyone."

"Happy to hear it."

"The new guy should be arriving any time. He's got an impressive resume. Frank sure knows how to pick 'em."

"So does Cole." I smiled when I looked through the glass doors and saw John laughing with Mike. "I can see why you've stayed here for so long."

"Nowhere else has ever called to me like Shadows has." He tucked his hands in his pockets as he looked out at the lake. "How are—"

"I'm okay." I cut him off, hating that he worried about me so much. "You know who I'm worried about?"

"Mm?"

"Keith and his kids."

"Yeah," he dropped his head, "me too."

I didn't need him to tell me the story, and I let him know that. I'd hear it from the source at some point. The way Keith drifted off during dinner several times made me wonder where his mind went. The past? The future? I hoped I could help in some way.

"Keith has always been a big brother to Savi ever since she arrived here. Maybe check in with her from time to time too. They're very close, and she might need someone to talk to about it."

"I can do that." I made a mental note for later.

"Someone else you might want to talk to is John's wife, Sloane."

"Yeah? Is she close to Keith's wife?"

"No," he shook his head and kept his eyes on the lake, "she might be able to help *you*, though." I cleared my throat and shifted in my seat. There was enough going on in this house, and I didn't want the attention to be on me right now. I was a fixer and enjoyed that role. It did not sit well with me when it went the other way around.

"Reid, I'm not sure how to tell you this any other way, but I'm holding it together. I know it's ingrained in us to get our patients to speak up and voice their internal struggles, but there's nothing to voice. What happened, happened. I can't rewrite it. What I can do is just get through the storm and come out the other end with a better mindset and a new sense of awareness."

"Mm," he grunted, not liking my answer. "You know the problem with being a psychologist, Ivy?"

"What?" I felt tired.

"We always know what to say to make us sound fine when we're nowhere near it."

"That's a subject up for debate," I countered but looked away because he was right. I could talk myself out of many situations, and this wasn't one of them.

His smart watch alerted him of a text, and his eyes narrowed in on it.

"Our newest recruit has arrived." He waited for me to stand, but I shook my head. I needed a moment to clear my mind. My uncle had probed at a door that I had been doing my best to keep shut, at least for now. I needed a few minutes to nail it back into place. "I'll meet you inside." He kissed my head and left me to my thoughts.

Once I was alone, I covered my face with my hands and used the tips of my fingers to ease the beginnings of a headache in my forehead. The moment I closed my eyes, the horrible memory popped up and filled my mind with all I'd tried to bury. The creak of the handle as the door opened. I flinched at the sound, and then the tapping. A nail on the side table, just *tap, tap, tap, tap*. It sped up and got louder. *Tap, tap, tap, tap*. It forced me to my feet with a rush of anxiety. I wrung my hands and paced the floor in an effort to slow my heartbeat.

"It's not real," I whispered as I felt my heart pound my chest. "It's not real."

"Damn!" Mia stepped out on the patio with a grin, and I immediately dropped my arms and morphed into *everything is fine* mode. "I can't even begin to describe how hot the new guy is." I chuckled, but she must have caught my uneasiness because she studied me for a moment.

"What's he, ahh," I stumbled and tried to think of something to say, "look like?"

"Like a sexier version of Marco Dapper," she cooed.

"Who?"

"Carmine Basco from *The Young and the Restless*," she smiled like she was picturing him, "but like more rugged and grittier."

"Oh, that's intriguing." I looked over her shoulder through the glass door but couldn't spot him, but I did notice Savi coming toward us.

"Oh, my God," she stuck her head through the door, "he's so frickin' hot."

"Right?" Mia gushed as I laughed at the two of them.

"Mark was right. He does look like Marco Dapper."

Savi made me chuckle. Mark was comical and wonderfully comfortable with who he was as a person.

"He's got this haunted look, though," Mia added, "like his smile doesn't quite reach its full sexy capacity. Oh, baby, but when it finally does… watch out!"

"We call it the dark, sexy brood," Savannah filled me in, and I laughed harder.

As far as I could see, these ladies were surrounded by male models as a part of their daily life, and yet here they were with me, gushing over the new hottie inside. I loved it because it was real. They were being honest, and there was certainly nothing wrong with appreciating and looking. Men did it all the time.

"You're single, yes?"

"Yes, but not really looking." I had way too much going on inside to even entertain the idea of dating. But, typical me, my head had already jumped beyond her words. It just might be a good way to distract my uncle and certain others from worrying about me. Also, if I appeared to be doing normal things, maybe normal would come find me again. That was something I would tell my patients because I believed it to be true. We have the power to control our own outcomes. We just have to be willing to fight for it.

"Well, you need to take one for the team and meet him." Savi looked me up and down. "Although I might get a little jealous." She winked. "I may just have a little girl crush on you, and all that's happening right here." She waved a finger to indicate my gray fitted skirt, white blouse with ruffles down the V-neck, and leather-print high heels.

"I'm not so sure the office look rates very high on the sexy scale for men who wear fatigues most of the time," I joked. I was comfortable in my business wear. I felt I knew the type of man I would look for. At least I thought so. I had taken a break from dating after my fiancé and I broke up a few years back. We just fell out of love. We were still friends, but we both wanted more than that, and it just didn't seem to be there. We broke it off before either of us got hurt. I thought our parents were more upset than we were. One thing that came out of it was I realized that dating someone in my own field was boring. Two psychologists in a relationship was like a punch line for a joke. I needed to shake it up a little, but I just wasn't sure if I was ready yet.

"Take it from me, you'd be surprised how opposites attract." Savannah wiggled her eyebrows. "Come on. Let me introduce you."

I followed her inside and scanned the room. I didn't see anyone I hadn't yet met.

"Ivy?" Cole waved me over. "I'd like a word with you, please."

"Of course."

"Now, Cole?" Savi's face fell, but she backed off as she read her husband's face. "Sorry. We'll meet out here when you're finished, okay?" She winked at me and gave Cole's arm a pat.

"Lead the way." I smiled and followed him through

the kitchen and down the hall to his office. He partly closed the door.

"I apologize for taking you away from the others, but I assume you'd like to keep your personal situation private from the others?" He gave me a moment as I pulled at the cuff of my blouse and composed myself. I pushed away my discomfort at the topic. It wasn't easy to speak with anyone about my private life. I knew, however, that Cole had been brought up to speed on it or I wouldn't be here at all.

"Thank you, yes. I appreciate your discretion." He nodded and tapped a key on his keyboard.

"Frank called and—"

"Has he shown up?" I didn't mean to cut him off, but I didn't need to be warmed up to what was going on. I just wanted it straight.

"No." He looked away for a moment. "I'm sorry, Ivy, not yet."

"Go on."

"Frank is arriving tomorrow, and you, he, and Daniel will make the official report." I let out a huff of air and moved my hands to my hips, needing some kind of anchor. "He's already made a few calls, so it won't just be the CID on the call. Criminal Investigations—"

"Department. I know." I cut him off again, so I closed my eyes and pressed my lips together hard as I realized I was being rude. I looked up and made sure to look him square in the eyes. "My apologies, Cole. I know you're only relaying information to me." My voice wavered, and

I cleared my throat. "I'm afraid I've discovered I'm not very good at being on this side of the conversation."

"No one is, particularly when you're generally on the opposite one." He smiled warmly. "Look, Ivy, I won't lie. This isn't going to be easy. It'll get worse before it gets better. But you're safe here, and you've got a bunch of strong women to lean on. Each of them has been through tough experiences of their own, and I know if you take time to confide in any of them, they'll offer you advice and will support you in any way they can." He stood and waved his arm. "And our entire property is guarded with some of the best trained soldiers the US Army has. No one can touch you here."

I had once thought I was completely safe in my office but held back that comment.

"Thanks." I forced a smile. "Are we finished?"

"For now, yes." He motioned that I could leave, and I rushed out and headed for some much-needed air. I zipped out the front door, and as I reached the landing, I felt something soft jump over me, but I was too rattled to care. I headed for the protection of the shadows. Once I was safely tucked away on a bench where I was sure no one could see me, I let my guard down. Tears streamed down my face, my heart raced, and I fought to breathe. I knew I had to do this. I knew it was the right thing to do. It was my job to do it, but that didn't make me any less human. Any less terrified of being in the spotlight in front of *him*.

Jesus, Ivy, breathe!

My arms started to shake, and I felt my control slip away. Panic tore through me, and I let out a small cry. Shit, shit, shit. I knew what was happening, but I couldn't stop it. My mind spun, my heart wanted to claw its way out of my chest, my knees went weak.

"Whoa," someone said from far away, "I know that look." Hands appeared in front of me, and he held them up. "I'm going to touch you now. Is that all right?" I somehow nodded. His warm hands covered mine and started to massage my palms. "Focus on your hands, channel all of the panic down to me, and let me get rid of it." His voice was low and raspy. A faint smell of pine found my nose and gave one of my senses something to focus on. "Good." He continued to rub my hands, and I slowly came back down. "Now, breathe with me, in and out." His breath brushed over my face, and I found myself drawn to it. The black spots cleared from my vision as I took in the man in front of me.

Damn.

The shadows limited my view of his features, but I knew he was tall, large, and solid.

"Are you okay now?" He still rubbed, and I wasn't sure where my voice went.

"Yes." I sniffed but still felt some of the rawness nip at my chest just to make sure I knew it was still there. "Thank you."

"Glad I was here to help." He slowly let go of my hands, and I looked down at them as I felt the loss of his warm touch. I let them drop to my thighs. "Panic attacks don't go away on their own, you know. You might want to see someone about it."

"Yeah," I chuckled darkly, using the back of my hand to pat my face dry, "maybe."

"Are you coming inside?"

"I think I need a minute."

"All right, then." He paused.

"Ivy," I said before he left.

"Ty." He used the same short introduction. I nodded as he scooped up his bag and disappeared toward the house. I wanted to follow him. I felt a need to see what he actually looked like, but my feet stayed rooted in place. Yeah, I needed another moment.

SIX

Location: Rosarito, Mexico
Coordinates: Cartel Operations

ERIC

Sweat trickled down my neck and soaked the collar of my shirt, which only added to the discomfort I was already in. The gold chain around my neck heated and seemed to burn my skin as the temperature continued to rise in the small room. I fingered my cross and adjusted the position of the chain. I hated the summer heat but was glad of the fact that I became more useful in the summer. The tourists who plagued the tropical coast looking for a good time constantly passed by the window. I curled my lips at the sight of them, so carefree. Little did they know what was happening a mere six feet away.

"Why is a gringo here?" The asshole client shot me a nasty look, but I gave no sign I even heard him.

"He's one of ours. He might look like a tourist but that's good, no? No one suspects he works for us," Alejandro explained.

I oversaw these meetings, but I liked to get a feel of who I was working with before I showed who I really was. That was where my buddy Alejandro came into play. He started the meetings, and I ended them.

"He looks like American beef." The asshole slapped his arm and showed a tight arm muscle as he laughed, making fun of my big build. "Doesn't seem like he has much for brains either."

"Are we here to talk about him or the job you want us to take on?" Alejandro tried to steer him back on course.

"I need five white and three exotics." He wiggled his bushy eyebrows. "Women between sixteen and nineteen. Nothing older. No track marks. I want clean, and I need them by this weekend." I shook my head and chuckled and wondered who he thought he was. His gaze quickly turned nasty at me. "I was told you could do the job."

"We can, we can," Alejandro assured him with a smile, "but you want these girls in three days? Man, we need at least four." Alejandro held his ground.

"I could just shoot you and your gringo instead." He smirked, and I decided it was time to speak up.

"Or I could just call Denton Barlow?" I spoke in perfect Spanish and watched his brows go up when he realized I could understand everything the entire time. I lifted an eyebrow back at him and rubbed a hand over my thick beard. I hated my beard, but it hid my facial expressions well. I looked young without it, and I needed to look old and weathered if I wanted any respect around here. It was the curse of my light skin.

"He's dead. Prison shakedown."

I smirked. "That's what they want you to believe." I gnawed on the toothpick I held between my teeth and felt sweat roll down my back. It was unbearably hot now, and the lack of breeze in this shit-smelling room didn't help. I caught Alejandro's gaze and shook my head slightly, so he'd look away.

"And how do you know Denton?" The man turned to see me better.

"He's my cousin. He's the one who got me into this business, and he's the one who can take you out of it with one phone call." I leaned forward to make my point. "We're good to make the extraction. You know that because you're here. But what you want is impossible in the time you're asking for. Like my buddy said, four days max and we'll have them for you. They'll be clean girls, top of the line, and ready for you to take back to wherever the hell you crawled out from." I used a rag and wiped my forehead.

"Three days."

"Look, I don't give a shit if you want this deal or not. I have other clients who know who I am and what I'm capable of. So, if you're done wasting my time, I'm done drowning in a pool of sweat while you demand something I can't give." I wanted to get out of this sweatbox of a room. When I stood, my men stood along with me, and we left the asshole to chew over what he wanted to do.

I walked the alley between the two buildings. I hated taking the streets because every local with some type of shell shit they'd glued or tied together wanted to make a few bucks from the tourists. They always tried to hit me up like I was here for spring break. I shook my head and wondered for the thousandth time what people did with that junk once they got it back home.

"Hey, I thought Denton was dead," Filippo, one of my newest guys, asked as he raced to keep up with his short legs.

"Yeah, he is, but that shithead doesn't have to know that," Alejandro explained as he walked with us. "He needs to think there's a small possibility he isn't. Stuff like that keeps us at the top of the tree." He tapped his head. "The fact that Eric is Denton's cousin helps us, dead or alive. That blood tie keeps the amateurs away."

At the end of the alley, I stopped near a vendor and turned on the hose next to him. I let the cool water run down over my head and back. I ignored the vendor's offer of a towel as I turned off the tap.

"And here we go." Alejandro held up his phone, and I

motioned for him to answer it. He stepped away while Filippo stood guard. He was young and smart; I'd picked him up at the border after watching him attempt to make some fast cash. I liked the way he worked. He learned fast and kept his head down. I'd tested him a few times since with cash laying around and a few expensive items left here and there. He never bit, so I took him under my wing and somewhat trusted him to have my back.

"Four days, eight girls, and we've made mega money." Alejandro grinned as he tossed me a shirt from a vendor's rack and handed the guy a bill. I knew these locals made very little. A lot of the guys who worked Rosarito would just take what they wanted, but I didn't do business that way. I found it helped to keep the locals friendly. Because…

"Mr. Noah, maybe have a look." The vendor handed me the phone I'd given him awhile back and pointed for me to skim the photos he'd taken. It was important for me to know if anyone was encroaching on my territory. I worked hard to build my business here and had proven myself time and time again to the Castillo family I worked under. They were ranked pretty high in the Cartel, and I intended to make sure I kept my seat at the table at the end of the day. Trafficking was a competitive business, and if you were smart, there was a lot of money to be made.

"Shit," I cursed in English when I looked at the photos. Juan and his three dumbass goons could be seen as they scoped out the spring break crowd. I knew they would be on the lookout for those who were well dressed and looked like they had money. I shook my head. You needed to be smart with who you plucked off the street. They had to be nobodies, wanderers, or at the very least girls who you could tell were on the run. It didn't take much talk to figure out which ones were safe to take.

"Are they still here?"

"*Sí*, they are staying over there." He pointed to a rundown building most tourists avoided.

"Alejandro, take Filippo and flush them out," I ordered and took a seat on an upside-down bucket and lit a joint. I didn't do the dirty work unless I had to. I'd learned early on to keep my hands clean of everything I could.

They rushed off, and I handed the phone back to the owner.

"Take a seat." I nodded.

"*Sí, gracias*." He did as he was told and tried to relax. I pulled a pile of cash from my wallet and dropped some on his table.

"You did good, so I reward you. See, I keep my promises."

"*Sí, gracias*," he repeated and tucked the money away.

"If you have any trouble, you let me know," I added. I liked the owner. I chose not to learn his name. Names were connections, and I sure didn't need any.

"*Sí*." He nodded as he stood and stepped aside when my guys pulled Juan and the others over behind some cars. I whisked over to them and pointed my gun at Juan's head.

"Why are you here, Juan? Looking for a death wish?"

"You don't own Rosarito," he hissed. "I was just visiting some friends."

"Funny, because I remember making it very clear to you before that this was my town." I dragged the tip of the gun over the scar I'd left him above his eye.

"Work has been slow, Eric." He used my name, and I cracked him on the skull for doing so. "Ah!" he yelped but didn't cower. "Those fuckers in the US, the army wannabes, are making clients jumpy. And there's been talk."

"Talk?" I repeated.

"That they're cracking down on that new operation, Los Débiles."

"Keep talking."

"I got word they're headed down here in a few days."

I'd heard nothing about this.

"Why? And speak faster." I knew I had only minutes before someone saw me and might start to record.

"Sources say—"

"What sources do you have?" I laughed in his face.

"My cousin, Tomás, he lives in Washington, got himself a job near the country's main Army hub. He's got ears everywhere." He ran his mouth like a canary. "He's got this girl whose brother works at a food truck, too. He hears all kinds of shit."

"Like?" Lord, he was dumb.

"Like that the wannabes are coming here, based off some tip they got that Los Débiles is being run from Rosarito."

I contemplated driving my fist into his skull, but now that he'd actually provided me with something useful, I figured I could use him for a bit longer.

"Congratulations. Today, you're not a total idiot." I pushed him backward, and he stumbled to catch his footing. I thought for a moment then tucked my gun away as a bunch of very white-skinned girls in bikinis walked by on the street. Juan practically licked his lips. "Don't be an idiot," I warned. "Listen, maybe for once you can be useful." He smiled like the dumb fuck he was and gave me his attention. I hoped I wasn't going to regret this. "If you want work, I've got some." I nodded at Alejandro to give him his number. He snatched the phone from his goon and typed the number in. "If you do this without screwing it up, I'll consider hiring you more."

"I won't." He acted annoyed, but I knew he needed this.

"Under one condition." I stepped closer. "You relay any information from your contact in Washington to me first. Understood?"

"Yeah." He raised his chin at me like he was hard, and I rolled my eyes.

"Good. Now get the fuck off my territory and don't even think of touching anything on your way out."

We watched them leave, and Alejandro looked up at me.

"You think that was a wise idea?"

"He's got something I don't. Yes, it's wise." I shot him a look for questioning me. I looked at my watch. "Let's go."

We headed back toward the alley, and the shade from the buildings was a sweet relief from the blazing sun. Once I had it in sight, I started to veer away from the others. I spotted Grim Gates as he stepped from his blacked-out 1965 Pontiac Catalina. He was expensively dressed as usual. I stepped back and watched as he nodded at some biker then walked over to him and they had a few words. I wondered what that was about. As the bike started up, its noisy engine roared, and as he pulled away, I noticed the striped snake on his back.

What Castillo was to Mexico, Grim was to the United States, and no one messed with him if they could help it. He was younger than me by about ten to twelve years and had more connections to the underground than most would ever want to know. I knew his history and was smart enough to keep plenty of distance between him and me. The thing about Grim was once you saw him; you'd never forget him.

I huffed to myself as he walked away. It rubbed me raw that he'd been seen with Talya. I hadn't spoken to her since I broke her heart, and keeping myself distanced from her had helped, but when Alejandro showed me a picture of the two of them the other day, I felt like I'd been hit by a truck. Grim disappeared into a house, and I shook the nasty thoughts away.

"I'll meet you back at the house," I ordered.

"Where does he disappear to?" Filippo asked.

"Church." Alejandro answered his question.

"But he only goes a few times a month. How's that even worth it?"

"Don't question the boss. I've only ever asked him once if he wanted company, and I'll never ask him again."

"Why?"

"Because he might just shoot you. He'll never answer you, anyway. If it brings him peace, what do you care?"

SEVEN

TY

I dropped my duffle bag on the floor next to my other belongings and took a breath before I entered the living room. I'd met a few of them outside, but it was time to meet the rest.

"Not a fan of crowds?" A guy came up behind me and smiled.

"Just getting used to being around people who don't want to kill me." I went with honesty as I held out a hand. "Ty Beckett."

"John Black." He folded his arms and looked back at the room.

"I've heard a little about you, Black."

"You as well. I'm looking forward to seeing you in action. Your resume is impressive."

"Don't believe all you hear."

"Spoken like a true soldier." He smiled. He was right. Most soldiers didn't want the attention for what we did. We all did the job for our own reasons, but mainly because we believed in making a difference. It sounded so patriotic, but it was the truth. "I didn't spend as much time away from the United States as you did, especially consecutively, but I can promise you this place is great, especially after being over there." I shifted uneasily and tried to push back the image of Brown's face. "Welcome to the family." He sounded sincere.

"Thanks."

"A word of advice, watch out for that one." He pointed to a woman who had just stepped out the door. She rolled her eyes, and he laughed as he hurried off.

"Don't listen to John." She grinned and held out her hand. "Hi. I'm Sloane, that big lug's wife. It's a pleasure to meet you, Ty."

"You too, Sloane." I took a step into the room and let my eyes adjust as I surveyed the exits.

"Hey, Ty." Dr. Roberts suddenly appeared, no doubt sensing my unease. "I can take it from here, Sloane." He smiled, and she inclined her head and moved away. "Let's make this really easy on you."

"Okay."

"That's Colonel Logan's wife, Savannah, now talking with Sloane. That woman pretending not to look at you is Catalina." He chuckled. "Lexi's not home right now, but she's Keith's wife. Keith's the guy in gray by the window." He pointed to each person as he talked. "They're all trying to give you some space while the women, on the other hand, can't wait to sink their claws into you." He laughed again, and I assumed this was the norm. I got it.

"I get that." I went for a smile. "My sister is the same way."

"The kids are out on an adventure with Abigail and her sister June, who you'll meet later. And," his smile softened as he looked over my shoulder at someone behind me, "this is the newest addition to the house, besides you, of course, Dr. Ivy Knight."

Ivy…

I turned to see her, that drop-dead gorgeous woman I'd met earlier in a sliver of porch light. If I hadn't already met her, I mightn't have caught her glossy eyes. This time I took in her whole look and not just those eyes. She was dressed in a sexy business look. Her slender shoulders and small waist were wrapped in a gray blouse that dipped just low enough to show a little cleavage. Her long blonde hair reached all the way down to her waist. I drank her in. I couldn't help it. She was incredible. I'd lived among soldiers for the past eight years, and it had obviously affected my judgement. I couldn't help my eyes as they traveled down her body. Her slender, tanned legs under that tight skirt ended in a set of incredibly sexy heels. I really missed the female body. I knew I had to speak, but my tongue was glued to the roof of my mouth. I managed to take a breath.

"Dr. Knight," Dr. Roberts coughed as I remained silent, "this is Tyler Beckett, our newest recruit."

"Nice to meet you, Dr. Knight." I found my voice, but it sounded odd even to my own ears. I acted like our previous encounter had never happened. No one needed to know.

"You as well, Beckett." Relief took over her face and she seemed to relax. Her pink lips stretched into a warm smile, and her green eyes lit up when she made eye contact again. "You just returned from Afghanistan, correct?"

My gut twisted, but I pushed past it.

"Yes, ma'am. I just came off a special ops assignment."

"Congratulations on your promotion." Dr. Roberts held his glass up to me. "Beckett was just promoted to major."

"Oh, you're a major now." She smiled. "That's impressive."

"And well deserved, too," Dr. Roberts added as he looked about the room. "Please excuse me."

We stood in silence for a moment.

"Thanks," she scrunched up her face, "for not saying anything about…"

"It was dark. I couldn't see your face, anyway." I winked, and she smiled with a nod. "So, what kind of a doctor are you?"

"Psychologist." She lifted a shoulder. "Might seem a little funny, given what you witnessed out there."

"Why?" I tilted my head to one side. "Aren't psychologists people too?"

"Yeah," she gave a little laugh, "I guess we are." She

seemed lost in thought for a moment, and I knew there had to be a story about what happened out there. It seemed to be weighing on her. "I worked in Washington and just recently moved over here to work at Shadows."

"You were working at our headquarters?"

"I was, yes. I worked with some of the soldiers who had come back from Afghanistan."

Interesting.

"What had you make the jump over here?" I wanted to spend more time with her, so I kept the conversation going. I felt comfortable with Ivy. We were both newbies here, and it gave us a connection. I could see that the others occasionally glanced our way and appreciated that they were giving us a little space.

"I just needed a change." She shifted her wine glass to the other hand as though nervous about something. "It will take a little getting used to, though. You know, all the trees, and wind, and wood." She fumbled with her words, and I hid my laugh.

"Well, I'm glad I'm not the only new person here."

"Yeah." She looked around and spotted Cole's wife, who gave her a thumbs up, but she quickly looked away.

Something hit me, and I looked back down at her.

"Will you be working with me and my team or with Blackstone?"

"Blackstone."

"Good."

"Good?" Her perfectly arched eyebrow rose, and I

found myself lost in her features again. She really was a beautiful woman.

"Mhmm," was all I offered, and she squinted like she was trying to read my mind.

"I'm not sure if I should be offended or not." She chuckled into her glass and took a long sip. She stood tall and pushed her shoulders back as if she'd found her confidence, and she seemed to enjoy our banter, which was even more attractive.

"Or not." I played along but found myself steering the conversation in a different direction. "Did you leave a lot of people behind when you moved here?"

"What brought you here to Shadows?" She pivoted around the question while she rested her wine glass against her breast and peered up at me. "Tired of living in a land of dust and Taliban?" she threw back.

"Ah, I hit a sore spot. Okay." I lightly laughed, and her smile twisted as she tried to hide that I'd hit the nail on the head.

"Or maybe it's time for you to answer a question, Major."

"You don't like me on the other side of the chair?" I challenged, and something flickered across her face, but before I could read it, she looked away. I wanted to reach out and tilt her chin to look at me, to keep her gorgeous eyes on me, but I forced my hand down.

"Beckett," Logan spotted me as he came into the room, "I see you've met Dr. Knight."

"Yes," I nodded, "we were just getting to know one

another." I gave her a glance, and she returned it. There was a strange sense of tug and pull between us, and I found it rather fun.

"Great." Cole looked around. "Let me introduce you to my team, and then we'll get you settled in your room. Wake up is zero-five-hundred, and we start training at zero-five-thirty." He glanced at Ivy. "Your things arrived this afternoon, Dr. Knight. I had Mark and Mike leave everything in your office."

"Oh, good. I appreciate that." She glanced down the hall like she was planning her retreat once Logan pulled me away.

"If you need anything at all, you know who to ask." Cole smiled at her.

"Will do." She stepped away, and I followed Logan to meet the others.

Team Blackstone soon put me at ease. It was like I was back with my team in Afghanistan. They were easy, light, and even when things fell silent, they were comfortable with it.

Mark seemed to be the life of the party and had no problem sharing stories about their adventures in Mexico. Keith was the quiet one, but he seemed to enjoy sharing what kind of weapons and equipment they used.

"I have a friend who knows how to find anything you want," Keith informed me. "If you need anything, let me know, and she'll find it." I noticed Mike gave John a knowing look and wondered what that was about.

"Okay, good to know." I got a rush at the idea of stepping back into combat. I craved the Army life, and it seemed these guys did, too. Cole was mostly all business until his wife Savannah came over.

"So, Ty," she leaned into Cole, and his face immediately softened as he kissed her head affectionately, "what do you think of Shadows?"

"He's seen the entry way and living room," Mike teased. "Don't be coming over here and doing your wifey thing."

"It's nine p.m., Mike. Do you know where your wife is?" She gave him a pointed look, and his face morphed into excitement.

"That's right, the kids are gone! Whoop! Tell the wife I'm on the way." He shoved his beer into Mark's hand and whisked out the door while the rest of us laughed.

"I know I'm gonna like it here. Thanks, Savannah." I nodded politely. "It'll just take some getting used to."

"I would imagine." Mark nodded. "When was the last time you slept in a real bed?"

"It's been a while."

"After training tomorrow, we'll give you a tour of the house and grounds, and then we'll walk you through our next mission." Cole read something off his phone as he spoke.

"When do we ship out?"

"We're on call. That's all we know."

"Can't he have one night off?" Savannah scoffed. "I'm sorry, Ty."

"It's all I know." I shrugged. "It's my comfort zone."

"Well, we're going to break you of that," she smiled, "starting with, I see you've met Ivy—"

"And that's enough from you, little lady." Mark pulled her from Cole's side and pushed her on her way.

"What?" She laughed all the way back to Sloane.

"They have the best intentions, but they love playing matchmaker." Mark pointed at someone who had just come into the room. As she approached us, Mark put a hand on her shoulder. "Please intervene with that one," he begged and pointed to Savannah.

"Provoke her?" She gave him an evil grin. "On it!"

"I swear to God," Mark chuckled, "they'll be the ones to take me down, not the Cartel."

"That's his wife, Mia." Cole filled me in.

John came up and joined us, adding his chuckle to show he'd overheard Mark's comment.

"Speaking of the Cartel, why don't you fill me in a little more on Los Débiles."

Cole looked over at me with a strange expression then glanced at Mark.

"Yeah, all right, let's do this." He waved at me to follow, and John leaned in.

"You're going to fit in well with us."

"Why?" I had to ask.

"You like to work, and so does Logan." He fell in step with me as we trailed Mark and Cole.

What he'd said was true. Besides, socializing, especially in groups, just wasn't my scene. I stepped into the office, and Cole closed the door.

By the time we were finished, I felt confident I had a better picture of what we would be dealing with. The Cartel was gaining speed with their new operations, and for us to have any effect, we needed to cover the whole country and work with our informants over there. Once my team was fully functioning, Frank wanted us to focus our attention on Rosarito and the rest of the west. Dusk's team would handle the east, and Blackstone would focus on mid-country.

I had much to learn and was glad Cole was an excellent teacher. He was a cut and dry detail kind of guy, and I liked it. The Cartels had many similarities with the Taliban, but on a much higher scale. They had endless amounts of money. They were ruthless with their kills, showed no mercy to their own people, and their government sounded totally corrupt, with a lot of politicians in their pocket. The fact that they were in our own back yard rather than in the middle of a third- world country starved for freedom made it that much harder to swallow.

"All right," Cole stood after he turned off the projector he'd streamed from his laptop, "let's call it for the night. Ty, stay for a moment."

"Yes, sir." I stayed in my seat while the others left.

"Fifteen minutes, boys." Mark chuckled from the hallway.

The moment the work talk stopped, my head shot right back to Hill and Brown. I blinked and tried to clear it, but it was a struggle.

"I appreciate your desire to jump right in and learn

this stuff, and I know you've been cleared by Doc Roberts, but I have to ask, will you be up for our next mission if they need us, say, by tomorrow?"

"Yes." I didn't miss a beat, and he rubbed his bottom lip while he thought.

"I can see it on your face." He studied me. "You're carrying a lot."

"I am." I nodded. "I'm sure you understand when I say it's the price of being a leader. You can't predict the outcome in our line of work. Shit happens at the worst of times." I took a deep breath to stem the rage that still threatened every time I allowed myself to go there. "I've been a soldier nearly my entire life. It's what I know. I've worked my way from the bottom up because I need to challenge myself. But I know my limits. I gave you my word I'm right for this job, and I intend to keep it."

He eyed me for a moment and seemed to come to a decision, and his face cleared.

"Okay, good to hear." He stood and checked his watch. "I have a few emails to send off, and," he smiled at the door that had just opened a crack, "Savi is here to show you to your room."

"See you tomorrow, then." I got up and smiled at Savannah, who took my arm as we walked down the hall.

"In case the guys forget to tell you, that's Dr. Roberts' office." She pointed to an open door on my left. "Don't skip his appointments. He *will* find you." She spoke in her soft voice and followed it with a laugh. "And this here," she pointed to a closed door, "is Dr. Ivy Knight's office."

"Got it." I peered down at her and saw her attempt to hide a grin as she eyed the door.

"I want to show you something else you might benefit from." I followed her to the kitchen, and we stopped at the island. "I've had my fair share of mind-numbing headaches." She closed her eyes and swallowed as though she pushed back a dark memory. "Right here, top shelf, are some pain meds. If you need something stronger, ask Doc Roberts, but it might require an extra session." Savi chuckled as she handed me a bottle of water and two painkillers.

"You sure have a pulse on this place, don't you?"

"They're my family and helped me through some very difficult times. It's the least I can do." She smiled warmly.

"It's in you, dear, to be mothering." Daniel Logan placed a hand on her shoulder as he set a radio on a charging block. "It comes naturally." He moved his attention over to me. "Headache?"

"Yes." I wasn't going to lie. "Nothing a few pills won't fix."

"Well, if they get worse…"

"I heard Doc Roberts was the man to see." I gave a pointed look at Savannah.

"Hey," John nodded and pulled a beer from the fridge, "did you get the tour?"

"I did." I welcomed the change in topic. Suddenly,

Mark came in, and John flew to the other side of the room.

"Was it something I said?" Daniel looked at the two of them. "What's going on?"

"The guys watched this ridiculous movie last night called *Tag*," Savannah explained. "Now it's exploded, and everyone is involved."

"It's true." Mark nodded. "We even got the staff in on it."

"Tag?" Daniel repeated and seemed confused. "Like, tag you're it?" He leaned over and hit Mark's shoulder.

"Yeah, but there's words to go with it."

"Oh, you mean," a long smirk drew across Daniel's face, "'suck it, sucker, you're it'?"

Mark's eyes bugged out, and Savannah burst out laughing as she fled the room.

"Your brother got me last night." Daniel rolled his eyes. "I thought I'd keep it in the family."

"That's cold, Daniel, cold!" He stood and pointed a finger in Daniel's face. "Be happy you're immune from me right now because—"

"Because what?" Savannah chirped from somewhere, laughing so hard she could barely speak.

"Savi!" He raced out of the room, and she yelped.

"Welcome to the house, Beckett." Daniel winked as Savannah raced back in and fixed her shirt, out of breath.

"Shall we continue?"

"That depends. Are you it?" I raised an eyebrow at her and thought how carefree and nice it was here. I hoped over time I'd get to that point of carefree living. Savannah smirked.

"Me?" She waved me off. "I just tossed Cole in his path."

"Ruthless."

"You'd be wise to remember that." She pointed to leave the room. "All right, let's keep going. Up here," she pointed upward as we climbed the stairs, "will be your team's wing of the house. The rooms are empty now, of course, Team Blackstone used to be there, but now they stay in family cabins farther out on the property."

I couldn't help but feel odd with all the vacant space around me. It wasn't the kind of space I was used to or that I enjoyed. I'd be glad when there were men here to fill the void.

"As team leader, you get this room." She continued as she pushed open a door. I was shocked at how huge it was. It looked like an apartment, with everything you could imagine in it, even a fireplace and mini fridge.

"This really isn't necessary." I felt completely out of place.

"It is to us, Ty." Her face softened. "You're to be the leader of a new team here at Shadows. Do you have any idea how many people we looked at for that position? Hundreds, until Frank came in and handed us a short stack and said he thought you were the best one for the job. I'm not sure how well you know Frank, but he never puts his name on anyone. Ever. You might not think you're worth this, but he does, my husband and I do. The entire team does. Though Cole made the final call, all those men down there had their say. Don't sell yourself short just because you've been living over there all these years. You're needed here now, and this is what you've earned. Besides, this room isn't all that different from the others."

I forced back my discomfort and nodded.

"Thanks."

"Good." She looked around while she held on to the door handle. "This room holds a lot of good memories for me, and I hope it will for you, too."

"This was Cole's room, then?"

"Yes. Later, I'll show you something cool about that wall over there." She pointed. "But I'm sure you're tired, so I'll leave you be."

"So, no other room is being used right now?" I looked down the massive hallway.

"They're mostly all empty." She smiled warmly and left me to get settled.

I looked at my bags. Someone had brought them up here, and I didn't know where to begin. The bracelet Halim made me was in my pocket. I pulled it out and hung it off the light on the nightstand. The wolf dangled in the air, and I thumbed the engraving. Hard to believe I wouldn't be going back there. I knew I had to get my head back on straight and gave myself a mental shake.

I reached down and grabbed one of my bags and tossed it on the bed. As I did, I heard a noise in the hall and went to check it out. Ivy stood in front of one of the doors. She seemed to be unsure and held out her hand and studied it like she was a bit shaky. I could hear her as she took a deep breath and let it out with a huff.

"Are you okay?" I called, and she gave a little squeak and jumped at the sound of my voice. "Sorry if I scared you."

"No problem. It's just been a day." She gave a small wave. "Good night, Ty." She disappeared inside the room and closed the door with a firm click.

So, I do have company on this floor.

———

Dr. Roberts' office was a lot different than I expected it to be. I'd been to enough sessions to know what the rooms were usually like. A cold room, with a clock on a table, and a maybe a plant for color. The Army wasn't known for anything warm and fuzzy, particularly in their spaces, so I did a bit of a double take when I walked into his room. It felt more like a living room, and it put me at ease right away. I guessed that was his plan, and it worked.

"Please take a seat." He pointed to a comfortable looking couch across from him, and I hesitated. "Or would that one be more your comfort level?" He pointed to the one against the wall. I headed for that one and leaned an arm on the armrest in an effort to look comfortable. "How are you feeling today? Head any better?"

"It comes and goes," I answered truthfully.

"Did you have headaches before?"

"Before what?" I shifted and cleared my throat.

"Before the death of Brown." He studied me, and I tried to hold still and not react.

"No."

"I see that on your last mission, you endured a lot of gunfire and explosives." He tapped his screen. "Seemed pretty intense." I shrugged. "Do you think any of that could contribute to your headaches?"

"Sure."

"Does noise or sound hurt your head?" I shook my head. "Does the mention of Brown's name bring pain to your head?" A laser noise pierced through my skull again, and I couldn't control my thumb this time. I pushed it into my eye to seek any kind of relief. "I see." He gave me a break for a second as he scribbled something down then studied me. I waited for it. I figured it was coming, those four haunting letters that surely would flip my entire life to shit. *PTSD*. "How are you sleeping?"

"Not too badly. The mattress is nice." That made him smile.

"Yes, I suppose it's a step up from the ground or a military cot. What about dreams or nightmares?" He sensed my unease and removed his glasses then pushed his iPad off to the side. "Ty, I've been working at Shadows for years. I've seen and heard it all. What you went through that day with the loss of one of your brothers has been experienced right here by men within these walls. We've lost good men and even had a traitor in the family. I'm not looking for a way to send you back home. I'm looking for a way to help you through this." He paused. "War is the ugly side of freedom. One most will never understand. Though you're wired to be a soldier, that doesn't mean you're not human. So, when I ask you these questions, I'm not looking for the right answer. I'm looking for a way in to help you heal."

I let out a long breath and let his words sink in. Frank said Doc Roberts was the best, and I was beginning to see he was right. Trust was hard for me, but I lowered my guard and let him in. Really, I had nothing to lose at that point.

"The nightmare doesn't just come at night." I cleared my throat. "It's whenever I let my mind idle or close my eyes or… you get the point."

"I do. You mentioned the nightmare, as in one. So, it's the same one?"

"Yes, the moment Brown was shot, murdered, and when I'm trying to stop the bleeding." I rubbed my palms into my fatigues. "Just a constant loop."

"All right." He pulled his iPad back onto his lap and started to write with his electronic pen. "Is it the only dream that you have, or are you soundly sleeping the rest of the time?"

"No," I rubbed my head, "it's just that." *All the fucking time.*

"Are you able to control it, stop the loop from spinning?"

"Sometimes, yeah," I shook my head and tried to find

the words to explain. "There's a place I go in my head. It's quiet, free of screams, like, you know." He nodded. "No bullets zipping by or angry yelling, that sort of thing."

"Do you see anything when you go there in your head?" Doc Roberts kept his voice calm and low.

"Yeah, I'm standing on the edge of a lake. I hear loon sounds way off in the distance. I've got my fishing rod, and I can see my lure just below the surface. I'm waiting for a bite. There's this smell, this fresh scent. I can't pinpoint what it is, but it makes me feel settled. Like I know that's where I'm supposed to be at that very moment." I rubbed my head again, uneasy with his eyes on me.

"Do you recognize the location?"

"No, but it could be anywhere. I mean, it's just trees and water. No landmark or anything."

"Your file says you're tapped into your sixth sense pretty well. Does anything at all about this place make you nervous or unsure?"

"No, the opposite, actually." I waited a moment. "All right, so what's it mean?" He continued to look at me. "I mean, isn't that what you docs do? You let me tell you about some strange moment that really didn't happen, then you tell me some kind of metaphor about it?" He smiled, and I suddenly felt vulnerable. "You're going to ask what do *I* think it means, aren't you?" I grimaced.

"Actually, that's not what I was going to say at all." He held my gaze as I waited for him to say something insightful. Something that was supposed to make me feel better.

It wouldn't. I knew that much. I may have left South Central Asia, but I was stuck in a war in my head. I wasn't sure what was worse. At least then I had something physical to fight. "Ty, I honestly think there will come a moment when all that anger and loss of control that loops over and over in your head will finally dissolve, and you'll find your peace. It will just take time."

"So, you're saying *you* can see the future?" I knew I was being a bit of an asshole, but my frustration with it all was overwhelming.

"Maybe?" He chuckled. "I've heard of crazier things. What I'm saying is that I think when you're ready, you're going to make that moment happen yourself. That place you go in your head, it's a happy, safe place for you, and the more you go there and allow yourself to relax, you'll find peace, and you'll discover what the smell is."

"Do we have a time stamp on this date with the loon?"

"I don't. It's when you're ready to find it."

EIGHT

IVY

There are no bugs, lizards, or snakes. There are no bugs, lizards, or snakes, I chanted in my head as I veered around a corner. *Nature is your friend if you let it in.*

My feet beat the uneven ground, and my arms pumped furiously as I ran. My mind was everywhere it shouldn't be. I ran because it cleared my mind, but not today. There was a battle going on in my head between insects, reptiles, and *him*. As hard as I tried not to let it, he once again won and took over my head, and I almost lost control.

Focus. Birds. I like birds. They chirped and perched on the branches that shielded me from the sun. Their pretty little songs flooded the forest with sound. The green leaves fluttered in the breeze and joined in with the melody. A squirrel scurried up on a rock and made a noise, mad that I was there, I assumed. The *tap-tap-tap* of a woodpecker could be heard. I shuddered as his face flashed in front of me again.

No.

I picked up speed and followed the narrow, beaten path Sloane had spoken so highly about.

She was a runner too and had asked me to join her, but I hadn't slept well and got up and left well before five. Cole had assured me it was safe at all hours to be out here. I knew there were armed men who patrolled the property, but I hadn't spotted any yet. I wondered if I would.

When my legs and lungs screamed at me to stop, I checked the time and saw it was nearly six. I turned to walk back and felt the buzz against my arm. I took a moment to see the text message that had popped up.

Frank: See you in an hour.

Shit.

I had run a fair distance, and I didn't want to be late, so I picked up speed and headed back. I managed to clear my head and began to enjoy the run. Suddenly, my nerves were set off. I felt someone or heard something, and I glanced over my shoulder. I couldn't see anything. The coast was clear, I told myself and forced back the uneasy feeling that had come over me. One thing I'd found about the situation I'd been in lately was that being alone didn't bring the same kind of peace it once had. No, I was riddled with uneasy thoughts and darkness. This wasn't who I was. I was a happy, loving person destined to help as many people as I could. My heart leapt in my throat again when the noise returned. I whipped my head around to look over my shoulder and did a double take at who, or rather what, was coming up behind me.

A huge German shepherd flew by me, and I slammed on my brakes as my lungs gasped for air. He stopped and turned to face me, then plunked his butt down in the middle of the trail and opened his mouth. His tongue flopped out like the dog in *Coco*. "Please tell me you belong to someone and you're not here to make me your breakfast?" I chuckled shakily. I loved animals, but cats were more my speed. Their dicky personalities, and the fact that they really couldn't give two shits about their owners made them super appealing. I spotted the gold-colored tag around his neck. "Well, you have a collar on, so that's a good sign," I nervously said to him. "I'm really not that tasty."

All seventy-five or so pounds of him suddenly stood, and he yelped. I did, too.

"Tripper," someone called, and I felt an immediate sense of relief. Keith emerged from the brush dressed in fatigues. He looked like he'd been on a stroll through the jungle. He whistled, and the dog was at his side in an instant.

"Hey, Ivy." He came toward me as the dog matched his steps. "I hope Tripper didn't scare you."

"I'm in the woods. A butterfly'd give me the creeps." I

dripped with sarcasm, and he chuckled. "So, your dog's name is Tripper."

"Yes, but he's not mine. He's John's. He just likes my hikes better." He rubbed the pup's head, and Tripper's tongue flailed around.

"Ah, yes, I've heard thick jungle walks are good for the soul."

"Ha," he chuckled again, "something like that." He motioned for me to start the walk back toward the house. "I see you and I have a session this afternoon."

"That's right, we do."

"Any chance we could have it now?"

I glanced at my watch and thought how very out of my norm it would be to not have my session in an office. I had to remember that these guys felt more comfortable outside.

"I have thirty minutes before I meet Frank, so sure, until then, I'm all yours."

"Thanks," he said then fell silent, so I took the lead.

"So, normally I'd ask you a bit about yourself, then I'd share that I've worked for the military since I graduated from university, so I'm not your typical psychologist. You know, the type who wants to wear gloves when dealing with their patients. People have real stuff going on, but soldiers have it at a whole different level. Anyway, let's skip all that for now." I looked up to see him nod and knew he'd heard me.

"I know you've worked with Dr. Roberts, so you've had the best from the best. But if I'm going to take over from him, I have to do things my way. I'm going to give it to you real, Keith, and sometimes it might seem that you've been through it all before with him. I know you guys are survivors, but I also know how important it is to talk things out after your missions. It's how you stay healthy in the long run. I make sure all my patients continue to make progress." I paused. "As for you, I could start this off by acting like I haven't observed a few things, but I'm not going to do that. I'd guess you're not one to bullshit around a topic, correct?" He looked at me with an unreadable expression, but I could tell he liked my approach.

"Correct."

"Tell me about your wife, Lexi." He wavered in his step but cleared his throat and took a deep breath.

"We were high school sweethearts. Had our life figured out. Then one day I joined the Army and didn't talk to her about it first."

"Why?"

"I don't know."

"Yes, you do. You just don't want to admit it."

"All right." He paused. "Because it made sense to me."

"And?" I knew there was more.

"And I knew she wouldn't like it, wouldn't want me to go."

"Okay, so you joined, and then what?"

"She flipped out, and I left." He rubbed his head. "We kept in touch for a while, but when her parents were murdered, and I couldn't be there, it broke her. I still feel guilty about it."

"Yeah, sadly, that's the Army life for you. If they weren't your parents and you two weren't married, they wouldn't give permission for you to go home."

"Nope," he huffed, "and when I finally did get back home, I discovered she and her brother had joined a local gang. The guys were a bunch of wannabe gangsters, way over their heads into trouble. I tried to reach out to her, get her to see me, but she carried so much hate and pain that I could barely get to her. It didn't help she was dating the gang president."

"That must've been hard."

"It was, but over time I wore her down and got her to see that I wasn't going anywhere. Lexi isn't like the other woman here. She holds on to stuff. She won't forgive all that happened with us. She says she does, but it's a lie. Even after I chased her to Canada and found out she was pregnant with Baby B, she still took a jab at me here and there."

"And she was seeing Dr. Roberts?"

"Yes. He made huge progress with her, and it was great for a while, but now, I don't know, it's like she's back to her old self again."

"How so?"

"She's not here." He lifted his hands. "I have no idea where my kids' mother is." He shook his head like those weren't the words he wanted to use. "I mean, she's around here somewhere, but she's mentally checked out. She avoids me at all costs, and when she leaves for trips to see her friends back home, she consistently extends it."

An SUV came down the driveway, and I knew our time was up. I could tell this guy was in pain, and it didn't take very long to know where it stemmed from. It wasn't a mission; it was his heart.

"What's Frank doing here?" He squinted.

"We have some paperwork to go over on one of my old clients." I looked away for a moment to conceal my fib. "I'm sorry to cut this short, Keith, but for now, I'll say this. Your kids are priority number one. It's okay to let them know that you're not happy mommy is gone or checked out, but you need to be both parents for them, at least for now. They need you to be strong. Spend extra time with them. Let them sleep in your bed if they want, because they're feeling that sense of loss, too. When you see her next, she needs to decide if she's a mother or not. Marriage comes and goes, but you're a mother forever." I squeezed his shoulder, and I saw such sadness on his face.

"Thank you."

"Any time, and I mean it." I started to walk backward then turned and jogged the rest of the way to meet Frank.

"Hey." I caught him at the stairs. He looked at my outfit and then over at Keith.

"Everything okay?"

"Yeah. Some sessions are just better outside." I held up a finger. "Can you give me ten, and then I'll be ready."

"Take twenty. I need to speak with Logan, anyway."

"Thanks, Frank." I rushed upstairs to my room where

I stripped off my workout clothes. I quickly showered, dressed, finger combed my hair with the dryer, and applied makeup like a champ. I hooked the bedroom door closed with my foot as I tucked my blouse into my skirt and found myself stumbling into a pair of strong arms.

"Oh!" I was steadied and placed back on my feet.

"Sorry, Ivy." Ty looked down at me and smiled in a way that made my skin heat. "I was rushing."

"Me too." I tried not to stare at his shirtless torso, but that was like not looking at fireworks. His shoulders were broad and defined, and his arms and strong hands felt like steel as they held me in place. Then there were his chest and stomach that would make any woman blush. He spoke, but I didn't hear him over the blood that pounded in my ears.

"Pardon?" His hand left one of my shoulders and pointed at my chest.

"You missed a button."

I blinked and looked down to see I was indeed giving him a good show. My lacy black bra was on display from above, and he took full advantage of his viewpoint.

"Thanks." I pushed the pearl button through the tiny hole. "Silk and pearls aren't always a good idea." I blushed and looked up at him and found him staring like he was trying to read my mind again. "Are you good?"

His fingers moved away, and he ran a hand through his short brown hair.

"Yeah, I'm good." He grinned.

"Well, now I'm really late."

"Me too." He stepped back. "See you later."

I smiled and made my way down the stairs but not before looking over my shoulder to find him watching me. Jesus, his intense stare stirred something deep inside me.

I spotted my uncle and Frank deep in conversation.

Cole had asked to be involved, so we all joined him in his office. Frank sat the speaker phone in the center of the table.

"Are you ready, Ivy?" Frank asked before he dialed.

No.

I nodded.

"And you understand what this means?"

I don't want to do this.

I nodded.

"This will ignite him to the max." Frank looked at my uncle, who looked at me.

I never asked for this.

"But you know that by law we have to do this."

Run, Ivy.

I nodded.

He nodded back at me and started to dial. My eyes stayed glued to the table as it rang. Each ring pulled me farther and farther away from the confidence I had built since I arrived here.

"Hi, Frank." The voice was harsh and all business. "Is she ready?"

I became stone, muscles locked in place. My fingers

dug into my palms with the need to feel something other than sheer panic.

"Ivy?" My uncle moved to sit next to me. "It's okay. You're safe here."

"You have my word on that," Cole said from somewhere in the room.

Just tell them what happened, then you can get out of this room.

"I'm ready," I barely whispered as the walls of the room seemed to get closer. Ever so slowly, I opened the door to that memory.

NINE

I looked out my bedroom window and watched the dogs chasing each other around like fools. They were a riot to watch. I shook my head as one of them rolled the other completely over then held him there with his paw. I could see the victor's tongue lolling out of his mouth as his tail wagged furiously.

Ivy came into view and slowed from her jog and stopped at the driveway. She leaned over to catch her breath, looked around, than dried her cheeks with the sleeve of her shirt.

What was going on with her?

I pulled my gaze away to give her some privacy and looked around at the view from the window. The afternoon sun hugged the mountaintops and made me miss the views of Afghanistan. Last night, I had barely slept on the huge mattress. It felt so strange, as I was used to a small cot. Doc Roberts was right; it was definitely a step up, but one that was still hard to get used to. I contemplated a move to the floor but knew I had to adapt. Every time I heard a sound, I found myself on high alert, and I kept reaching for a weapon that wasn't there.

Instead, I used the hours I lay awake to relive every moment of that day in the village. I revisited every decision I'd made, but I knew in my gut I'd done everything right. I had the situation under control, and Brown's weapon was no longer pointed at the family when I started to talk him down. My words were having an effect, and I knew if Hill had just backed off and shut up, I'd have gotten Brown through it and brought him home. His needless death burned like acid.

I sank into my chair and must have finally fallen asleep for a few moments, because when my phone rang, I sat up abruptly and fumbled for it. I struggled to tune in to Moore's voice as he talked.

"What do you mean, he didn't take the job?" I shook my head to grasp what he was saying.

"He was bragging about how he got it, then suddenly he was gone." Moore sighed. "Dustin said it was family related."

"Bullshit. Hill doesn't give a shit about family," I growled. I knew Dustin was gullible and would believe whatever anyone told him.

"I agree, but shit, even Rivera disappeared for a few days, but he's back now."

"Do me a favor."

"Yeah," he replied, and I heard him grunt as he sat down. I could picture him in his tiny computer chair. "I'll do some more digging."

"Thanks."

"Ty?"

"Yeah?"

"Are you good?" I could hear he wasn't, so I wasn't about to lie. "I mean, shit, we've seen so much go down. It was always the three of us at the end of it, though, you know. But now..."

"Yeah, I know." I rubbed my face and felt my eyes prickle with emotion. "Now it's like part of us is missing. We're left feelin' like shit, our hearts ripped out. It doesn't make sense."

"Exactly." He cleared his throat and went silent for a minute. I knew we were finished with that topic for now. "I'll do some digging."

I hung up and pressed my hand on the sides of the window. I wanted to punch something.

I changed out of my boots, tugged on my sneakers, and raced downstairs. I needed to burn off some tension. I discovered that Cole liked us to wear black t-shirts and fatigues for the most part during the day and whatever in the evening. I liked that he kept things simple but consistent.

"You look really pale, Ivy. Are you feeling okay?" I heard concern in Sloane's voice.

Ivy? I pivoted and headed toward the kitchen.

"What's going on?" I tried to read the situation.

"Really, I'm fine. I just didn't get much sleep." Ivy forced a smile. "I think a run will do me some good."

A run? I eyed her fib. She had already gone running, but I kept my mouth shut.

Sloane looked at me, worried. "Do you need something?"

"Just going to grab a water. Going for a run myself."

"Okay, ah," Sloane stumbled and looked at Ivy, "some of us are going to Zack's for dinner and drinks tonight. I was wondering if you'd like to join us. It's our favorite place in town."

"Yes, going out actually sounds good." Ivy checked her watch. "I'm running late for a session, but let me know when and I'll be ready."

"Great." Sloane watched her leave then tilted her head on one side with an expression as though she contemplated Ivy's answers. She looked like she might comment but stopped herself.

"What?"

"Nothing." She brushed their conversation off. "So, you up for tonight? Dinner and drinks at a restaurant in town."

"Town? We can do that?"

"Yes. The owner is Cole's father's best friend and a former Blackstone teammate. Us wives, Abby, and June are the only ones who need escorts when we go out. We're like chum for the Cartel." She gave a dry laugh and hopped off the stool. She almost reached the door when she swiveled on her heel. "Ivy too." She inclined her head. "She can't leave without one of you with her. Blonde and gorgeous, she'd be prime meat on the black market."

For me, too.

"That's some dark humor you have there."

"It's a lot easier to make fun of the danger we're in than to try to repress it." She shrugged. "We keep it casual at Zack's unless it's a holiday. The guys normally wear jeans and a t-shirt. Just no fatigues."

"Copy that." I grabbed a water bottle from the fridge and left for my run. I ran until my breath came in short gasps and my shirt was wet with sweat. I neared the house and allowed myself to slow to a walk.

"Hey, Logan wants to see you in his office," Sloane called as she caught sight of me.

"Thanks."

I noticed Ivy's door was shut when I zipped by, heading to Cole's office. I heard Keith's voice and slowed, not wanting to interrupt.

"Feedback?" Cole asked.

"Straight shooter, logical, and fair. I couldn't have asked for a better replacement for Doc Roberts. I like her, Cole. I think I might ask her to take on the whole family."

I hoped Cole would share Keith's praise with Ivy at some point.

"I like that idea, too."

"Thanks." Keith hurried out of the room and gave me a nod as he trotted by. I liked Keith. He was quiet but fit with everyone else here. He obviously had a lot going on in his personal life, something about his wife. I'd figured out that much, but I wasn't about to ask. Whatever it was, I hoped it would end soon. A guy in our line of work didn't need that kind of stress in his life.

"Hey, Logan." I stood in the doorway and waited for Cole to ask me in.

"Beckett." He registered my presence. "This'll only take a sec," he said with his eyes on a file. "Come on in."

I moved just inside the door and stood still. The Army life was ingrained in me, and the casual style of the others would take time.

"At ease." He tossed the file on the table and looked up at me. "You coming to Zack's tonight?"

"Yes, I think. Sloane just gave me the invite."

"Good. So, here are some things to know. Zack used to work on my father's team, but his passion seemed to be more behind a stove than behind the scope of a gun." He chuckled at his own words. "Anyway, he's got a restaurant in town that's safe for us all to relax and have a bit of fun. The town is used to us and pretty much give us our space. Still, we don't often venture far when we're out with the girls. We take turns watching over them if they decide to move about, but we don't hover. We make our presence known, but that's about it."

He took a moment, and I thought he was done, but he continued. "Zack's place is big, and though most of his staff keep their eyes open for strangers, that doesn't mean we can't be spotted or that our girls are safe. The Cartel would love to get one of us, but they know our weak spot would be our wives and children. That would hurt us the most. All of us keep our eyes on our family all the time. Ivy is new here, and so are you. I'm going to ask you to do the same for her."

"Understood." I was fine with that order.

"Ivy might not be in danger with the Cartel specifically, but between you and me, she could use a little extra protection." *Oh?* "So, if you can help keep an eye on her and report back if anyone stands out, that would be great. That being said," he got up and stepped close, "you have my permission to do whatever is necessary, depending on the circumstance. Just remember, you're not in Afghanistan anymore."

"Not a problem."

"Suck it sucker, you're it!" someone screamed from outside the door, and Cole smirked but quickly regained his composure.

"Good. We convoy into town. I'll warn you now, the girls haven't been out in a while." He gave me a *God help us* look. "The kids are all back from Abby and June's tomorrow, so they'll want to blow off some steam."

"I'll be ready." I smiled and tried to remember the last time I'd gone out for drinks in public. "If there's nothing else, I need to check on a buddy."

"Moore?" he asked.

"Yes."

"Are you considering him for a position on the team?"

"Yes, sir, I am. I trust him with my life."

"Excellent." He nodded. "I'd like to take you to Camp Green here soon. Give you a chance to see who else might be coming up the ranks. Ray, my father's teammate from years ago, helps run the place. He's good people, and I want you to meet him. Plus, I want Dr. Knight to check on a few of our men."

"I'd like that." He motioned permission to leave with his head.

I grabbed the small towel from my belt loop and wiped my face as I walked toward the stairs to my room. A young voice drew my attention, and I moved toward it.

"Riddle me this. I'm green, I spend most of my days trying to blend in, and I can make a bubble." She stood next to the window with her hands on her hips and a serious look on her face.

"A grasshopper," Mike guessed.

"Seriously, Mike? What grasshopper do you know blows bubbles?" She rolled her eyes, and I had to smile at her wry expression.

"Fine, a cricket."

"Mike, you're not even trying."

"A frog," I called out, and she turned to look at me. *Ha!* She was Savannah's daughter, no doubt about that. She was a dead ringer for her gorgeous mother. Only the serious expression she wore was all her own.

"Thank you, a frog. Beckett got it right." She reached over and held out her hand. "I'm Olivia Logan."

"Ty Beckett."

"Oh, I know." She smiled wide, and I saw her mom. "Major Tyler Beckett, eight years in Afghanistan, saved a boy from the Taliban and managed to return him to his parents in one piece. Singlehandedly preserving our relationship with an important ally. You're a legend around here."

"You know your stuff."

"She knows all," Mike warned me. "She's a Logan."

"Mike, you flatter me." She stood up straight. "How are you adjusting to life here?"

"Better than I thought." I spoke to her like she was one of the guys, and she seemed to like it.

"Happy to hear it. If you need anything, I'm the girl to ask."

"Good to know. It was a pleasure meeting you, Olivia."

"You as well." She shot Mike a look then grabbed her bookbag and headed out, saying she was going to her father's office.

"She's ten going on thirty." Mike chuckled. "She runs a tight ship with the rest of the kids and an even tighter one with us."

"Ten?" I shook my head. "I wish I was half that quick at fifteen." I stopped a second to send a text off to Moore, who texted back he was on a call. He said he'd call back later when he found something.

"Tell me about it." He glanced at the time. "We're officially off duty, minus being on call, of course, but we have hydrating IVs for that if need be." He stood and tucked his phone away. "Time to go have some fun. No fatigues," he called over his shoulder.

"Sloane already caught me up to speed." I chuckled.

"Yes, when you go into town, you need to blend." Olivia came up behind me. "Fatigues are fine during the day here, but they seem to provoke the rowdy crowds showing off for the girls." She rolled her eyes.

"You sure know a lot that goes on here, don't you."

She nodded then opened her bookbag and pulled out a notebook and iPad.

"Why aren't you out with Abby and June and the rest of the kids?"

"I needed a break."

I chuckled quietly at her answer and tapped the side of my water bottle. "Are you cool with us going out tonight?"

"A house to myself? Yes, please. Besides, there's always someone here, really." She pulled out her Apple pen. "I need to keep my grades up if I'm going to take over this place someday."

"Riddle me this." I grinned at her. "What's ten, smart, and will make a badass boss someday?"

She smiled at me. "Thanks, Beckett."

I rushed up the stairs and saw Ivy coming out of her room. She looked unbelievably good in her outfit. She seemed to have shaken off her earlier sadness as she grinned at me.

"Hey." Her cheeks pinked. *Interesting.* I liked how her body reacted when I was near. I decided to let my own guard down and slowly circled her to drink in the view. Her white shorts hugged her bottom, and I could see if she so much as bent over her cheeks would show. Her shirt left nothing to the imagination, and with one flick of my finger, her breasts would spill out. My fingers twitched.

"Do you think you should change?"

"What?" Her hip popped out. "What's wrong with this?" She craned her neck to see me.

"It's too sexy." I watched her from behind and studied the way her body moved under her clothes.

"No, it's not."

"It is," I countered and hid my amusement, "and stop wearing silk."

"I love silk." She turned.

"So do I. That's the problem." Her eyes flared with interest, and she raised her chin and gave me a smirk. I could see the fire behind those eyes, and my body instantly reacted. "Here's the deal." I took a step toward her. "You are *mine* to keep an eye on tonight." Her lips parted as she contemplated my words. "So, you can change and make my life easier, or you can wear that and have to deal with whatever comes your way."

"Is that so?"

"It is."

She waited a beat then twitched her brow, popped a button on her top to give me a better show, then headed for the stairs. I could hear her laugh as she went down the steps.

My smile grew as she disappeared. I walked to my room with a grin on my face.

I stood in front of the closet and eyed my unpacked bag. I shook my head to free any negative thoughts and focused on the fact I was about to go out and have fun. Normal fun. That seemed so odd.

I thumbed through the bag and tugged out some perfectly pressed jeans then decided on a darker pair and tossed them on the bed behind me. I found a gray t-shirt, white sneakers, and my beloved ball hat. I grabbed my watch, wallet, and phone, then headed downstairs where the guys waited.

"The girls are in the van impatiently waiting for Mark!" John called.

"It takes time to look gorgeous," he called from some-where, and the guys chuckled at his sense of humor.

"Come on." Cole waved us out, and I spotted a glimpse of Ivy getting into the other van. I caught sight of her blonde hair and long, bare legs. *Seriously? She might kill me tonight.*

"This is us, unless you want to be in that one." Mark slapped my shoulder. He was as bad as the girls.

Zack's was as big as Cole promised. It had a restaurant on one side and a full-on bar on the other. He came up to us, and Cole introduced me and explained that Zack was like a second father to him.

"Order whatever you want and let me take care of the rest," he said over the music. "It's not like this on weekdays, but on the weekends, we like to open it up, so people have a place to let off some steam."

"Sounds great to me." I shook his hand then noticed Sloane, who waved me over to a seat next to her and conveniently directly across from Ivy. I went along with it and made a show of looking around when really that was something I always did every few minutes on the mark.

Pitchers of beer were placed in front of us, and I saw the ladies had either wine or fruity drinks. A line of about a dozen shots appeared, and Savannah waved to get our attention.

"This is the game of 'where's the penny.'" She spoke loudly to be heard over the music. "A penny is passed along through every hand. Everyone needs to make the action of passing the real penny or they can fake the pass. Whoever's turn it is calls a stop when they want, then everyone slams their hands down on the table. You have to guess where that penny is. If you lose, you share your worst date. It's a *get to know you* kind of game."

Two rounds in, and I noticed it wasn't about trying to guess where the penny was, but more about whose face slipped when the penny hit the table.

Mark lost and took a shot, Mike won, and then it was Ivy's turn. The penny began its round until stop was called. Cole had the penny. The only reason I knew was because Savannah tried hard not to look at him. Cole, on the other hand, had a face like stone.

"Umm," she glanced around.

"Come on, now Ivy. You crawl inside people's brains for a living," Mark joked.

"That's completely different, Mark." She smiled, looking at each of us.

"Ty?" She tugged her lip in, and I slowly rolled each hand. "Oh, no!" She smacked her face.

"It's Cole." I nodded at him.

"How could you know that?" Savannah's mouth dropped open.

"Don't forget who we're sitting with." Cole tossed the penny in the middle of the table. "I'm impressed, Beckett." I nodded at him with a grin and listened while everyone tried to get Ivy to share.

My phone buzzed on the table. I flipped it over and saw her name. I declined it and tuned back into Ivy's story. She glanced at me and kept going.

"That's about it, really."

"Not near enough." Catalina gave her a shot. "That's not how this game works. You lost, so now you have to give us the goods."

"All right." She laughed and made a face at the shot before she downed it. "I'm going to hate you tomorrow." She sighed and leaned back in her seat. "All right, worst dates. Well, I tend to attract real winners, so this isn't that hard for me." She ran a few fingers through her hair, and I found myself intrigued with her movements again. She was smooth and graceful. She looked put together, but somehow, I didn't think she tried hard at it. Her navy silk tank top was cut low in the front, and I noticed she'd done up the button she had popped open earlier. She had a delicate silver necklace around her neck which she often played with. And the fact she wore heels made me realize just how much I'd missed the little things.

"Let's see, there was Brian, who told me he was in a motorcycle gang, and later on I discovered what he really meant was more of a *moped* gang." She shrugged and made a face, but I noticed the other women winked at each other. "Needless to say, the sexiness went out the window pretty fast on that one." All the girls laughed, and the guys groaned and rolled their eyes, unimpressed.

"Wait," I raised a hand, "what was with the looks between the ladies?"

Catalina went to say something, but Mark slapped a hand over her mouth.

"There's a reason we don't visit California," Mark hissed at Catalina.

Mike rolled his eyes. "He's not that bad!"

"He really isn't." Savi avoided a nasty glare from Cole and high-fived Mia. "Sorry, Ivy. Continue."

"I'd like to circle back to this later." She pointed at Savi. "Okay, then there was Dale, who talked with his mother on the phone almost the entire time." She sipped her drink while everyone laughed. "Oh, then there was John, who decided to walk me home after dinner, and when a sketchy guy approached us to ask for money, he panicked and practically pushed me into the guy's arms and ran away scared."

"Thank you for not being that John," Sloane said and laughed to her husband.

"Oh, then there was Billy, who couldn't stop staring at the woman who sat at the next table long enough to notice I had called a cab to go home." She shook her head. "Like I said, I pick the winners."

"So, no mommas' boys, no moped gangs, no chicken shits, and someone who will actually see you?" Savannah held up her fingers. "Anything else you'd like to add to the list?"

"I don't know." She played with the stem of her wine glass. "I just want to feel safe, be seen and heard, and have someone who's witty and enjoys banter."

Savannah caught my eye and wiggled her eyebrows, and I chuckled quietly. The ladies really had no shame when it came to people's love lives.

"Sounds like you need to date a soldier," Mark chimed in. "We check all those boxes."

"Amen, brother." Mike tapped his beer. "A woman should be cherished and loved."

"But not in the bedroom." Catalina made the entire table breakout in laughter.

"Certainly not." Ivy shrugged when the girls high-fived her. I shifted in my seat and avoided Savannah's knowing look.

"Well, this conversation just took an interesting turn." John smirked at me. "Welcome to the family, Beckett, where nothing is too private to be talked about, even in public."

"Love is a wonderful thing," Mia held up a hand to speak, "and trust and respect always need to be there both ways, but in the bedroom…well," she winked at Ivy, "there's a reason we date soldiers. They are resourceful, strong, demanding—"

"Don't forget alpha." Savannah grinned at Cole, who grabbed her head and kissed her hard.

I missed kissing, the feel of a woman's soft lips, her taste, the little sounds they made when they were lost in the moment.

"Yes!" Mia hit the table, clearly enjoying her buzz. "Toe-curling alpha males who make you scream in the night for all the right reasons."

"That's the best kind." Ivy smiled into her glass then held it up to the ladies. "To savage love, anywhere, anytime."

"Ahhhh, yes!" Sloane clicked her glass to Ivy's, and the other girls did the same.

"Oh," Mia shot up, "and Ty is only one syllable. That makes life easier."

"Seriously?" Mark snatched her drink and finished it off.

"How would you feel about an open relationship?" Savannah grinned at Cole, who raised an eyebrow at her. "Because I think Ivy could be really magical."

"And she's had too much." Cole laughed and pulled the glass out of her hand. "Remember, I don't share."

"To not sharing." Mike held his beer up, and all the guys joined in.

"To not sharing." I repeated the three words while I held Ivy's gaze. I relished the sight of her blush; it climbed up her neck and told me she liked what I said.

"So, let's see," Mia looked around the room, "who meets these qualifications that you could go on a blind date with?" She looked around, and Ivy's eyes widened.

"I don't know if that's such a good idea, Mia."

"A girl has needs. Ivy, when was the last time you had a good slap and tickle?"

"Good or in general?" I huffed, which drew her attention back to me. "What about you, Beckett?"

"Don't turn this around on me, Ivy. This is all about you." I held up my hands, which made the women hit the table in excitement. "I've spent the last eight years with men. There weren't many opportunities for *my kind* of slap and tickle."

"Ah," she leaned forward, which tugged on her shirt, "but you would have been on leave a few times. You're telling me that you didn't find some *savage* love somewhere?" I grinned at her then tipped my ball hat down to shade my eyes.

"Don't hide those gorgeous eyes behind that hat of yours." She pointed her finger and leaned her head to the side.

"Drinks, anyone?" I stood, and Mark looked at Cole.

"I believe he's asking for a scotch, neat." Mark chuckled as he spoke.

"I think so, too, brother." Cole laughed. "Run, Beckett, and get me another while you're out there."

I didn't wait for any more orders. I'd just get everyone another round. I stopped at the bar and waved the bartender over.

"You must be Beckett." The guy offered a hand. "I'm Jake. A friend of your group over there."

"Nice to meet you, Jake. Could I buy the table another round?"

"Sure thing." He took my card. "Leave it open?" I noticed he didn't swipe it.

"Sure." My phone rang, and I saw it was Demi again. I pointed at the hallway, and Jake nodded that he understood I was leaving.

"I heard you were back," she purred when our call connected.

"I am."

"I wondered if you'd found someone else to replace me," she gave a little laugh, "but when I saw your folks the other day, they said you jumped into another job in North Dakota."

We are told to tell people we work in North Dakota; Montana was strictly for training.

"I did." I glanced around to be sure I was still alone.

"Well, I just so happen to be free the next while. Maybe we could catch up."

I closed my eyes, knowing I could do about six rounds with a woman right now. I glanced at the table and saw Ivy wasn't there.

"You know me, Ty. I'm not looking for anything more than a ride. I know what you like, and you know what I like." She lowered her voice to a husky tone. "I know that you need a woman who can give it up to you, let you take control. A woman who can take whatever you give her." I felt my stomach coil and my head cloud. "And I also know that you really need it when you come home. I'm what you need, Ty." I leaned into my arm on the wall and pressed my forehead into it as my erection grew.

"I'll text you where to meet. Let me know when you arrive?" I grunted.

"Three days from now." She giggled, and I fought through the fog well enough to think straight.

"I'll be in Montana at that point training for work, anyway."

"Just tell me where and when." She kept her voice sexy.

"Yeah." I took a controlled breath, not because she turned me on but because I needed the release, and I knew she'd brought it to me before. It had been too long, and lately being around Ivy, it was almost unbearable. "Demi."

"Yeah?"

"Stretch first." It was our inside joke, and I could hear her laugh as I hung up. When I turned around, I found Ivy behind me. She tapped her fingers on the wall as she stood there and studied me a moment then walked by me into the restroom without a word.

As I watched her disappear, I saw John coming toward me. I tucked my phone away and cleared my head and prayed the music had been loud enough that Ivy hadn't overheard my conversation with Demi.

"Hey, man, the restaurant is filling up, and Cole said you're on Ivy duty. Could you walk her back to the table? I need to piss like no one's business."

"Yeah, of course." I leaned against the wall and waited. I felt incredibly pent-up and agitated. If I was still overseas, my mind would be focused on the business of staying alive, but being here in this town and being around her...I felt like I might explode.

"Hey," she looked up at me as she came out, "were you waiting on me?"

"Yeah," I pushed off the wall, "the place is filling up, and Cole wanted eyes on you."

"Ah, yes, you mentioned that earlier." She shook her head. "But I'm not one of the family needing protection from the Cartel," she said quietly for only me to hear.

"You're associated with us." I motioned for her to start walking. "I'm going to assume that makes you a target."

"To who?" She looked down the hallway. "No one knows me here. I'm just some woman in a bar. Really, Ty, I don't need an escort." She forced a laugh.

"Rules of the house. And you're sexy as shit, Ivy, so you're stuck with me. Deal with it." I urged her forward and glared at the men who stared at her.

"Someone's cranky," she muttered.

"I wouldn't be if you weren't wearing that."

"Hey," she turned and placed her hands on her hips, "no guy is going to give me a problem with you hanging around me. You scream either military or police," she wiggled a finger at me, "so, relax and enjoy yourself. God knows we both deserve it."

"I don't do crowds well." I glanced around the room.

"Well, lucky for you," she stepped closer, "I do." The light scent of her perfume found me, and I breathed it in deeply. "Come on, Beckett."

She turned to walk as a group of guys came by and forced her to step back into me. My hands quickly landed on her hips as I moved her out of the way. I nearly moaned when my thumb grazed her bare skin.

"See," she looked up at me, "you got this."

"Come on." I flexed my hands and steered her toward the table. I wasn't ready to let go yet, but I did. I took my job seriously and did what I'd been told. I made my presence known. Maybe, just maybe, I loved every minute of it even if it did almost kill me.

TEN

The smell of dirt and tobacco swirled around my senses as I listened to the sounds of the sophisticated tunnel we had built between San Diego and Rosarito. It utilized a rail system, steel shoring, and an electric ventilation system. It was one of best designs to date and something a lot of others had tried before but failed. When we weren't moving girls through here, I'd rent out the space to the other side of Castillo's operation and they'd move cocaine, meth, and heroin through. But I oversaw everything; that was my number one rule. I knew what was coming through, when it came through, and who the buyers were.

"Eric?" Alejandro held up his phone as he came closer. "The buyer is here, and the girls should be arriving within the next few minutes."

"Here?" I looked over his shoulder toward the bright outdoors. "Okay, stay here while I go out and speak to him."

"*Sí*, boss." He wiped his forehead free of sweat and tried to catch his breath.

"Over there." Filippo pointed to Chili, my buyer, and I told him to stay put. I didn't trust the guys with the women, especially not at the last leg of the trip when they'd gotten this far. I always offered the best. I never dipped into my own product and kept my guys away from them as well.

"Mr. Noah." Chili pushed away from his very expensive car where he'd leaned casually in his flashy suit and snakeskin boots. He reminded me of Denton, who always showed off what he had just to boost his own ego. That was typical of these guys. Personally, I chose to lay low. I didn't get flashy with my money, and I had a lot of it. I didn't need to display it. That only brought the sharks. "I thought I'd come and see you in action."

"I see." I was curious what he was really doing here. It was not the way things went.

"I hear you have some prime product waiting for me." He looked over at Filippo, who was within earshot of us.

"You expect anything less, Chili?" I took the cigar he offered me and stood next to him to watch the entrance to the tunnel. I watched the open hatch and waited for my motion sensor to go off that they were getting close.

"After today, when's the next shipment?" He turned away from Filippo in an attempt to keep his business private. It was smart not to trust anyone in this industry, so I understood his hesitation to speak freely.

"I heard sometime next week."

"Where from?"

"East LA."

"Ages?"

"Eleven to twenty-four." I looked down as my sensor went off. "They're here." I grunted, and Chili lit the tip of the banana leaf and handed me his Zippo so I could do the same. Filippo started to walk toward us with his phone to his ear.

"Eric," he lowered his voice, "there's been talk about Castillo having a mark at his house."

"What kind of mark?"

"Not sure yet. But I think something big might be going down." I tossed down the cigar that I'd pretended to smoke and squashed the ember into the dirt with the toe of my shoe.

"You should make sure you get a handle on that. I'd like to have first pick of what's being moved through."

The fact that Chili was telling me this right here at the tunnel and not back at my place had my head spinning at just what my boss was up to. It wasn't how we usually handled business. I knew something was going on. I didn't like it.

"You have my word I won't sell to anyone else as long as you don't buy from anyone else." I gave him a look as he puffed away on his cigar.

"My concern isn't your loyalty, Eric, just that I want to have first dibs."

I nodded and rubbed my evening stubble as I wished to hell it wasn't a billion and fuck degrees out. "I'll see what I can find out."

"Good."

"Boss, they're here." Filippo lowered his phone, and I watched as a string of girls, bound at the wrists and ankles, shuffled out of the tunnel. They squinted and cried when they saw us. I motioned for the men to back off so I could inspect them.

I reached up and moved the first girl's chin side to side and checked her for bruising. Her frightened eyes shifted over to one of the men, and it told me something had happened. I'd spent over a decade trafficking females, and even some men, to know the signs that something was up.

"Are you hurt?" I asked the next girl.

"No," she wouldn't look at me, "but she is." She pointed to a small girl about thirteen or fourteen. "It was him." She pointed to a man. He stepped forward, and I reached for my gun, and he stopped in his tracks.

"You," I nodded to the small girl, "where are you hurt?" Slowly she raised her shirt and showed me black and blue bruises on her stomach. "You did this?" I asked the man.

"She tried to run," he spat in disgust.

"As opposed to voluntarily getting in the car with you?" I dripped with sarcasm.

"Bitch tried to scream."

"Scream? Like this?" I shot him in the kneecap, and the girls jumped and huddled together at his scream. I grabbed him by the hair and yanked him off the ground. "What is my number one rule?"

"Don't touch," he moaned through the pain.

"And you touched?" He nodded, so I shoved my gun down his throat and pulled the trigger. I looked at the rest of them, and they all nodded like they got it. "You touch, you die."

I tossed the asshole away from me and waited for Chili to come up and inspect. Filippo and Alejandro stayed close but quiet. They knew better than to get involved with Chili and me.

"Anyone else hurt?" he called, and they all shook their heads.

"You want me to take them back to my place and wait until she heals?" I asked Chili. That was normally what we did. I'd keep the girls locked away in the basement if they were injured, to give them time to heal. That way, we'd be sure they'd sell for top dollar.

"No, I can deal with that one myself." He signaled for his men to move the girls into the two awaiting vehicles.

"So, we good here?"

"*Sí.*" He handed me a wad of cash. "I'll be in touch." He slipped behind the tinted windows and left us in a cloud of dust.

"Jesus, why did he show up here?" Filippo whispered to Alejandro as I poured gasoline over the dead Cartel's body and motioned the other men to return to the US through the tunnel. I knew my contact over there would give them their payment when they got back. I didn't need any murders over money happening in my fucking tunnel.

Once the body was soaked, I tossed the container aside and went to the back of my truck to wash up.

"He's just making sure we're keeping our end of the agreement," I heard Alejandro explain.

"Why doesn't Eric use a different buyer?"

"Why do you ask so many questions, Filippo?"

"I'm trying to learn."

"Fuck." Alejandro grabbed the water jug from the ground and poured it over his sweaty head. "When there's something to learn, I'll teach you, but asking questions in this line of work will get you killed."

"Fine." Filippo plunked to the ground with a heavy sigh. I think the kid saw a life in this business, but Alejandro was right. Asking too many questions only made me more paranoid than I was already.

"Learn this now, kid," Alejandro huffed as he moved around his bad shoulder. He glanced at me, no doubt wondering if I could hear them. "It's like why he only goes to church once in a while. No one knows, and no one asks. He's the boss, so keep your mouth shut, eyes down, and continue to show your loyalty. That's how you stay alive."

"Got it."

"Let's go!" I hit the truck to get their attention as I lit the match and tossed it. The body burned.

ELEVEN

IVY

I was pleased with how my office turned out. The lavender walls were calming and matched the elephant tusk colored plush couch and chairs. A decorative waterfall in the far corner provided white noise and brought the outdoors inside. I wanted to create a place where people who had spent most of their lives out in the elements could feel safe inside with familiar sights and sounds. If that didn't work, I'd haul all the stuff outside and that would be my office.

"Ivy?" Mia held out a plant as she tried to disentangle herself from her daughter's tight grip on her leg. Tabby's arms were wrapped around Mia's leg, and a snorkel hung around her small neck. "I love flowers, and I thought maybe you'd like some for your office." She smiled at my transformed room.

"So do I." I took the big green plant from her arms and set it next to the window. "It's lovely. Thanks, Mia."

"Okay," she took a step inside the room, "I didn't come here just to give you the plant."

"No?"

"Tabby, wait outside for a moment, please." She peeled her daughter off and gave her a little push toward the door then came closer to me. "Screw my dad, screw the law, just screw it all." Her face was serious. "I know how he operates. Dad has his reasons for bringing people here. He did it with Sloane too. I also know that as much as my dad tries to help, he doesn't take into account that you might need someone to talk to. I know I'm not around as much as the others right now, because of the classes I'm taking, but you can talk to me, to any of us. We've all been through scary stuff. We also know how to keep our mouths shut. I just want you to know, we are here for you anytime. Okay?"

"Okay." I nodded at her with a smile. I deeply appreciated Mia's offer; I knew it came from the heart. "Thanks, Mia."

"Of course." She gave me a hug, then she glanced at the plant. "It looks great there." She sounded very matter-of-fact. Then she scooped up Tabby, who waved at me over her mother's shoulder as they left.

I chuckled at what just happened then sat down and admired the room again. A movement caught my eye, and my door slowly opened. A moment later, a white ball of fur hopped up on my couch and a pair of round eyes stared at me.

"Well, hello there." I grinned at his scowl and was pleased to see someone here owned a cat. "What's your name?" He blinked then flopped on his back, spread his legs open, and looked at me. "No shame, hey? I dig that."

"Hey," Savannah popped her head inside, "I checked, and since you aren't seeing anyone for another hour, I hoped maybe you had some time for me. I cleared it with Doc Roberts too."

"Always." I felt flattered and waved her inside. "Please take a seat."

"Wow, you really transformed this room, Ivy. It's lovely."

"Thanks, but to be fair, I had a lot to work with when I arrived. So, really, I should be thanking you." She seemed to enjoy that compliment as she settled into her seat.

"I see you've met Scoot." She pointed to the shameless cat. "He thinks this is his room, so yeah," she rolled her eyes, "you need to share."

"I'm fine with that." I laughed and watched her play with her fingers, uneasy.

"Do you mind if I just jump in?"

"Not in the least. Please do." I pulled my iPad on my lap and waited for her to start. Scoot jumped off the couch while she got settled, and he strode over to sit on the armrest of my chair. I guessed we were holding this session together.

"Well, the wives and I had a chat, and we thought you should get a little background on Lexi from our point of view. It's also important to know that I've always been very close to Keith, and I was a little nervous when she first arrived here."

"How so?"

"I'm not sure how much Keith has told you, but Lexi beats to her own drum." She raised her eyebrows and pressed her lips tight. "She's a bit of a gypsy and has never really fit the Blackstone wife mold, if you get my drift. Not like us other girls do, anyway."

"How do you see the Blackstone mold?"

"It's maybe not just a Blackstone mold but more of a Shadows mold." She squinted as she tried to explain. "We're targets because of who we're married to, just like our children are, and well, just like everyone else who lives here. But then there's Abby and June. They have escorts whenever they leave the grounds and go into the town. They're not married to anyone here, but they have inside knowledge of what happens here. Therefore, they're a target too."

"I understand that." I nodded because I totally got it. I indicated she should go on.

"We're all warned from the very start what life will be like here." She shrugged. "Cole, Daniel, Frank, they gave it to us straight. So, you had to weigh the pros and cons to living this life. You had to change your mindset if you wanted to make it work for you. Every one of us has done that. Each of us has found our place within this world. For the most part, we're happy and enjoy life here and all the perks that come with it. Everyone but Lexi."

"That's what I've been hearing." I wanted her to know I understood and had heard the same things. "Why do you think that is?"

"I have my theories." She struggled. "It's not like we didn't welcome her in, show her the ropes, made her feel like family, but there's that old saying you can't make someone like you if they don't like themselves."

"You think she might be unhappy with herself?"

"Look, Lexi has always been looking for more. Even after she got Keith back, had adorable babies, a safe place to live, she never really seemed to settle. I mean, she even had us, her sisters. I know it can be overwhelming at times, but we've all been there and were victims from something. We know she really missed her brother." She paused. "He committed suicide." She looked uneasy while I digested that. "We would never try to replace him, but we all feel connected almost like siblings. With Lexi, it just never seemed to be enough."

"I thought for a while she was good." She lifted her hands and shrugged. "But now," she stopped herself and caught her lip between her teeth to stop her emotions, "now she's hurting Keith, my best friend, and their kids. Not to mention putting everything the Logans have worked to create at risk. Like when she decides to change her trip plans and goes partying in Vegas last minute. Davie," she paused to explain, "one of the Dusk teammates in North Carolina, is the one who watches over her when she travels and has to run all over the place because she just 'needs a break from it all.'" She did air quotes. "I'm sorry. That was rude, but she has no idea what that means for Davie and the rest of the team trying to train." She rubbed her chest for a moment in thought.

"We're free to come and go as long as we have someone with us, but all of us wives are very aware of what it means to pull one of the soldiers away. It leaves a hole the other guys have to fill. I hate to judge, but she's being selfish to everyone, not to mention her family." I handed her a tissue and gave her a moment to gather herself.

"Sometimes having it all is the problem." I spoke carefully, not wanting her to think I agreed with Lexi's behavior, because I didn't. "Sounds like Lexi really went through a rough time, the loss of her parents, joining the gang life. Keith did tell me that it was to discover who killed her parents, but then her brother commits suicide. Sometimes when you fight through enough of the rough times that life throws at you, you almost need it to feel alive. The fight brings more of a comfort than a happy, stable life does. Grit versus frills."

"As in it feels better to hurt than to feel good?"

"Exactly."

"Do you think she feels guilty for feeling good when her family isn't alive?" I could see Savannah try to piece her thoughts together as we talked. That was good. People needed to make sense of things before they could see a situation clearly.

"Perhaps, but she also could just be someone who likes to be or needs to be on the darker side of life to really feel alive."

"I've been there, but only because I was so scared," she confessed. "I'm not sure what to do. None of us does."

"Well," I removed my glasses and took a second to think, "I would just keep being there for Keith and his kids. They need a lot of help right now. And when Lexi tries to include herself in your daily life again, let her, but give her some space. She'll most likely be prepared for you to come at her. She'll be defensive about her behavior, so deflate it by backing off."

"Makes sense." She nodded. "What if she stays checked out, and continues to distance herself from everyone? Oh, Lord, what if she leaves again?"

"Let's not go there unless we have to, and if we do, we'll all be in it together."

"You sound like Cole." She chuckled as she wiped a tear away. "Thanks, Ivy. I just needed to get it off my chest."

"I'm always here to talk, Savi, truly."

She checked the time. "We have fifteen minutes. Any chance we can chat about something off the record?"

"Sure." I grinned and put my iPad aside and joined her on the couch. "What's up?" Scoot moved to my chair and curled up in a ball.

"So, Ty…" Her eyes lit up, and I shook my head with a wry smile.

"You don't give up, do you?"

"Not when I see something that could be. Just answer me this. Do you find him attractive?"

"Extremely." I covered my face, feeling fifteen again. I forgot how fun it was to gush over a guy. Sometimes, being an adult, you suppressed the little things in life like having butterflies brought on by the opposite sex. "But look, I have some things going on right now that are making things complicated—"

"I fell in love with Cole while I was being hunted by the Cartel that my own father sent to kill me."

My face fell at her words. I'd wondered if what I had heard was true. There even had been whispers of a book written about her experience.

"That's for another conversation and a bottle of wine." She waved me off. "If I may, can I offer you some advice?"

"Yes, please," I huffed.

"It's okay to just lust after someone. That's the best part. You get to ask yourself those delicious questions like, did he just look at me? Did he just touch me on purpose? Ugh! Those are the best times." She squeezed her eyes shut with a moan, and I found myself relaxing a bit. "It doesn't have to be love at first sight, or even at all. You'd be surprised how much just letting it happen can help distract or heal you from other things. Life hands us many wonderful things, sometimes at the worst of times. Ty seems great. Give him a chance, get to know him a little. Lord, if anything, you might get the best sex of your life!"

"I can't tell you how refreshing it is getting sound advice from another female, but I've got to share something with you. Last night at Zack's, I overheard him talking to someone named Demi. I think he already has someone, or at least has an interest in someone else."

"Oh," her face twisted, "I'm sorry. I thought I heard Cole say he was single."

"It's all right, but I do think you're on to something. I do need to get out there and try this dating thing again. If you know of anyone?"

"Oh," she wiggled her eyebrows, "I'll start the hunt."

"Hey, Ivy." John came walking in but held his hand up when he saw Savi. "I'm sorry. I can come back."

"No," Savi jumped to her feet, "I have work to do, and you need to get on with your day." She winked as she left the room.

"Please, take a seat, John." I moved off the couch and slipped into work mode.

I spent time in my office after hours sorting through my notes from my talks with Savi, John, and Mike. I appreciated how each had opened up and shared their feelings, concerns, and just random things with me. It really helped to get to know them better. Mike's story about his troll tattoo nearly had me in tears, and I loved how he and Catalina found one another, especially when you considered her connection to the Cartel. I planned to pick his brain more on that later.

Scoot found a new spot to perch, right up behind my shoulders on the couch. Occasionally, he'd prop his head on one of my shoulders and peer down at my iPad.

I swiped the screen and brought up my notes on Lexi. I read through all the comments I'd typed in from those I'd interviewed.

"Hmm." I rubbed my forehead as Scoot purred loudly in my ear.

What really stood out and bothered me the most was that each of them truly had tried hard to reach Lexi, in spite of the fact that she'd pushed the limit with the number one house rule, that you couldn't leave without an escort, more than once. I had a feeling Cole might have bent that rule for her once, and now she pushed the limits with each of her stays by extending them. I was looking forward to hearing Cole's view on that topic and wondered how open he would be with me.

"You can't hide in here all night." Sloane stood in the doorway in her swimsuit. "The littles are back, and we're all heading down to the lake for an evening swim. You want to join us?"

I unfolded from my chair and thought how nice it would be to stretch my body.

"That sounds like the perfect way to end the day." I shut my iPad with a snap and followed her out, closing the office door behind me.

"So, Ivy," Sloane stopped hard at the stairs, "is everything all right with you?"

"Me?" I gripped the railing, so my body language wasn't as obvious. "Of course. Why?"

Her eyes narrowed in on me, and she thought for a moment. "You just seemed a little off yesterday."

"Oh, that. One of my patients from home isn't doing so well." I realized my hand ran through my hair and forced myself to drop it. She caught it and let me know she had. It was a tell that I was lying. "I guess it got my head going," I finished with a lame smile.

"I'm sorry to hear that." She stepped back and gave me a look. "Okay, I'll meet you down at the lake?"

"Sounds good." I whisked up the stairs to get changed.

I choose a white bikini and a pair of wedge heels more for height than look. I slipped on a loose, oversized button-up shirt and headed out the back door and went down to join the others.

I'd already noticed that whenever the house did anything, it was never subtle. Sure enough, there was a huge bonfire, and I passed a table with bags of marshmallows and chocolate for s'mores. The kids ran by with drippy popsicles, and John and Mike were singing as they strummed their guitars. The best part as I came down through the yard was the laughter. My uncle always said the best thing about where he worked was how happy everyone seemed. He said he didn't know whether it was from his mandatory psychology sessions, or the extreme way Blackstone lived their lives. Many were on their second chance at a better life, but it really didn't matter to me. It was a beautiful scene.

"I'm loving all of this." Savi waved her finger up and down my outfit. She linked arms with me. "Your bikini makes your eyes pop."

"Thank you." I eyed her pink one and made a sound of approval, and she smiled at me.

"Come. I want you to meet Abby and June. If you thought I was bad for meddling, just wait until you meet these two. Abby is sneakier and quieter, but June has no shame. I love it!" Two older women turned around when Savi called out to them.

"Oh, my, you must be Ivy. I'm June, Abby's younger sister." She winked.

"Hi, Ivy. I'm Abby, Mark's mom. I've heard such wonderful things about you." I remembered reading his file and the story of how Abigail adopted him.

"That's nice. Thank you."

"She's also dating Doc Roberts," June added, and my chin nearly hit the ground.

"June!" Abby swatted her.

"Oh, my God," I studied Abby, "everything just clicked for me." I chuckled. "We need to spend some time together because I just have so many questions."

"No questions," Mark huffed. He balanced Tabby, his youngest, on his shoulders. Both her hands had a tight grip on each of his ears like handles. "There'll be no questions." He cringed.

"Relax, Mark." June waved him off. "No man is taking your mother from you."

"Listen, you little gecko," he yelped. I watched as he peeled one of his daughter's hands off his ear, and just as quickly, she latched a hand over his eye like a sucker fish. As fast as he moved it, she grabbed his chin.

I laughed as he continued the battle and spotted Ty as he walked down the hill with Cole and John. Ty was in black board shorts, a ball hat, sunglasses, and flip flops. His arms flexed when he reached down to pat Butters, who insisted on some attention. His body looked like sculped steel.

"Sometimes I pinch myself when I see my husband." Savi sighed. Her words forced me to rip my eyes away from Ty. "There's just something about an Army body that speaks to me."

"Well, there goes my dinner," her daughter, who I hadn't even noticed was behind us, groaned.

"Oh, please." Savi pulled her in for a hug. "It just means your parents are happy."

"I love the happy part, but talking about Daddy that way..." She made a face. "Besides, the littles are back." She waved at the kids who were all younger but not that far from her age. "Show some self-control, Mom."

"I have none when it comes to your father," she called, which made Olivia run up the hill as fast as she could. "I really think I have this parenting thing down pat." She grinned at me.

"I'm taking orders." Keith came up next to us. "What can I get you?"

"White wine for me." Savi looked at me.

"Same, please. Thanks."

Ty made a little small talk then gave me a sexy smile, and I tried hard to act like it didn't affect me at all as I returned it. I huffed out a breath as he went to help Keith, who was balancing all the drinks as he made his way toward us. Then he handed Savi and me our drinks, playing the part of a waiter with a napkin over his arm.

"You're a psychologist, Ivy," he whispered as he fiddled with the napkin. "Surely you know what that bikini can do to a man." I felt a jolt as he growled under his breath.

Jesus.

"Dad?" Keith's son, Brandon, came up with his hands tucked in his pockets. "Do I have to be here? Can I go?"

"Okay, son, that's fine. Go if you want." Keith looked at me, and I gave a small nod, agreeing with his decision. Right now, his son didn't need to be forced into a social situation when he was dealing with so much already.

"Miss Ivy?" I heard a small voice next to me, and I looked down to find Reagan, Keith's daughter. "Could you help me?" Her lips were dyed blue from her popsicle. It had slid down the stick and needed to be pushed up to the top so she could eat it.

"Of course." I set my drink down and grabbed a napkin from the table and helped clean her hands. "Here's a trick, Reagan, you put one finger like this," I put my finger on the top of the stick, "and you use your thumb to push the popsicle up like this, so it doesn't pop right off."

"Oh, cool." She giggled then bit off the top of the popsicle. It made my teeth hurt as I watched. "Thanks."

"Anytime." She raced off, her pigtails flying in all directions.

"Thank you," Keith mouthed and then tuned back into a story Savannah was telling as I moved toward Ty.

"Here." Ty grinned as he handed me my drink again. "You're good with kids."

"They're just tiny adults." I sipped the cold wine and felt it slide all the way through to my core, easing the hot flash that came on when he was near. "How was training today?"

"Good. We did the element circuit today, mountains, water, parachutes, mud." He shrugged, and I chuckled. "What?"

"You just make it sound like a walk in the park."

"It's not, but that's why I crave it."

"So, you crave what challenges you?" I didn't mean to make it sound the way I did, but I felt that wonderful jolt as his gaze locked on to mine.

"I crave very few things in life, but when I do," his gaze dragged down my body, and I felt the heat right down to the center of my stomach, "I sink all of myself into it."

"Sounds like you know what you like."

"I do." His jawbone flexed and his neck contracted, drawing my eyes to his shoulders.

"Ivy," Savi was suddenly beside me with her phone, "his name is Patrick, and he's a yoga instructor in town." The picture she showed me was from his website, and he was sitting on a mat doing a pose. He looked good, though a bit short and small for my liking. "I had a friend of a friend call him. I don't know anything about him, but my friend assures me he's very nice. Anyway, long story short, he wants a date tomorrow night."

"Tomorrow?" My jaw nearly hit the ground. "Oh, um…"

"Let me see this guy." Mark popped out of nowhere and leaned over Savi's shoulder. He made a noise in his throat. "Okay, so, he's like her height with manicured eyebrows and a shiny face. Look at his bio. He likes vegan food, cats, and musicals." He shook his head at me. "Oh, and look at his quote. 'Kale is the key to living the best life.' Pass!" He snorted.

"He cares about his body," Savannah argued. I caught Ty's perplexed expression as he turned it on me, and I looked around for an exit.

"I care about my body," Mark said as he shoved nearly an entire hamburger in his mouth as she glared at him.

"He might be perfect for you, Ivy." She turned her attention back to me. "So, yes? Just say the word and I'll send this text."

"I, ah…" I stumbled again.

"Okay, look, go on the date. One of the guys will be with you, anyway, and you can have a signal if you need the date to end." She waved his picture at me. "Just think about it, and in the meantime, I'll keep searching." She leaned in. "Maybe you can find out how bendy he really is." She grinned hopefully. "Think of the stories you can tell on our wine night!" My gaze shot over to Ty, and I recalled what I heard him say to Demi that night on the phone.

"I'll get back to you, okay?" I bit my lip as I nodded, and she raced off to talk to Catalina, who was on her way down the path to us.

Ty's phone went off, and he glanced at it and excused himself. I looked around and spotted Brandon sitting on the grass several yards away from us, looking over the lake. I finished my wine and headed over his way. A part of me just needed a moment to think straight.

He waved when I got closer, and he didn't seem to mind that I was encroaching on his quiet time.

"Any chance I could sit with you?"

"Okay." He shrugged and kept his gaze forward. We sat in silence for a moment. "Are you here to give me a session, too, like my dad?"

"Do you have five hundred dollars to pay me?" That made him chuckle and look at me.

"Maybe I should be a doctor like you when I get older."

"It can be hard." I shrugged.

"Actually, I'm going to be just like my dad."

"An Army kid, are ya?"

"I guess, but I want to be a hero just like Dad. Mom

says nothing gets by my dad." I was pleased to hear he had love and respect for Keith. It was well-deserved.

"They're the best of the best." I watched his dad and the guys down by the picnic table next to the barbecue. Ty was smiling at someone on the phone. I couldn't help but wonder if it was that Demi girl.

"Did you have fun with the other kids on your trip?"

"I guess," he pulled at a blade of grass, "but when we got back here, everything was the exact same. Mom didn't come and tuck me in." He stilled. "Reagan cries at night, but Mommy doesn't come and talk to her the way she used to either." He pulled at the grass again. "I don't think she likes us anymore. She seems sad."

That made my heart hurt, and I kept my gaze forward like he did. I knew that kids talked more without eye contact.

"Oh, no, Brandon. I'm sure you're wrong about that. I'm sure your mom loves you." I patted his back gently.

"I'm sad. I'm mad at..." He cleared his throat and tried to hold it together. "What did we do to make my mom not love us anymore?"

And this was why I worked with adults. Children in pain broke me in the of worst ways. I took a moment to think of how I should answer him.

"Have you ever seen a snow globe?" He nodded. "You know when you shake it all up and it makes a blizzard, and you can't see the people inside anymore? Well, that's what it's like for your mom. She's just lost in a blizzard. But the storm will go away, and the snow will settle. She'll see you again, I'm sure of it. Just give it a little time. Do you understand what I mean?"

"Yeah. Okay." He looked down and seemed to shake off a little of stress he was holding on to.

"Should we eat?" He nodded, and we walked together down to the others. Daniel called him over to the grill and fixed him a plate.

Later that evening after the cleanup, everyone was sitting around the fire, and I decided to slip down for another quick swim. The water was black. The sun low in the sky made a brilliant orange path that led to the mountains. I stripped down to my bikini, sat on the edge of the dock, and slipped silently into the cool water. I knew from my earlier swim there weren't any big rocks or debris to worry about. I duck-dived under the surface and with a strong stroke glided along under the cool water. It felt heavenly. I popped up a few yards away and took in everything around me.

My ears picked up the sound of the crickets as they chirped from the shore, the loons called to each other from the distance, and the soft strums of John's guitar floated along in the breeze. I closed my eyes and let it flow over me. It was incredibly relaxing.

"You know," Ty popped up in front of me, and I nearly screamed, "it's not safe to swim at night without letting anyone know where you were going."

"How did you— I didn't even hear you." I treaded water in front of him.

"I've many skills you've yet to discover." He grinned.

"I've spent days hidden in the dark water, barely above the surface just to stay alive." He moved in circles around me like a predator, hardly raising a ripple in the water. "You learn how to be quiet and not draw attention to yourself." He circled once more with his eyes just above the surface.

"I can see that." I continued to move to face him. "Well, so ya know, I wasn't trying to be reckless. I just wanted to cool off."

"Tell me next time."

"You don't need to watch me here too, Ty."

"I wish I couldn't." He waited a beat letting his comment linger in the air between us. "I figured the kids would have worn you right out." He chuckled and stopped and effortlessly began to tread water. "They sure kept you busy."

"I hoped I'd be tired after all that exercise. Sadly, sleep hasn't been my friend for a while," I muttered without thinking.

"Got a lot on your mind?"

"Yeah." I tipped my head back into the water to allow my long hair to flow with it down my back. The sun was just about to drop behind the mountain peak, casting a palette of colors across the sky.

"Want to talk about it?" He looked into my eyes as I shifted my gaze to him and saw he watched me intently.

"I wish it was that simple."

"It can be."

"It's not." I shook my head. "I'm legally not allowed to talk about it."

"Oh." He nodded like he understood. I rubbed my face in frustration, and he motioned for us to swim back to the dock.

I held on to the side and took a breather. It had been a while since I'd been swimming.

He swam to the side of the dock until he could stand. I followed and could just touch on my tippytoes where he had stopped. We were in a place that gave us some privacy from the others.

"Can I ask you something?"

"I can't promise I can answer," I warned.

"With this thing that you can't talk about, are you in any kind of danger?"

I instantly looked away and felt the knot build in my throat with the topic of conversation.

"You know, my job is about reading people, too, Ivy," he said softly, "and even with the little I do know about you, I can see you're scared of something and maybe it's for a good reason."

"And what is it that you know about me?" I tried to move the spotlight to him.

"I know you were having a panic attack the first time we met. I know you want a man in your life who will make you feel safe." He stood in front of me, and I was caught between his body and one of the legs of the dock.

"Who doesn't want that?" I tried to play it off as nothing. He pressed his chest into mine, and I wanted to moan at how good it felt.

"I know you want a strong man," his hand slowly slid

around my hips then quickly tugged me into him. My hands flew to his arms as he leaned down to stare into my eyes. The moon reflected in his eyes which made his stare that much more intense. "And I know that I've only been around men for almost a decade, so hearing what a beautiful woman might need makes me feel like a caged animal around you."

Animal.

The word nearly tipped me over the edge.

"And what is it that you need, Ty?" I pressed my breasts into his chest, needing some sweet relief from somewhere. They ached with need. He chuckled, and the vibration traveled through him and right into the center of my coiled stomach.

"I've been a leader my entire life. I'm not one to hold back. I fight to stay alive almost every damn day. I need—"

"Control." I slid my hands up to his shoulders and felt his muscles flex under my touch. He seemed to like it, because his eyes hooded and his throat contracted.

His hand on my lower back slid down over my bottom, to my knee, and then hiked my leg to rest on his hip. Gently, he leaned me back against the dock leg as he pushed his erection into my pelvic bone, and I tilted my head to expose my neck.

"You give it over so easily," he groaned as he leaned forward and sealed his hot mouth to my sensitive neck.

It was a completely reckless and inappropriate way for the two of us to behave, but I just needed to feel something. Though the others might be okay with us being together, I wasn't sure what my uncle would think. After all, it had been only a week or so since I arrived.

His tongue teased the lobe of my ear while his warm breath, combined with his stubble, drove me wild, and all I could do was take. I shamelessly pressed myself harder into him, molding to every groove in his body. I hopped up and wrapped both legs around his waist, tired of the struggle to stay above the water's surface.

"Jesus, Ivy." He pulled down the top of my suit to uncover one of my breasts and drew in my nipple. My legs squeezed tight around him. He nipped and sucked while his hands slid around the inside of my bottoms. I combed through his hair and rubbed his shoulders, lost in the moment.

Though the lake was cool, my skin felt licked by fire. I could tell by his grip on my hip and breast he was trying to control himself. Suddenly, he pulled back, reached up, and cupped my chin with his strong fingers and turned my face to look at him.

"I'm a good guy, Ivy, but I want to do so many bad things to you."

I forgot how to breathe. Finally, a man I could see myself having some real fun with.

"Oh, yeah?" I raised an eyebrow, heaving my chest in his face. "Like what?"

"Ivy?" Savi called and snapped me from my bubble. "Where'd you go?"

"Shit." I tried to push by him, but he held me tight as

he tugged up my top, and my hot breast was instantly cooled by my wet suit.

"This isn't over." He kissed my neck then grabbed me by the hips and lifted me effortlessly out of the water and placed me up on the dock in one fluid motion. My legs were mush as my head tried to calm down.

I grabbed the first piece of clothing I saw and tugged it on. I was totally frazzled as I hurried up the path. I could hear Ty just behind me.

"Hey, Ty," Mark called from the firepit and held up a phone, "someone named Demi has called several times, and there's a text."

"Okay," he called. "Thanks for monitoring my phone." Ty laughed sarcastically as he snatched it from Mark.

"Glad to be of help." Mark grinned.

That was all I needed to know. Ty was indeed taken, or at least was entertaining someone else. Clearly, it wasn't too serious because of our moment in the lake, but regardless, I needed to take a step back. Lust could be a real bitch sometimes. To say I was disappointed was an understatement, but we were grownups and that was life. I totally understood. The man had been away a long time and had needs. I knew he was attracted to me, but I certainly didn't want to be up against someone else.

"Savi! Hi, were you looking for me?"

"Yeah!" She kissed her son, who had fallen asleep on her lap, and handed him to Abby. "I just wondered where you'd gotten to. Are you enjoying yourself?" She joined me while I dried my hair with a towel. I could see Ty on his phone and tried to ignore the ping in my chest. In fairness, we never asked one another if we were dating anyone else. I knew he was aware I was single from our previous conversation. "I was wondering if you were tired, or—"

"I'll go on a date with Patrick." *Where did that come from?*

"Yeah?" She grinned.

"You're dating?" My uncle shot off his chair and looked at me in surprise, "I'm shocked to hear that, but I'm pleased to know you're getting some normal back in your life."

Yes, see? All is fine in the world. I'm being normal and going on a date.

"I'm pretty sure I can handle a date with a yoga instructor."

"Just sneeze and he'll fall over," Mark teased.

"You just seem to be everywhere, don't you?" I tossed my towel at him, and he laughed.

"Consider it taken care of." Savi grinned as she rubbed her hands together.

I had to laugh at her matchmaking then rushed off toward the house so I couldn't change my mind. I caught a glimpse of a woman walking out of the woods with her hands around her midsection. I waited for her to get closer before I spoke.

"You must be Lexi." I kept myself natural. "I was wondering when we'd meet."

"Ah, yes," she seemed almost annoyed, "you're the new doctor."

"I am." I offered a wave. "Ivy Knight. It's a pleasure to put a face to the name."

"Is it?" She checked her watch. "Because I'm guessing you've heard a ton of shit about me." Her defenses were on high.

Wow, okay. I changed tactics.

"If you're so worried about that, why don't you have a session with me, then I can form my own thoughts about you," I challenged. She let out a heavy huff and dropped her arms.

"Got any openings soon?"

"Yeah, but if you don't show, I won't give you another chance." I held my ground, knowing how people like Lexi worked. The more time they had to think about things, the more chance they'd talk themselves out of it. "Thursday, five p.m. sharp." She shook her head but then nodded.

"Fine." She rushed off, and I headed toward the house. My first impression was she had an edge to her. I just wondered if it had always been there. I hoped the second impression would give me a clearer picture of what was going on with this woman.

Once inside, I saw John and Mike and their wives sitting in the living room enjoying a nightcap before bed. I waved and rushed up the stairs. I needed a moment to process what Ty had awoken inside me. Once I was alone in the hallway, I sagged against the wall by my door. God,

I felt like a tightly wound toy ready to go but never released. I leaned my head back against the cool wall and pressed my legs together as tight as I could and shut my eyes. Memories of Ty flickered before me, and I groaned as I wished his hands were still on me. His mouth on my skin, my breast, his…

"I don't think I've been jealous of a hoodie before." His raspy tone nearly had me in tears.

What? I glanced down at what I was wearing and remembered I'd grabbed something to put on at the dock. I had on his zipper hoodie. I let go a chuckle. *Smooth, Ivy.*

"Sorry." I started to slip it down my shoulders, but his hand landed on my mine as he tugged it back in place.

"Don't. It's incredibly sexy seeing my name on you." His eyes flared as his thumb brushed over my collarbone.

"I'll return it tomorrow."

"Dr. Knight." Keith was suddenly in the hallway, and I noticed Ty didn't attempt to put any space between us. "Beckett, good. Zero-six-hundred, we all head to Camp Green."

"Copy that," Ty responded, and I nodded.

"Maybe, ah…" Keith struggled to say something to me. "Speak to Savannah about what it can be like there for females."

"Meaning?" I chuckled and wondered exactly what he meant.

"Young soldiers tend to be inappropriate around women such as yourself."

"What exactly am I?" I rather enjoyed watching Keith

trip over his own words. I really wished Savannah would come right about now.

"Beckett?" Keith looked at him for help, but there was no help there except a huge grin. He retreated to safety downstairs. I choked with laughter as I looked back at Ty, who watched me while he shook his head.

"That was mean." He chuckled.

"No, that was fun." I waited a beat. "Well, goodnight, Ty."

"Goodnight." His gaze dropped down me one last time before he went to his room.

"No." I stood in the doorway of Ivy's bedroom when she opened it the next morning. "No way."

Her skintight white dress with its thin brown belt showed every single one of her gorgeous curves. The little cleavage that showed was enough for my mouth to run dry. She turned a moment to glance back into the room, and my eyes went to the slit up the back of the skirt.

"How long have you been standing there?" She looked back at me then made an attempt to brush me off.

"Wear this." I handed her one of my t-shirts and she held it up. "Wear it with jeans and do one of those knot things Sloane does with her t-shirts."

"As flattered as I am that you care, the answer is no. This is way too big, and I don't wear jeans on the job."

She took a step back and set it on the table inside the door.

"Ivy." I rubbed my head and tried to suppress my urge to command.

"Tyler," she used my full name, and that grabbed my attention, "I think you're forgetting that I'm a professional and have years of experience. I often work one on one with soldiers in my office, alone. I am quite capable of choosing the appropriate attire."

"I'm a grown man and also a professional, but I can barely handle myself around you," I grunted.

"You're horny," she shot back, and I held her gaze.

"Can you blame me after last night?"

"Come on." She grabbed her phone off the table. When I went to reach for my t-shirt, she stopped. "No." She pulled it from my hand and held it to her chest.

"Are you going to wear it?" I felt a glimmer of hope spread through me.

"Yes," she tossed it on the bed, "just not right now."

"Ivy."

"I know you're used to getting your own way, but not this time." She grinned and pointed with her head to show I was to follow her toward the stairs.

It wasn't too long before we turned off the highway and down the long side road to where the camp was nestled in the middle of the woods.

Camp Green was impressive. I didn't expect anything less once I heard Cole oversaw the place. The Logan name had a reputation for a reason. They thought of everything.

Cole and Keith gave us a tour, and like Keith warned, every friggin' pair of eyes was on Ivy. Why couldn't she wear fatigues and a black shirt like the rest of us?

"These six, here." Cole handed me a clipboard with printed profiles. "They're in there running drills. I've had them on my radar since they arrived." I scanned the first few and was pleased to see they had excellent track records. "Dr. Knight, I'd like you and Beckett to spend a few minutes with each of them. I want a first impression. What's your feel?"

"Of course." Ivy looked over my shoulder at the first picture and scanned the room to find him. Cole called the men together and explained that they were to meet us in a room down the hall. He and Ivy followed the guys as they fell out. Keith put a hand on my shoulder.

"When you're done, I'd like you to meet someone who might be of use to you."

"Oh?"

"Yes. I like to think of her as a wizard."

"Roger." I watched him leave and noticed Ivy had stopped to speak to someone. I came up behind them and caught part of the conversation.

"Yes, there's a place in town, and if you'd like, I could show you," he explained. I noticed his rank on his shirt. He was young and probably just got promoted, by the way he was nervously watching the door for either Cole or Keith to come back. She must have sensed me because she turned.

"Are we ready?"

"Yes." I stared at the kid.

"Thanks for letting me know." She waved politely as I joined her. "Lead the way."

The interviews went well. Each soldier was respectful of Ivy and looked her in the eye whenever she addressed one of them. They answered the questions without hesitation, and it left me with a good gut feeling. Though it would take time to think of them as my team, I was certainly open to the idea. Ivy interested me the most, though. She was professional and spoke with ease, but her voice commanded honest answers, she didn't allow them to bullshit her. For someone so small, she could be quite mighty, and the guys surprised me by their immediate reaction to her.

"So, tell me, Gear." Ivy was on the last candidate. She was through the standard questions, but for some reason she didn't let this one off as easy. "From what you've been told about this position, how do you feel about being away for lengths of time?"

"Ahh," he stumbled for the first time, "fine."

I watched her face; I knew Ivy hated that answer.

"You're the youngest, yes?" He nodded. "Two older sisters, and you're the baby."

"Yes, ma'am. I'm not ashamed to say I'm a momma's boy."

"Me too." She smiled back. *Hmm, interesting detail.* "I bet your mama makes a mean southern dish."

"The best in three counties."

"Family dinners must be a real treat. Iced tea, fried chicken, apple dumplings."

"Don't forget peach cobbler," he added with a smile.

"I bet you're excited for Christmas this year. I hear the peach crops were divine."

"Best in years." His face lit up. "I've never missed a holiday dinner." He suddenly caught on to what she was implying and chewed his lip.

"I see your sister's in a wheelchair."

"Yes." He looked up as she changed topics without warning. "She fell when she was young, severed her spine."

"I'm sorry." Ivy reached out and squeezed his arm. "That must be hard on the family."

"It is. But I help out and take her to her appointments and physiotherapy."

"Who's helping her right now?"

"My cousin, but he'll head back when I've done my training."

"And then?"

"And then…" He looked at her again as he wet his lips. "And then I take her to her appointments. My mama isn't capable of driving her, so I do it." The kid was bright, and he could already see the writing on the wall as Ivy went on.

"So, tell me this. What happens if you're on call this Thanksgiving or need to fly out at Christmas and spend your holidays under fire, covered in sweat and mud instead of with your family? Is that something you can live with?"

"It's just food," he said defensively and glanced at me. I could see him trying to find a way out. "I can miss a few meals."

"And your sister?"

His face fell and his shoulders slumped. He opened his mouth but then shut it again.

"Gear, you're a great candidate. You passed all the standard questions with flying colors, but this job is more than just being a badass soldier. It's about everything else that you'll have to give up along the way. A job like this means you have to be ready to go at the drop of a hat with no explanation. You have to keep everyone you love in the dark for their own protection. Even dating someone will be a major challenge, not to mention a future with a wife and family. That would have to be put on hold. I can see your family needs you. Your sister needs you."

"Yeah." He nodded, and it was obvious it was the first time everything had sunk in for him.

"I won't pull your file from the stack, but I want you to make sure this is what *you* really want. If you decide it isn't for you, just call Logan, and he'll pull your file quietly and no one will be the wiser."

I watched him leave, and when the door shut, I looked at Ivy.

"How'd you know?"

"By how many emails he's received from his mother." She scribbled down a few notes. "Most candidates email a lot at first, but then it tapers off once they're settled in. Gear's mother writes him several times a day, and he replied to every one of them."

"That's impressive, Dr. Knight." God, she was sexy even when she worked.

Keith popped his head in the door. "Ready, Beckett?"

"Yes." I hesitated as I looked at Ivy, who was gathering up her iPad and water bottle.

"I'm good, Ty. Go ahead." She chuckled and shook her head at me. "I can handle myself."

"Take a left outside the door," Keith said, "and at the end take another left and you'll find us."

"Sounds good." She smiled at him, then at me.

Keith's mouth had softened a little as we started down the hall, but a few minutes later it morphed into a full-on smile when he approached the cute little strawberry blonde behind a counter.

"Liza Forrest, this is our new team commander, Major Tyler Beckett."

"Nice to meet you, Beckett." She offered a firm handshake and a bright smile, which swung immediately back over to Keith once she'd acknowledged me. Her cheeks pinked, and she tucked a small piece of hair that had escaped from her loose ponytail behind her ear. I stifled a smile of my own. Seemed Keith had an admirer.

"Liza here can find anything you need from anywhere in the world." Keith beamed.

"Now I see why he calls you the wizard," I added.

She chuckled. "He's exaggerating. I just don't stop until I get what I want."

I couldn't help but catch Keith's gaze at that one, and he cleared his throat and moved his eyes back to her. Everything about him looked alive. His body had an energy I'd never felt before. I hadn't met this Keith yet. He was more like the man Savannah talked about. The guy seemed completely different. There was confidence in his voice as he spoke to her. I liked this guy and enjoyed listening to them talk. We discussed some things I hoped she could get for me.

"It was really nice meeting you, Liza. I'll be in touch soon."

"Sounds good." She waved as I left the two of them alone and made my way toward Ivy, who stood in conversation with a few soldiers.

"How is someone as pretty as you not snatched up yet?" one of them asked. "If you were mine, I wouldn't let you within ten feet of this place. We wolves can sniff a female's scent in the air." He lifted his nose and gave a demonstration. I rolled my eyes at his nasty attempt to flirt.

"Oh, trust me, I have a wolf who doesn't let me get ten feet away from him," she warned as I came up behind her.

"That she does." I glared at them as I slid my arm around her waist and kissed her neck, letting my lips linger for a moment. They all stiffened when they caught my rank on my shoulder.

"Sorry, sir," one said. "We didn't know."

"Now you do," I grunted and relished how great her body felt against mine. "Dismissed."

They all scurried off, and Ivy chuckled.

"Good timing." She patted my arm that was still locked around her. She tilted her head back and looked at me. "They're gone now."

"Wolves travel in packs." I glanced around, making sure everyone saw my claim. She wasn't theirs. Well, she wasn't mine either, but still.

"Then don't go far." The corners of her mouth tugged, and I slowly let her go but kept her within arm's reach for the rest of our visit.

Once we got back to Shadows, the wives were into the margaritas. Mark handed me a beer.

"Did you meet Liza?" Savi asked me quietly as I sipped my brew.

"I did."

"She's good people. Whenever I go to the camp, we try to get a moment to slip away for a bit. We have a little place we love to go for a drink and a chat." She tapped her finger on her glass. "How was Ivy's visit?" Her expression turned mischievous. "I love Camp Green, but it's hard to get away from Cole. He doesn't let me get too far from him if he can help it."

"I can understand that."

"Mm, so, they got to her?"

"They tried." She seemed impressed by my answer.

"I like you, Ty." She smiled then spotted Cole and headed toward him.

I spotted Ivy in the kitchen and locked my gaze with hers. Her lips went up in a smile as I started toward her.

"Beers down!" Cole's voice boomed throughout the house, and suddenly the entire mood changed. Gone was the lingering party vibe. It was as though the wind had shifted direction. "Suit up. We ship out in one hour."

My eyes never left hers, and for a full minute I couldn't break the hold…didn't want to. She nodded. I shifted gears in my head, stood taller, and left.

Here we go.

———

The winds were strong as we swept over the Mexican border and deep into the unknown. The buzz of the chopper seemed to help the guys focus on what awaited us on the ground. Our mission was to locate a group of missing teens who had last been seen three days before in the company of one of the local Cartel runners, Juan. Cole explained that one of the girls taken was connected to a politician in Wyoming. Frank's informant said he had eyes on them somewhere in Rosarito. Juan was an idiot, according to Mark. He was a guy who loved the idea of being what he saw as a big-time Army informant. He would puff himself up and give the scoop on any of the Cartel guys he encountered. They kept him around because he was harmless for the most part and ran his mouth for nothing more than a bottle of tequila.

I went over and over what was expected of me. I knew exactly what the plan was when we touched down. After being team captain for many years, I knew I had to know every second of the plan and account for any problems that might arise.

Once I felt confident with everything, I closed my eyes to find Ivy waiting in my thoughts. She was so incredibly submissive when I touched her, and it took every bit of me not to lose myself with her at the dock. When she wrapped her legs around my waist, and I felt her heavy breast in my hand, it just about undid me. The sensation of her nipple in my mouth still filled my senses. I was a strong man, but one taste of her and I became someone else. The moment she put on my hoodie with my name printed on the back, it was as though I had claimed her as my own. I never needed a woman in my life. I was content with my choices. I loved my job and would die happy doing it. But since I first met Ivy, something had awakened inside me. Like a primal force I wanted to protect and devour all at once. I could barely handle being in the same room with her, let alone at a camp where all the guys flirted with her. My mind went back to the nervous way she looked when Logan announced we were to ship out. It made me want to get inside her head to see what was happening in there.

I shouldn't have made plans with Demi, not when I couldn't keep myself away from Ivy.

I felt a tap on my knee, and my eyes popped open to find Cole signaling that we were ready to go in three minutes. I gave him a thumbs up and moved to stand behind Mark. At the signal, one by one, we descended the ropes and slipped quietly into the night.

We followed a street called Justicia that ran north of Rosarito then moved southwest into the city. We moved quietly on our feet along the narrow alleyways. As we went, we had to weave through the sea of trash that waited to be dealt with in the morning. I scanned the buildings, windows, rooftops, anywhere a sniper could hide. The Taliban and the Cartel had the same motive—to kill those who weren't their own. I'd lived with that mentality for years, and it had trained me well.

We came to a building where we believed they were being held. Mark checked the door, while Mike and John scanned the perimeter. Keith stayed tight at the door, and Cole communicated with Frank, who had our informant on the other line.

"Clear," both Mike and John confirmed over the radio.

One by one, each of us scanned the rooftops one last time before we stepped inside. We stopped just long enough to let our eyes adjust to the dim light. Instantly, my gut twisted, and my head slipped into survival mode.

Something was off.

It was a general store, with rows of canned food. Refrigerators against the back wall held milk and eggs.

The place was empty, and I could hear water as it dripped from somewhere. Nothing else could be heard.

"Something feels off," John's voice crackled over the radio. "This isn't what it seems."

"I second that," I added.

"Eyes on alert, boys. Gut is everything." Cole didn't dismiss our feelings, and I was glad because something wasn't right at all.

The guys started to clear the aisle while the hair on my neck prickled incessantly. There was more to the situation.

Mike tapped his foot and held up a hand that he found something. He used the tip of his shoe to push back an old rug to expose a raised ridge. Slowly, we joined him, and we saw part of a trap door. With a thorough check, Keith and I silently counted to three and lifted the counter over to expose the rest of the door. Mark bent down and inspected the perimeter while I signaled to Cole that I wanted to step back to check something. The milk cartons had caught my attention. He nodded.

What am I not seeing?

Careful not to disturb anything, I nudged a box of the milk with the tip of my rifle and noticed it easily rocked backward before it sat back in place. It was empty. Odd. I did it to the others, and they were full. My eyes went back to the empty milk carton, and I focused on the faded expiration date, three years old.

Then I saw it, a wire, running from behind the eggs into the wall. It was out of place and looked all too familiar to me. Quickly, I pulled out a sensor that I was given by a commander years ago. It allowed me to follow the wire through rock or, in this case, plaster. It had a screen that gave me a readout of explosive materials, wire types, and other details…My boots scuffed as I made quick work around the room. The three red lights that had saved my life countless times before blinked brightly at me.

Shit.

I looked over at John, who had just slid his micro camera underneath the hatch.

"It looks empty—"

"Stop!" I commanded, and the entire team came to a standstill. "Black." I directed all my attention to John. "Don't move your hand. Look over Lopez's left shoulder. Do you see the cracked tile in the corner there?"

"Yeah."

"There's a wire coming out of the wall headed in your direction."

"Shit, I see it." He stayed perfectly still as I came over, scanning the floor as I went.

"The entire door is rigged with C-4." I showed Cole the readout. "It looks to me," I knelt on the floor and scanned the perimeter of the door, "yeah," I said more to myself, "this entire thing is rigged. We're standing on a makeshift bomb." I moved carefully next to John and bent to peer under the crack in the trap door. The camera was just about to trip the wire. I looked around and spotted Mark's pink gum in his pocket. He'd been popping gum in his mouth earlier. "Lopez, can I have a piece of your gum?"

"Yeah." He carefully unwrapped it and handed it to me. I put it in my mouth and chewed the nasty goo. Once it was sticky, I looked at Cole.

"We'll lose the camera." I eyed him.

He nodded. "Do what you need to."

"Okay, Black. Steady, my friend. If that camera even so much as wiggles forward or backward a hair, you might get a lot more than a close shave. I need to stabilize it right where it is."

"Copy that." He held totally still while I secured the bubblegum around the neck of the camera, so it was plastered to the trap door. I bent down and blew on the gum, hardening it before I trusted John to let go.

"Give it a sec," I cautioned. "The Taliban would run wire all over the place and sit and wait for us to trip it." I decided to share where my head was. "After three months over there, we got sensitized to it. It's almost like I can feel it." I blew again. "Black, remove your hand very slowly." John released each finger and carefully let go of the wire that held the tiny camera. "The sugar in the gum crystalizes around the wire, holds it in place better than tape or putty."

"I think Frank needs to double check his informant is working for the right team," Mike grunted with a relieved sigh. "That was too close for comfort."

"Yeah, I rather like my face attached to my body." John chuckled, more out of relief.

"Good catch, Beckett." Keith looked at Cole, and he nodded.

"They're not here." Cole pulled out his satellite phone. "We're leaving."

Cole made a call, then we slipped back into the night and raced back the way we'd come. Just as we were getting close to the only open area, we heard tires squeal and a few men shouting, so we slowed our pace and glued ourselves to the wall of the alley.

Cole, who was in the front, signaled there was a truck full of Cartel ahead. Mark groaned and dropped his head.

"They know we're here," he whispered over the radio. "Withdraw. Use alternate route."

"Roger that." Mark struggled to turn in the narrow space with all his gear on. He waved us to follow. Plan B was the longer way back to the chopper. Just like before, we heard tires come to a stop up ahead, and we froze. They had scouts giving our location.

I shut my eyes, and in my head, I pictured the way we had moved to this location. We'd traveled in a perfect Z shape, which would mean the two turns were most likely being blocked by them as well.

"Logan," I pointed upward, "rooftops might be a good choice."

"Go," he ordered.

I pressed my hands outward against the wall on either side and hopped up, using the toes of my boots to hold my legs taut, and started to shimmy up the wall. The others followed, and soon we made our way up to the top and sprung onto the roof. Laying low, we carefully zipped across the buildings, hoping to hell the scouts wouldn't spot us on the rooftop. Once we made it as far as we could, we scanned the perimeter, slid down a pipe to the ground, and dropped into the tall grass.

We eventually made our way safely back to our chopper. As we lifted into the air, we could see several trucks in various areas along our route. Thankfully, we'd outsmarted them. As I looked at the faces of my fellow teammates, it was clear this mission was not how things normally went.

The moment we crossed the United States border, I could feel the tension lift. Mark popped gum in his mouth, Keith kicked his feet out, John fell asleep, and Mike nudged Cole, who no doubt was replaying every moment of the mission in his head. It was what you did as a leader. I'd always analyze every moment of what happened. No matter if the mission went perfectly or went wrong, there was always something to learn.

"Logan, did I hear Quinn is back in town?" John asked as we flew over the Montana mountains. We were almost home, and I was impressed with the magnitude of changes in vehicles and the deviations we'd had to make to get there. Cole didn't mess around when it came to the location of the safehouse.

"Yes, he's back," Mark chimed in, "but we might miss him." He looked at his watch. "Ivy's got a date, and since we were gone—" He made a face.

"Copy that." John nodded.

A date? I noticed Mark moved his attention to me

and wiggled his eyebrows. "Mr. Bendy Yoga," he mouthed, and I looked away but caught his smirk.

Really? She agreed to go on a date with that yoga instructor?

Once we got back home, the wives came out to greet the guys, and the kids cheered and hugged their fathers. Daniel and Sue stayed back with smiles, and Abby and Doc Roberts watched it all from the window. I wondered if it was always like this, but my gut told me it was. It was quite the sight and made me pause for a moment as I wondered if that was something I'd want someday.

"Beckett?" Daniel stopped me at the door. "Your parents called the contact line. They'd like you to call them as soon as possible."

Oh?

"Copy that. Thank you, sir." He nodded as I went inside and headed to my room.

I tossed my bag on the bed and removed my phone from the charger. Normally, I'd wait until after my shower to call, but the fact they called the house line made me wonder what the urgency was.

"Hello, my sweet boy." I smiled at her greeting, I could be fifty, and I'd still be her sweet boy. "Your father and I have news."

"Good, I hope." I eased into the chair by the window and watched Mark's twins as they played with Butters.

"Demi told us she's having dinner with you tonight. She invited your father, sister, and me to join you."

My stomach dropped, and I held my forehead with sigh.

"That's great, Mom. I can't wait." I'd wanted tonight to explain to Demi that the agreement we had needed to end. But now, it would be a whole lot trickier. Not to mention my sister would be there. She had eyes like a hawk and could read me like an open book.

"Demi told us you're training in Montana this week, so we booked this adorable little Airbnb right in town so we could have a drink or two and not worry about driving. Oh, dear, I just can't believe we get to do this. Your father and I have waited so long to see you."

"I'm looking forward to it, too, Mom. See you tonight." I hung up and leaned my head back against the chair and mentally prepared for a night with my family and Demi.

When I arrived, Zack's was busy, and I was happy that Mark told me he'd called ahead to let them know we were coming. Though there were a few other restaurants in town, he assured me we'd be taken care of here. I was starting to see the perks of this job, and this was one I was truly thankful for. My family was casual, so I was pleased that I only needed to wear jeans and a t-shirt to meet them. I wore a ball hat so I could shade my eyes while I watched the room. Crowds were not something I was used to, and I was instantly on alert.

"Good evening, Mr. Beckett." The host smiled up at me after I gave him my name. "Zack told me you were coming, and I have a table in the corner for you and your party. But I do have a table by the window about to open up. Mark mentioned you might prefer that one.

"No, the corner's great. Thanks." I nodded for him to lead the way, and I settled in my seat to watch. A short time later, my family and Demi walked through the door.

Here we go.

My mother practically elbowed a customer aside as she raced to hug me. I knew I'd hurt them when I went from Afghanistan, to Washington, to Shadows without stopping for a visit, but this was the part of life I was bad at. Family.

"Look at you!" She wrapped me in her arms and nearly sobbed. "You're so big!"

"Work out much? Shit, brother, look at you." My sister squeezed my arm then peeled Mom off me and came in for a hug. "God, it's good to see you."

"You too, Shelly." I hugged her back. I knew she'd been through a lot since I'd been gone. Her ex was an asshole, and I was counting my days to get my hands on him. "You look great."

"Son," my father held my shoulders to look at me, "I'm so happy to see you're in one piece."

"I am, Dad. Only a few scrapes," I joked. Then Demi stepped up, and I felt my mood shift.

"What, no hug for me?" She gave me a hurt look, so I leaned in and hugged her. "I'm all prepped," she purred in my ear. "Just say the word, and we're out of here." There was a time when I would have faked an illness just to get her alone. There were never feelings involved; it was an understanding. We both had needs, and we enjoyed each other satisfying those needs. Demi was pretty and a nice girl but was high maintenance. She liked to be waited on and wanted to be on a pedestal when she was outside the bedroom. All things I hated. A woman should be loved, cherished, and cared for, but it should never be something to demand. It should happen naturally.

"Come, let's all sit." I sidestepped her comment. Demi had known my family for years. I assumed they thought we were more than we were. I really needed to set the record straight tonight. The fact that they seemed in good spirits told me they hadn't heard about Brown's death yet. I tucked that topic away, not wanting to deal with it tonight. I needed a mental break.

My sister went for the corner seat, and I eyed her hard. She tossed her hands up with a grin and a nod.

"Sorry, it's been a while." She shifted seats and beamed at me. "How is it that you've been through hell and back in a third-world country, yet you still look twenty-two?"

"I don't have a kid." I winked, and she lifted her water glass to mine.

"That's true."

"Well, maybe kids are in your future." Mom gave a side glance to Demi, as I nearly choked on my water.

"We haven't talked about that yet." Demi squeezed Mom's arm, and I felt like I was drowning.

Yet?

"Come on, Ty, we aren't young anymore."

What the fuck was this crap?

"I don't want kids," I chimed in. "You know kids and Army don't mix."

"Maybe it's just the act of making kids?" Demi whispered, and her hand landed on my thigh. I grabbed it and sat it back on her lap. She just chuckled and went back to the conversation with my parents. I wondered just what kind of conversations they'd had while I was away.

"You seem off." My sister turned in her seat. "Something's different."

"Nope." I sipped my water, but I felt her probes burrow into my head.

"You know, Mom was mentioning spending the week here. Spend some time with her boy." She played dirty. "Maybe I could convince her not to if I had a little incentive."

"I hate you."

"Oh, I know." She snorted into her glass. "So, what gives, brother?"

Something pulled my attention to the window, and I clenched my fists when I saw what it was. Now I knew why Mark made a reservation for me here.

THIRTEEN

I was shown to a seat in the front by the window and handed a glass of Josh cabernet sauvignon. *Nice.* Then I was told I looked lovely this evening by Zack. He was genuine, so I greatly appreciated his compliment. The truth was I had changed at least a hundred times, trying to find an outfit Patrick might like. Then the girls came in with something called a Marcus Martini, and soon after, I let my insecurities go and decided to wear one of my favorite outfits. The black flowy skirt hit tastefully mid-thigh, a pink silk blouse with gray buttons, and skinny gray heels, and I was ready to go. I had a small obsession with the color gray, and silk too, I guessed.

Savi suggested I should sweep my hair into a loose,

low bun with a few strands left to frame my face. I agreed and felt more confident with that than Mia's suggestion of boho pants and a long shirt that just wasn't my style.

Sloane, who I found very intriguing, stayed in the background and watched. I wondered if it was her professional background that caused her to be that way or just her nature. I knew JAG lawyers were a different breed, as were military psychologists. Perhaps we had more in common than I knew. I made a mental note to get her alone for a walk sometime and get to know her better.

"You're more confident in that outfit, Ivy," Sloane had said. "You'll be yourself in that."

I was a confident woman, so her comment hit home. I just hoped the fact that I wasn't myself with this from the start wasn't a sign that it was a bad idea.

I left the house earlier than I had planned to, as Quinn had a few errands to run and my nerves were getting the best of me. Savi was in the kitchen trying to get an ETA on the guys when I left, so I slipped out with a quick wave in her direction.

I checked my phone as I sat and sipped my wine and realized Patrick was fifteen minutes late. *Not a good start*, I thought as Quinn caught my eye and gave me a warm smile.

"Sorry," I mouthed, and he pointed to the menu with a smile. He was very sweet and didn't seem to mind being given the task to watch over me this evening. It was odd having someone always there, but at the same time, given what I had gone through back in Washington, I felt like I could really relax a little.

I scanned the restaurant and watched a mother try to feed her baby boy mashed potatoes, but every time they went in, they came right back out again. Her husband laughed and handed him a dinner roll, and that seemed to please him. She smiled, and they went back to eating. I loved that they worked as a team.

"I bet you thought I stood you up." A skinny man dressed in yoga pants and a tank top that had a ring of sweat around the collar and armpits dropped a hemp bag at my feet. "Ivy, right?"

"Patrick?" *Okay…* I stood to greet him.

"That would be me." He wiped his hand on his shirt then thrust it forward for a shake. "Sorry for my outfit. I had to step in for my co-worker at the last minute, and well, if I went home, I bet you would've left." He pulled his eighties sweatband off his forehead and shook out his shaggy, wild hair. He could have called, too, but here we were. "I can take a quick run back to my place and change, if you don't mind waiting."

"No problem. That won't be necessary." I tried not to wipe my hand from his clammy handshake. "Please take a —" He sat down, broke off a piece of bread, and shoved it into his mouth. "Seat." Just as I was about to sit back down myself, I locked eyes with Ty across the room. He sat at a table of people with a woman at his side. Why of all places was he here tonight? I hadn't realized they'd be back so soon. The woman pulled his attention just as Patrick spoke up to draw my attention back to him.

"I have a love affair with carbs." He smiled with an open mouth. The bread rolled around his tongue while I slowly slid down into my seat and dragged a napkin over my lap. I wasn't a prude at the dinner table, but, come on, first date impressions were everything.

I took a quick glance at Quinn, who tried everything to hide his grin. I was thankful it was him and not Mark who was with me tonight. Though now I wished I had listened to Mark's warning teases.

"So, Patrick, why don't you tell me—"

"About myself?" He grinned. "I have a knack for finishing people's sentences," he bragged.

"That's quite the gift," I muttered and downed a little more wine. I spotted Ty staring at me through the crowd. God, even his stare was sexy. My skin heated just knowing his eyes were on me.

Focus.

"Well, I've been a yoga instructor for nearly five years, and before that, I was a busker. I played everything from the spoons to the washboard, and before that, I was cardio instructor at a gym."

"I see." I eyed the bread and wondered if any of his shaggy hair had gotten in it.

"I know what you're thinking, but no, I'm not a gym rat like some of those Army guys in town. My muscles are all natural."

Muscles?

"Shall we—"

"Order?" He grinned again, and I sighed inwardly. I hated that he did that. I found my gaze once again moving away from him and over to Ty, whose eyes found me again. "Yes, but I have to say this wouldn't be the place I'd have chosen to eat." I glanced at Patrick as I replayed his words in my head. He turned up his nose at the menu, and I scowled at him. Zack's was impressive and seemed to be the busiest place in town. "I like the salad bar down the road more. I mean, meat is murder, and don't get me started on how he prepares his potato balls."

"Well, why don't you start with a drink?" I was going to kill Savannah.

"I don't drink." He eyed my glass. "Do you know what that does to your liver?"

"Nope, but I know what it does for my tolerance." I downed the rest as the waiter approached.

"Hi there. I hope your evening is going well." He smiled at us. "I'm Adam, and I'll be your waiter this evening. What can I—"

"Get us?" Patrick cut him off, and my eyes bugged out at how rude he sounded. "The menu is limited, so I'll have to go with the kale salad, and double wash the lettuce. I like the tomatoes julienned, the cucumbers diced not sliced, and the dressing on the side, not on top like last time." He held the menu in the air, and I just about died.

"Of course." Adam remained professional, but I could

see this wasn't the first time he'd dealt with Patrick. "And for you, miss?"

"I'll have the slow-roasted chicken with the garden salad on the side, please. Oh, and another one of these, perhaps larger." I smiled and held up my glass.

"Not a problem." He smirked, leaving me with the worst date I'd ever had.

"I must like you, because normally I'd never stick around and watch someone eat something that was alive last week." He laughed at his own comment.

Lucky me.

I reached for the glass of wine that Adam quickly returned with and smiled my thanks. It was filled to the brim. I took a long drink.

The couple next to us left. They held hands and smiled as they walked to the door, and I was suddenly envious of them. They got to leave. Their table was cleaned and reset in a flash, and someone else sat down next to us.

"Savannah tells me you like to run." Patrick looked directly at me for the first time.

I nodded "I do. I find it—"

"Relaxes you. Yes, it does. You know, most people run incorrectly. There's actually..." I tuned him out and relished my slight buzz. It calmed me enough to sit there. At least I knew with the wine, I could do it. Even the part of my brain that would normally psychoanalyze him wasn't even interested. In a normal world, I would have already made an excuse and left, but I couldn't because of

Quinn and the house rules. He would have to leave as well, and he didn't have his meal yet. Patrick's mouth moved as he mansplained the art of running, and I gave in and looked at Ty, only this time the woman, who I could only assume was Demi, had her hand on his shoulder as she smiled lovingly at him.

Damn.

Sexy or not, at that point in time, Ty had someone. I decided it didn't mean I couldn't look, though. I told myself there was nothing wrong with appreciating the male form and all that came with it. I could feel his hands on me, the way his erection dug deliciously into my lower belly as he held me tight. He seemed to know exactly what to do and how I liked it. He was so intense. My thighs squeezed together at the thought, and my throat became dry. Suddenly, birds and whale sounds could be heard through the noisy restaurant. My body jolted back to the present. What the ever-loving hell was that sound?

"My sister." Patrick held up his phone. "I have to take this."

"Please do." I watched him leave then sagged into my chair and hoped the floor would open up and swallow me whole. Maybe he'd have to leave, and I'd be free of sweaty Patrick forever.

Quinn grinned at me, and I glared back as I tried to control my blush. "Savannah's dead," he mouthed as he drew a finger across his throat and laughed. He bent his head and went back to reading something on his phone.

He'd better not warn her what was happening. She didn't need a head start.

"Here you are." Adam placed my dinner in front of me. "Zack thought you might like the rest of this?" He took an open bottle of wine from the other waiter who had helped bring the food over. "Or," he held up the cork, "maybe just keep it for the road." He winked.

"He's a good man, Adam." I watched him leave then admired my delicious looking dinner.

"Ah, I see you got the slow-roasted chicken," someone said next to me. "I got that, too." I looked up at the rather good-looking man at the table next to me. He wore a suit and expensive shoes. I knew my shoes.

"I heard it was the best."

"Well, you're at Zack's, so everything's amazing." He leaned over. "Without sounding too forward, I'm Carson Holden."

"Ivy Knight." I lifted my glass and thought how he was more my speed. He looked at the dinner plate across from me.

"Are you on a date?"

"Sadly, yes." I closed my eyes. "Sorry, that was rude. It was a blind date, and, well, I'm sure you've already noticed his ringtone." I rolled my eyes. "He isn't exactly what I hoped for. He's on a phone call."

"He took a call during your date?"

"Trust me, I could use the break."

The door opened, and Patrick returned. He sat and scowled at his food. Carson leaned back and thanked

Adam for his drink. Patrick slumped in his chair and lifted a piece of kale with his fork.

"This hasn't been washed."

"Welcome back." I stared at him, beyond annoyed at his rudeness. "Perhaps you'd like to learn a little about me?"

"Oh, I know you." He dropped his fork with a cocky smirk.

"Please, enlighten me."

"You eat meat, and not just chicken. I can tell by your skin pigment that you eat red sometimes too. I'll look past it because you're pretty." He winked, and I supposed I was to find that funny. "You're a psychologist, so chances are you've already formed an opinion of me, and the fact that you're still here when I got back means you're interested in me." I blinked at his gumption. "I've been out with women like you before. You're easy to read."

Don't snap, Ivy. He's not worth the outburst.

"Really?" I cleared my throat. "Well, I bet you didn't see this coming." I stood up, grabbed my plate, my purse, and my bottle of wine and looked for an open table or even an open seat.

"Please, Ivy." Carson pulled out the chair next to him.

"Thank you." I took the seat. Patrick's face dropped as he looked around, unsure what to do.

"There's a reason you're single, Ivy," he snapped as his face turned red.

"Yes, because of rude men like you." I turned to Carson, who smiled.

"How are you enjoying your chicken?" he asked as he cut a piece from his own.

Patrick grabbed his stuff, glared at me, and left, hitting Adam with his bag on the way out.

Adam gave me a huge thumbs up, and I sighed, thinking how happy I was he was gone.

"I'm sorry about that, Carson." I began to get up, but he held up a hand.

"I'd actually like some company. Eating alone is over-rated, so please sit."

I smiled and settled back in the seat and thought how nice it was to have a do-over. After all, I had spent the afternoon getting ready. Why should all that effort be wasted by going home early? I knew I'd just eat chocolate and watch Nicholas Sparks movies into the morning. I spotted Quinn, who had Zack's ear. I was sure he was about to order popcorn at this point. The evening must have been quite entertaining.

Conversation came easily, and I didn't even notice when our dinner plates were cleared and a chocolate mousse dessert was placed in front of us. We happily ate the creamy deliciousness while Carson told me about his job.

Wiping his mouth with a napkin, he leaned back and scanned the room with a grin.

"What?"

"I just can't believe I'm here with the most gorgeous woman in the place. How lucky am I?"

"You." I sidestepped his flattery. "I'd be stuck with

Patrick telling me about how our date was going." That made him laugh.

"I'm sorry for cutting this evening short, believe me, but I have a long drive ahead of me in the morning. I'll be in town for the rest of the week, though, and I'd love nothing more than to spend more time with you."

The woman at Ty's table laughed and pulled my attention. Ty was no longer at the table, and the woman was talking to the older couple. Oh, well. If Ty could have someone, so could I. I wanted to be truthful with Carson from the start.

"I have to be honest. I'm interested in someone. It's incredibly new, and I have no idea where it might go or if it's even going anywhere. But I really enjoyed tonight and would like to do this again."

"Then let the best man win." He chuckled. "You're refreshing Ivy, so," he scribbled on a napkin, "call me old fashioned, but here's my number."

"All right." I took the napkin with a smile and programmed his number into my phone. I sent a quick message off to him. "Call me modern." I laughed, and he grinned at his phone as my info arrived. He stood and touched his upper lip in thought.

"I want a fighting chance, so does Monday, here, at seven work?"

"I believe it does."

"Then it's a date." I watched him settle his bill with Adam at the front, then he whisked out into the rainy night.

Did that just happen? Yes, it did, Ivy!

"Well, you had quite the night." Quinn chuckled next to me.

"I sure did." I laughed as I folded the napkin Carson had given me with his number on it and tucked it away in my purse as a token. I left enough money on the table to cover the tab for myself and Patrick. It was worth every penny to be leaving without him.

"I'll tell you, Quinn, I've had all the fun I can endure for one evening. I'm totally ready to go."

"Let me." He pulled out my chair. "Since it's raining, I'd like to bring the car around. Zack is at the bar waiting for you to join him. He'll stick around until I let him know I'm out front."

"Sounds good." I headed to the bar and waved at Zack. He was helping the bartender, who looked swamped. With a quick glance over my shoulder, I spotted Ty's table was empty.

A pretty woman stepped in front of me. "Without sounding too forward, who are you?" Her eyes narrowed in on me, and I tried to place who she might be.

"I'm sorry. Do I know you?"

"No, but I'd like to know who you are." Her face softened, and it eased my nerves. "I want to know why my brother's mood changed the moment he spotted you in the restaurant."

"Ah, you're Ty's sister," I said more to myself. "I'm Ivy Knight, a team psychologist for the Army. I work with Ty."

"A psychologist?" She lifted an eyebrow. "Please tell me you can finally get him to leave Demi. Seriously, it's been years, and he's—" My face must have fallen, because she stopped herself.

"I'm not Ty's doctor. I'm with a different unit. I'm just in the same building."

"Oh," she nodded, "well, I'm Shelly." She pointed to herself. "Are you sure you just work with him? Because he barely took his eyes off you once."

"I'm really not sure what you think you saw." The topic got awkward for me, and I wondered where the hell Quinn was. "But I don't really know him all that well."

"He was just distant at dinner, but when he spotted you, he couldn't keep his eyes off you and your date. I'm sure it wasn't your date he was interested in." She made a face. "It was almost like he was upset or something. It just made me think there was something there."

"No." I waved her off. "We're just friends."

"I see, and I might believe that if he hadn't rushed out after that Richard Simmons workout type left your table and made such a scene when he left." She laughed. "Ty took off through the back, and I even heard him talking to the owner about what happened. FYI, Ty never cares that much about anything. Well, that's not military related, anyway. So," she folded her arms, "you can imagine my surprise when I get a look at who he'd been watching all night. A pretty blonde with a smokin' body."

I chuckled. "Thanks." I appreciated the insight.

"Truth?" She nodded. "Things are a bit complicated with

my personal life right now. My attention's a bit scattered. I won't bullshit you." I figured she was like the rest of them and liked things straightforward. "Your brother is great, but he's clearly got some stuff going on with Demi, and I just met someone tonight who seems pretty nice."

"That Richard Simmons wannabe?" Her mouth dropped open.

"No," I laughed, "another guy, Carson. He just happened to be there. Right place, right time kind of thing. Anyway, I want to give him a chance. I mean, he was great at having my back after the scene my blind date caused."

"Ty's a better catch." She winked, and I shook my head as she went on. "But yes, I get it. Demi and Ty go back a long way. They always seem to hook up again." She smiled sweetly. "I only think it's fair you know that."

"That's actually really cool of you to be honest about that, Shelly. Thanks." Zack caught my attention and pointed that Quinn was here. I held up a finger to ask Quinn for a second.

"Ty doesn't know this yet," she looked at Quinn, "but we're coming back the week after next. Our parents fell in love with Redstone, and Ty mentioned he'll be running back and forth to Montana for training. They're so desperate to spend time with him. We all are, really. And they're retired, so they thought it might be fun to spend some more time here."

"And you?"

"Well, right now I'm living with them, along with my little girl, so I might just tag along."

"I hope you do." I pointed over my shoulder. "I'm sorry, but I have to go. It was nice meeting you, Shelly."

"You too."

"Who was that?" Quinn gazed back at Shelly as I walked by him for the door.

"Ty's sister." I stepped out into the rain to join Quinn. I was more than ready to go home.

FOURTEEN

When we reached the house, it was well past one a.m., and I wasn't tired in the least. It was lightly misting, and it made it difficult to see very far.

"What am I hearing?" I asked Quinn as I shut the truck door.

"The guys are over there." He pointed, and I squinted to see the low light off in the distance.

"What's going on?"

"My guess, they're checking their gear for a trip out."

"They just got back."

"The Cartel aren't on a punch card, Ivy. Welcome to life at Shadows."

"But at this time of night?" I didn't like that they

were leaving again so soon, so I headed over. Careful to avoid the puddles, I used their voices to lead the way. I stepped up the stairs and took in the sight. The guys looked like they were suiting up for a battle. Guns were being checked and cleaned; items were being put in packs. I spotted Ty as he strapped a piece of gear around his leg.

"Impressive." I wrapped my arms around my midsection, feeling the cold seep in. Ty looked over and dragged his gaze down my front.

"How was your date with Mr. Yoga?" Mark smirked.

"It was interesting."

"Is there a second date in your future?"

"Not with him, but I did meet someone else." They all looked over at me. "Relax, boys. Quinn was there the entire time."

"Does this guy have a name?" John cut a glance at Ty, who stood straighter with a knife in his hand.

"Yup." I didn't offer anything else. "So, are you guys training tonight?"

"We've been called out," Keith said. "The last mission was shit, and we only have a short window to make things right."

"Oh." I felt my stomach twist at the thought of them going back out again, after what seemed a disaster last time. "You just got back. Isn't there a rule about sleep or something?"

"Nah, we've done worse things." John grabbed a bag. "Glad you had a good night."

"Thanks." I moved aside while he headed out the door.

I turned to Ty, who'd just finished packing his bag. He looked good in his tight black t-shirt, combat pants, and belt full of tactical gear. I stepped inside the small structure and admired their ammo on the wall. I picked up a piece of a pistol that had been taken apart and looked at the pieces around it. It was like a puzzle.

"Did you have a good evening?" I kept my back to him as I spoke.

"It was nice to see my family." I heard Velcro tear.

"That's nice." I held two metal parts and tried to piece them together. "Are you nervous about the mission?"

"This is what I do."

"That's doesn't mean you're not scared." I hated that kind of answer.

I heard the click of a belt, a thud, and footsteps while I dropped a pin. I scooped it off the floor and gave up. It was impossible to put together.

He pressed against my back and slid his hands down my arms. His body was hot and hard. His breath smelled fresh and inviting. "Slide that in here." He waited for me to do it. "Now pick up the spring and place it in the slide. Now do the barrel." I dropped another piece, and he took over. "The barrel goes in like this." His muscle flexed and made him squeeze me tighter. I closed my eyes for a moment. "You compress this with your thumb, then this slides onto the top like this." He did it effortlessly as he spoke. "Then you pull it back to fire it." He took my hand

and wrapped it around the pistol grip and aimed it at a target on the wall. "Now you aim and fire." He squeezed my finger, and the click of the gun made me jump. My heart raced at how incredibly sexual he made everything.

"You never answered my question," I whispered.

"No." He removed the gun from my hand and set it on the table. "I'm not scared." He kept me in front of him as he ran his hands along my waist.

"I would be."

"You're not trained for it. It's a mindset. You need to control that part of your head." He turned his nose into my hair and breathed deeply. "It takes all my control when you're near me."

"I'm not the one with a girlfriend."

"She's not my girlfriend."

"But she's your something." I pushed my palms into his thighs, needing to feel him. I was glad he'd removed his gear. It allowed us to be closer.

"I told her tonight that nothing would ever happen between her and me."

Shelly's words came back to me, so I pushed away and tried to clear my head. I ran a hand through my hair as I walked around the room. I was incredibly pent-up. I wasn't sure what to do with myself.

He leaned against the counter and watched me.

"So, you met someone?"

"I did." Air shot through his teeth when I leaned over to pick up his camo jacket. "May I?" The damp air was chilly.

"Mhm," he muttered quietly. I hesitated for a moment, then pushed my arms through the sleeves and wrapped it around me. "What's this guy like?"

"Nice," I shrugged, "I told him—" I stopped the rest of the sentence, unsure I wanted to say more. Was this lust or more with Ty?

"Told him what?" When I didn't answer, he pushed off the counter and stalked toward me. He twisted a piece of my hair around his finger then watched as it slid away. He let his finger trail into the jacket and down the collar of my shirt. "Ivy?" His tone had a bite to it. "Told him what?" His hand raised my chin, so I'd look at him straight on.

"That I was *also* interested in someone else." His gaze moved to my lips, and I felt a pull deep down in my stomach.

"And what did he say?" He tugged at my bottom lip, and I fought to close my eyes.

"He said he wanted a fighting chance," I lowered my voice, "so we're going out Monday."

"Monday?" His hand fell away.

"Mm."

"That's ambitious."

"He knows what he wants." I shrugged. Ty needed a reality check that if he wanted me, he needed to step up and decide. "It's sexy."

"I'm protective, Ivy." His hand glided around my neck. "I don't have a right to be, but I am."

If any other man had said that, I'd flip him off and

leave. I didn't do games. But with Ty, it was different. I wanted him to crave me just as much as I did him. The sexual tension between us was fun and exciting. It helped turn off all the crap that had come my way. Crap I still hid from. I knew Frank's phone call was coming soon, but right now, with the hungry expression on Ty's face, I didn't care.

"Maybe he's protective, too?" I challenged and his expression darkened.

"Not like me," he promised. "But, if you're giving him a chance, I'm getting one, too." He grabbed my head and caught my lips before I could think. His were strong and commanded the kiss. He tasted like mint with a hint of scotch. I molded my body to his as he pulled me tight against him. His tongue danced with mine, and I moaned when one of his hands moved from my neck to my bottom, giving it a good squeeze.

"Ty," I pulled away, "what if someone comes?"

"Then they see us." He backed me up to a counter full of weapons. Using his arm, he slid some aside as his lips found my throat.

"Don't you have to ship out?"

"Ivy," he pulled back, "I watched you on a date with some asshole who had no idea who he was sitting across from." He lifted me and sat me on the smooth stone counter. "It took everything in me not to tear him apart in the parking lot." He spread my legs and pushed up my skirt as he moved between them. "Then I find out someone else caught your attention." He gripped the backs of my knees and pulled me closer. He adjusted the coat to give us some privacy. My panties were soaked through, and he seemed to like it, by the way he groaned when he brushed over them.

With his fingers, he pressed and gently massaged the very spot that ached for attention. I leaned back and sighed with relief. We were both weak around one another. We knew what we needed but also didn't want to move toward it too quicky. Savoring each other's need.

"If I'm leaving," he used his free hand to unhook my buttons free, exposing my bra, "you're going to remember me until I get back." His fingers moved faster over the thin fabric and heightened my arousal.

"And what about you?" I outlined his erection with my finger, and he let out a strangled breath.

"I have this memory of you in my jacket, my fingers deep inside you, soaking wet, building toward a climax that I made happen." I tried to think straight as he pushed aside the fabric and slipped a finger inside me.

"Would Demi be all right with your fingers inside another woman?"

"I've never wanted her the way I want you." He pushed another finger in, and then a third. "I get hard the moment I think of you." My eyes rolled back at the delicious fullness.

I had never been emotionally connected to someone who was in such a dangerous profession. I always played it safe and stuck to the nine-to-fivers in suits. The thoughts that suddenly intruded were scary, and I had to push them aside to focus on the moment.

"Ty…" I grabbed his arm as he pulled me in closer. His teeth grazed my neck, then he drew in my skin. My orgasm built as I rocked against his hand, my breasts swelled, and my stomach coiled. His skilled fingers drove me wild, and all I could do was take it.

"When you're on your date, remember this feeling and how I don't give up on something I want." He pinched my nipple, and I lost it. I came. He kissed me through it. Not once did he break his rhythm. His hot breath brushed across my face as he huffed. "It physically hurts how much I want you, Ivy." I tried to catch my breath while my body hummed. "Every inch of me is tearing apart at the seams." I rested my head on his chest and breathed him in, knowing I felt the same way. "But once I get inside you, I won't be able to stop and—"

"Ten minutes, boys!" John shouted.

"Why?" I cried at the terrible timing these people had. I squeezed my eyes shut and willed my body upright. I pushed his hands away quickly and went to hop down, but he stopped me. He looked down at me and felt the fabric of my shirt.

"Don't wear silk on your date."

"Ty, that's ninety-five percent of my clothes." I chuckled. "The rest is workout gear."

"Please." He gave me a sardonic look. "I know what it does to me and, therefore, what it'll do to him." That caught me off guard.

"Are you seeing Demi anymore?"

"Just to explain things to—"

"Please be careful out there and don't lose a finger." I winked, not wanting to seem like I cared as he caught my arm.

"What's the name of the guy taking you out?"

"Why? Do you want to do a background check on him?" He brushed the back of his hand down my face while he stared intently into my eyes.

"I just want to know who I have to kill if he touches you."

———

"Sorry, sorry, sorry, I'm here." Savannah burst into the entertainment room with a drink in her hand and, without a drop of wine spilled, she landed gracefully on the pillows on the floor. "Brandon and Olivia had a thing, and Cole needed me to do something while he was away." She closed her eyes and dramatically took a breath. "I'm here now, and I'm ready for story time." She grinned and wiggled her brows.

"You're not late." I handed her the platter of homemade pizza. "I was just talking about what I'm going to wear tonight."

"Tonight?" Her eyes bugged out. "Patrick? Are you two going out again?"

"No. He was train wreck." I glared. "Seriously, never again. He was so sweaty and rude."

"Really?"

"Yes. Oh, my God, Savi, so bad. And what is with him and finishing people's sentences?"

"I thought he just did that with me!" Catalina looked shocked.

"Nope. I think he thinks it's sexy, or God forbid, smart." I made a face.

"I'm so sorry, Ivy. I'd never have set you up if I knew he was like that."

"Don't be. I got to meet Carson." I sipped my wine while her face went from mortified to intrigued.

"Um, have we gotten to the Carson bit yet?" she asked the others.

"Nope. We were waiting for you." Mia grinned behind her margarita.

Savi wiggled herself into her spot on the pillow. "Okay, so you saw him, and go!"

"The gist of the meet was that he sat at the next table, and when Patrick left to take a call from his sister, he commented how he'd ordered the same thing. He asked if I was on a date, and I knew he could tell it wasn't going well. Moving forward, I couldn't take Richard Simmons anymore." The girls laughed at my reference to the old seventies fitness personality. "So, I joined him instead."

"Wait, when was this date?" Mia asked. "Two days ago, right?" I nodded. "Wow, my husband *is* bad." She giggled.

"What?" Sloane looked confused.

"Mark made sure Ty and his family ate at the same restaurant as Ivy and Patrick that night."

"So, Ty was there?" Savi's excitement grew. "Did you see him?"

"Oh, I did." I laughed to relieve a little tension. "Anyway, Carson is nice and light and funny." I picked at my pizza. "He works for a medical company and travels a lot. He says he usually stays at inns or hotels because he's away so much."

"Do you think he has a family somewhere?" Cat cringed. "I'm sorry for the stereotype, but someone needs to ask."

"I won't lie, it crossed my mind, but I didn't get that impression. He's more 'I'm married to my job' and doesn't seem to be a settling down kind of guy."

"Well, that can change," Sloane cut in. "I mean, it's been known to happen. Look at who we married."

"I guess so." I shrugged.

"Are you really into this guy?" Mia handed me a napkin. "Because you seem unsure. I know it's new and all, but you seem hesitant, almost." I glanced at Savannah, and her smile broke and quickly made the other girls tune in to the mood change.

"Ah," Mia grinned, "maybe our work here *has* paid off, ladies." We all broke into laughter like a bunch of girls at a teen sleepover. The whole thing was fun and refreshing, and the more time I spent here, the more I felt free and youthful. I loved my life in Washington, but here in the wide-open Montana mountains, in the entertainment room of an Army safehouse, I felt closer to these four girls than I had with anyone in my life.

"I'm moving this story forward, ladies." Sloane cleared her throat. "Carson seems nice. You should go on a date with him tonight. He sounds fun, and there's no reason you shouldn't. So now it's time to hear the Ty story."

"Story or stories?" I raised an eyebrow, and Savannah grabbed the blender, ready to hear more.

———

If I was to rate my date that night, I would say it went pretty well. Great, actually. Carson was nice and asked about me and seemed interested in my profession. He drank a lot but seemed to be able to handle his liquor. I would guess it was the downside to being on the road a lot. Eating out often went along with having a drink. Only for Carson it meant having several drinks before our entrée even arrived. His dark beard was thick and made his chocolate-colored eyes even darker. He was handsome, and he made an effort to pay me some lovely compliments, so why did I keep finding my head slipping back to Ty more times than I could count?

I thought back to Savi's comment earlier in the evening while she hung out with me as I changed. Demi had called Ty's cell phone at least four times that morning. Savi only knew that because my uncle had found Ty's ringing cell phone in the couch. Her words to me were, "Go out, live, and enjoy life." Demi's still not totally out of the picture. I took her advice, which was why I was going for it with Carson.

"Ivy, this was fun." Carson's voice brought me back from my thoughts. "You're making an otherwise lonely trip to Montana very enjoyable."

"I'm happy to hear it."

"You know what would make this night even better?"

"What's that?" I played with my napkin under the table.

"A boat ride on the lake." I hesitated, and he started to nod. "Um, I don't want to scare you, but there's a guy who was here last time I met you, and he's here again today. Every so often, he looks at us. Do you know him?" He pointed over my shoulder, and I saw he was referring to Quinn.

Shit.

"No, I've never seen him before." I tried to control my tone. "I have one of those faces that people think they know."

"Maybe." He let it go. "So, what do you think?"

"About?" My mind was jumbled.

"The boat ride." He chuckled. "There's a place by the lake you can rent rowboats. I'd just like to do something different. Zack's is great, but there's something romantic about being out on the water."

"Sounds fun. Just let me use the restroom first."

"Of course." He nodded politely as I grabbed my purse and headed for the bathroom. I skipped the bathroom door and headed into the kitchen where I waved at

Zack, who was coming out of his back office. Jake the bartender walked in, and Zack pointed at me and made sure Jake stayed where he was so he wouldn't overhear.

Quickly, I called Quinn.

"Where are you?" Quinn's voice was low.

"In the kitchen out back. Jake's here, and Zack knows I'm here too. Look, Carson thinks you're watching me like some creepy guy."

Quinn came in, and we stepped out of the way of the busy kitchen. He opened the door to Zack's office and closed the door behind us. I could tell Quinn was uneasy by the way he cleared his throat.

"Shit," he barked through clenched teeth. He was probably concerned about being spotted. I felt strange. I was a grown woman asking permission to go out with my date. I had to swallow back my discomfort as we talked.

"He wants to take me out on one of those boats, you know with the long paddles." Quinn started to laugh. "You mean a rowboat?" He laughed again.

"Yes, and I know but he's trying, and it feels kind of nice that he is."

"It's very romantic."

"Yes, he mentioned something about that."

"You can't mention being romantic and then be romantic." Quinn groaned. "Where is Mark when you need him?"

"Whatever." But he had a point, or maybe I just wasn't overly romantic myself. "Are we good to do this?

"You need to drive with me, and we'll meet him there.

Any questions he might ask about me, remember what we went over."

"I can't have him see me with you. It'll only make him more suspicious."

"Maybe this isn't a good guy for you."

"Seriously, Quinn," I rubbed my head, "look at it from his point of view. He's just looking out for me."

"Maybe, but I'm under orders, Ivy."

"I know that, and I'm not asking you to break the rules, so here's my idea." I told him my plan, and there was silence.

"Cole isn't going to like this," he huffed, "but I know your situation is slightly different than the usual. Give me a minute to fill Zack in."

"It is, and thanks, Quinn." I hurried out of the kitchen ahead of him.

I headed over to the door where Carson was waiting.

"I'm ready, but I would feel more comfortable driving myself over."

"I understand that." He shrugged and didn't seem to mind.

"Thanks." He held the door open for me, and we split off toward our cars. Zack was outside, puffing away on a cigar, and watched me until I got to the truck. Quinn had the doors unlocked, and when I jumped in the driver's seat, he groaned from where he lay in the back.

"This isn't in my job description."

"I know, but think about how working with me will increase your resume." I chuckled as I eased out of the parking lot in the giant Escalade. "Damn, she drives like a dream," I purred, shifting the big beauty into drive. "Yeah, I need to get one of these."

"You owe me for this."

"Yup, a case of beer and some steaks. Would that be fair?"

"Maybe a cake too." He shifted his position on the back seat. "And Mark can't have any."

"Deal." I smirked. "He just pulled out in front of me, so stay low."

"Yes, ma'am."

A short time later, I was in a rowboat with Carson, who had propelled us out into the center of the lake. A few other couples were already there to enjoy the starry night. The sound of the water against the wooden boat was peaceful, and the squeak of the oars filled the odd silence that had fallen between us. Normally, I was better at making conversation on a date, but tonight I was a bit off.

"It's so beautiful." I sucked in a deep breath of fresh air and tried not to think about anything else but the moment I was in.

"Yes, the view is pretty great." He grinned at me, and I smiled. "I'm pleased to get you alone. Even if that creepy guy probably has a pair of binoculars trained on me."

"I'm sure he's harmless." I wrapped my sweater around me and had a flashback of Ty's jacket. I squeezed my eyes shut to stop the memory. "Oh!" I jumped when Carson touched my bare thigh.

"Sorry," he whispered, "there's just something about two strangers in the moonlight in the middle of a lake that just makes things…" He trailed off, and I remembered more of what Savi had said. *Have fun, let loose. You're not looking for love.*

"Special." I couldn't think of a better word as his hands moved down my thighs. *Relax, Ivy.* Only I couldn't. He seemed to sense it and instead moved one of his hands up to stoke my cheek.

"That other guy you mentioned before, has he kissed you yet?"

Oh, shit. Images of Ty and me together flooded my head and momentarily blocked my view of Carson. I nodded.

"I hope to be that lucky." He leaned back, and I took a breath once his hands were off me. *Seriously, Ivy, live a little!* I mentally kicked myself for not living in the moment and thought I should make it right.

"Tomorrow night," I blurted. "But let's meet somewhere different."

"Yes, let's lose your stalker."

"Yeah," I laughed lightly, "that's a good idea." I'd ask one of the others to take me instead. I knew his friend Dell or Davie were supposed to arrive soon.

"It's a date." We spent some more time chatting about nothing, and I relaxed a bit. Thankfully, he said he had a meeting in the morning, so we weren't out long. I was very thankful that he kissed my cheek and not my lips when we parted.

How could I know that the very next day I would be in my office with a very upset Lexi and a very pissed off Keith? Keith, who had nearly had his shoulder ripped off by a Cartel member, was in considerable pain. I certainly hadn't prepared myself for such an unexpected meeting with the two of them. And Scoot, who I was sure now thought he was a professional, had draped himself on the armrest of my chair and stared at them with the same intensity as he would a pair of mice.

"Well, this is unexpected," I began. "I'm sorry your mission was cut short, Keith. I heard about your injury."

"It happens." He shrugged, but I'd heard him speaking to Daniel earlier about how bad it was over there and how he wanted to be sent back.

"All right, well, one of us has to start," I quit the pleasantries, "so it'll be me. You two have a problem within your marriage. The only way to fix the problem is to know what that problem is. Lexi, why don't you start? What's bothers you most about your marriage with Keith?"

"Pass." She shook her head.

"That's not how I work," I shot that shit down immediately, "because what that tells me is that you're finished with your marriage. Are you done with Keith?"

"I don't know," she whispered, and Keith looked away from me. I figured I'd give Keith an opening to air his feelings now in case she walked out on us.

"Okay, Keith, your turn." He rubbed the side of his neck, obviously uneasy. I nodded at Lexi because now was his time for him to speak his truth. His lips pressed in a hard line, and his hands moved to his lap. I could see his knuckles were white as he clenched his hands together.

"I feel she blames me for all the bad things in her life." He cleared his throat, and she shook her head. "Blames me for all that she's lost. I never meant to hurt you, Lexi, leaving years ago, but I needed to do that for me."

"And I need to do this for me!" she shot back.

Okay, progress.

"You need to leave me, us? Every chance you get?" He used her same tone.

"It's smothering here. I'm not like rest of the Blackstone ladies." She made a distasteful face. "I don't fit in this world, stuck here on a mountain, with sister wives, and an escort every time I want to go have fun. I'm a free spirt. I crave a life of independence. I don't want to be here like them just waiting for my man to come home after every mission. You're out there living life, experiencing the excitement, the challenges. I want that for me. I want some fun, too."

"Wow," he turned with a wince to look at her, "I never knew you felt like that. I guess I never thought of what I did as fun." He looked down at his sling. "I sure never meant to smother you. I guess I thought you knew how important what we did was and why we did it."

"That's just it. It's all about you," Lexi shot back.

"Okay, I guess I get that." He licked his lips, and his voice went soft. "But tell me this, Lexi. In your visions of living a life like a twenty-year-old looking for fun, just where do our children fit into all that?"

"I don't know." She whispered the last word. "I'm detached from them." She looked at me. "I think I've always been."

"How so?" I tried to help her along when I noticed Keith's face had gone pale.

"When I look at them, I don't feel like they're my kids." She pulled a tissue from the box as she started to cry. "The rest of the women love their kids. I can see it, but when I look at mine, it's like looking at one of theirs." She looked at me as if to make me understand. "I think I was born without a maternal gene." She trailed off and looked at the floor. Silence filled the room while her words sank in and did their damage to him. I couldn't even imagine how much this was going to affect their children.

"And me?" Keith's voice cracked as his world shattered around him. "Is there anything left for me?"

She put a hand to her chest as tears rolled down her face. "I don't blame you, Keith, for how my life turned out. But I've never really forgiven you for leaving me all those years ago. I've tried everything to get past it, but I just can't."

"Lexi!" he shouted, and even made me jump. "Push aside everything else, right here, right now. I need to know. Do you still love me?"

"I," she cried harder, "I don't think I do." Keith went very still then nodded and slowly looked toward the wall.

"I think too much damage was done, and the more I'm here, the more I'm drowning."

"Maybe we could try some daily sessions, Lexi. I could help you—"

"I don't want help, Dr. Knight." I knew that, but I felt like I needed to try if I could. Truth be told, Lexi was finished with it all, and we all could see it. "I want out. I can't live this life anymore."

Ouch. Even though I saw it coming, I felt the sting of her comment hit home with Keith. He pushed to his feet and rubbed his cheeks dry. Heartbreak. I knew it could tear a person in half and leave them to drain out on the floor. It was heartless and irreparable.

"If you leave, Lexi," his tone was eerie but justified, "say goodbye to our kids, because you will not walk in and out of their lives ever again." He pulled off his ring and placed it on the table. "Thanks, Dr. Knight, but I think I'll cut this session short."

FIFTEEN

Rain beat our shoulders as we slugged through the thick terrain that had been our home for the past three days. Heavy mud clung to our boots, and drops of water constantly ran into our eyes. To say I missed the desert was an understatement.

Keith was on all our minds; it was hard to put it aside. This mission was hard both mentally and physically. I'd finally begun to understand the depth of the Cartel. They just never stopped coming. They were an army of thousands with endless funds to replace any who fell. We had been ambushed at one of the locations we'd thought we had already cleared. One of them came out of nowhere, and Keith nearly lost an arm. I popped two in the guy's back even as I wondered where they'd come from. We had been so careful to clear every inch of the land we were covering. Our scouts were in constant communication, so either something was going on we didn't know about, or Cole was right—they were just getting better.

It was clear to me why Blackstone needed another team. They were up against impossible odds.

We came to a road, and Cole put his hand up to indicate that someone was communicating with him. He leaned his head to the side and listened to his radio.

"Copy that." He turned to us. "Our informant says he last saw the girls in a house in a town to the west of us. I've got the coordinates."

"Why hasn't Frank given us the lowdown on this informant?" Mike chewed a piece of gum as he spoke. "Hey, Logan? I mean, it's not how we operate."

"Frank must have his reasons," he nodded, "but yeah, I'd like to get my own read on him myself."

While the guys took a breather, I pulled out a length of tubing from my bag along with two thin air pumps. I connected a piece to both pumps and slipped one into each of my boots then loosely tied them. I stood and threaded the rest of the tubing through my fatigues attaching the end to a clip I'd sewn in before we left.

"What in the hell is that contraption, Beckett?" John sucked down a protein gel.

"One winter, it rained more days than I could count," I explained. "We were so wet that we nearly lost our minds. So, I got creative and made this." I pointed to my boots. "As I walk, the pumps shoot a puff of air under my clothes. It helps keep me dry."

"So, you're telling me that every time you take a step, your nuts get a shot of air?" Mike grinned. I could see the piece of green gum he held between his teeth.

"Yeah, and it feels fucking phenomenal." I chuckled, and the rest joined in.

"That's brilliant." Cole studied the tube under my shirt as I held it up in the back. "But doesn't it make sound when you walk?"

"No. It took some time, but I worked the kinks out. It's pretty well silent now."

"And now we know one more reason they picked you for the new team commander." Mark fist bumped me. "And that you like your nuts to be fondled."

"Every guy has their thing."

"I'm impressed, Beckett." Cole checked the time, and I knew we needed to move. "I want to see that when we get home."

"Hooah."

―――――

We made it to the target destination in good time and without encountering any more Cartel.

"Clear," Mark whispered over the radio.

"Clear," Mike repeated.

John checked in. "Both rooms by the stairs are clear too. Anyone find out where that smell is coming from?"

"Negative," Cole spoke up, "but someone was here. Stove's still hot."

"Affirmative," Mark confirmed.

The house was massive, and it required patience and focus to clear each room. There were so many spots a person could hide. We couldn't miss a thing and kept our sweep tight. The smell John referred to was odd and overpowering, and my sense of smell was down for the count. I eyed the photos on the wall carefully, as I knew they could be used as peepholes. I walked by a small table and reached down to check it out. A piece of furniture could be nailed to the floor to hide the top of a trap door. Nothing could be overlooked.

Slowly, I moved light on my feet in and out of each room. The rooms were small with tiny windows, but the lights from the hallway flooded each room. Again, that was something that caught my attention. Why were there so many lights on at an empty house? Did they leave in a hurry, or were they still here somewhere?

The floors were dirty, and when I felt confident enough and we were in the clear, I'd get down and study the smudges on the tile.

I nudged the second to last door in the basement open and scanned the room through the scope of my rifle. Two doors on opposite sides of the room were partly open. There was many times in the past that it was me on the other side of those doors with a clear shot of any company entering the room. I blocked everything out and tuned in to my sixth sense. My throat contracted to the point of pain when I swallowed.

I wasn't alone.

Suddenly, someone yanked me from behind and tossed me down the hall just as a fireball ripped through the door. The blast that followed would have killed me in a half a second. Heat washed over me as I protected my head, then I scrambled to my feet and looked straight into the eyes of the guy who just saved my life.

"The girls are dead. The entire place is rigged," the guy yelled over the ringing in my ears. "It's controlled by a phone. Get your team out now!" He shoved me forward and disappeared in the opposite direction.

"Abort! Abort! Abort!" I yelled as I choked on the smoke and tried desperately to clear my vision. "Everyone out!" I fought my way to the stairs and out the back. My brain was in a frenzy to clear itself. John grabbed my shoulder, and we ran toward the others just as the next set of explosives went off.

"Well, that fucking sucked." John winced and held his arm. Mike used his flashlight to get a better look then popped an ice pack and handed it to him.

"Stop being a fucking hero, then," Mike grunted and slapped him on the shoulder.

We were hunkered down under some brush as we waited for the chopper to return.

"Speaking of which," Mark eyed me, "how did you know it was going to blow?"

"One minute I'm clearing the room, the next someone hauled my ass backward out the door as a flash of heat nearly took me out." I shook my head, remembering the bright light. "Back in Afghanistan, we called it the devil's hand because you didn't see it coming until you felt the burn."

"Good name for it," John said. "What guy?"

"No idea. I couldn't get a good look at him." I rubbed my head and ignored the ringing in my ears. "But he confirmed the girls are dead." I glanced at Cole, who cursed silently.

"Time to make another call." He kept low and moved away from us.

Thirty minutes later, Mark and John were passed out, and the rest of us took the time to mull over the night's events. It was heavy and played on my head.

"Who's *it*,' anyway?" Mike chuckled, breaking the silence.

"Aunt June." Cole smirked.

"Don't let her sweetness fool you." Mike directed his warning at me. "I've seen that woman hide behind a coat rack for an hour, waiting out Keith." We all laughed quietly.

"How do you win?" I was curious. "I mean, when's it over?"

"We have a scoreboard, in the barn," Mike explained. "Once you get tagged three times, you're out, until the last man's standing."

I snorted out a chuckle, and Mike joined in. I liked

the way they kept things light. I hadn't expected anything like that.

"Yeah, well, the girls got rid of our Furby and replaced it with their own, so now that's a friggin' shit show. No one's safe."

"Do I even want to know?" I raised a brow at him.

"Do you know what those are?" I nodded, remembering the creepy toys in the stores a few years back. Made you jump every time you walked down the aisle. "Well, we'd record dumb shit and hide it in spots to scare each other. It was all fun and games until the wives had enough, made a bet, and damn it, won. They tossed the little guy into the lake. Mark took it the hardest." He laughed at Mark, who was dead to the world. "Then like a dirty nightmare, they got another, more high-tech one. They got a passcode on it so only they can change the sayings and sound levels. Needless to say, they now have the advantage."

"I'm working on something," Cole chimed in, and I laughed because it was the last thing I expected from Cole.

"This job weighs on you. It's our way of trying to keep sane, make sure we still laugh." Mike's tone switched to a more serious one.

"I get that." I fiddled with the tab on my jacket. "It's certainly needed."

"I'm sorry about your friend." Cole's face turned sympathetic.

"Yeah, me too. He was a good guy." I looked at Cole.

"He shouldn't have been on that last mission. Physically, he was there, but not mentally. I saw the signs." Cole nodded. I knew he'd get it. As a leader himself, he'd know how I felt. "I know I could have gotten him through it. Fuck. That one of our own would take him out like that…right between the eyes, like he was the enemy and not our brother." I lowered my head as the painful, high-pitched sound screamed through it. A tightness wrapped my torso, and it felt like my head would split in two.

"Raven-One to Fox-One," Cole whispered. "Come in, come in, wherever you are." I looked questioningly at Mike.

Mike leaned back and looked up at the sky. "Staff Sergeant Paul, one of the best guys we had the honor to serve with at Shadows. John and Paul had a long history. They were very close. He still struggles with it."

"What happened?" I pushed my own hurt aside.

"Took a bullet to the chest during one of our missions here," Cole answered for Mike as he shifted to lean against a rock. "We knew it was bad, but…he died in the chopper. At least he didn't die alone."

"Shit," I breathed out.

"A hero to the end." Mike closed his eyes.

"I'm sorry." I fingered Halim's bracelet in my pocket. I knew how hard a loss like that would have been on everyone in that house. "I know losing not only one of my best friends but also a brother has become a serious dark turn for me." I spoke quietly as I felt the need to share my own pain. "I was, after all, his captain, and I didn't bring all my men back home. It's the worst kind of pain to know he's still back there."

"Beckett," I rolled my head to looked at Cole, "John's wife is a JAG lawyer. If you want to get that son of a bitch, you tell her I give you permission to proceed."

"Copy that."

SIXTEEN

ERIC

"You seem off," Alejandro played with his switchblade, "extra quiet."

"Thinking." I used a rag to wipe my face. A fan pointed directly at me but provided very little relief from the heat that smothered every inch of this Godforsaken place. Castillo had called while I was out, and when I got home, I was escorted to a location and told to wait. We didn't normally operate like this, and it bothered me. Martin Castillo didn't step off his property in fear he'd be shot. He had more protection than the fucking Pope. *So, why here? Why now?*

"You think Castillo's brought us here to whack us?" Alejandro's voice sounded matter-of-fact.

"With any luck." I dripped with sarcasm. "I'd do

anything to escape the heat of the devil's asshole." Sweat dripped from every pore, blurring my vision.

"Yeah, it's a hot one."

"No, Ale, this is hell."

The sound of an engine as it pulled up the driveway had me on my feet. I stood in the corner, leaned against the desk, and crossed my ankles in a relaxed manner.

"Out," Castillo ordered Alejandro, who looked at me before he ducked outside with the rest of Castillo's men. He motioned for the door to be closed and then removed his jacket and lit a cigar. He took a deep inhale.

"We have a problem." He examined the cigar before he cast his gaze on me. "Someone in our circle tipped off that filth in the north." He spat on the floor, and I could tell his temper was barely under control.

"What happened?"

"As you know, my plans are flawless." He settled himself on a chair and rested a leg on his thigh. "So, imagine my surprise when we have all the little Army men in perfect position to be blown to bits, and at the last second, poof, they're racing out unharmed into the night. All those perfectly placed explosives wasted."

"Could they have spotted something to tip them off?"

"No." He held my gaze. "Like I said, my plans are flawless."

I shook my head as I thought about how to handle Castillo. He had a reputation for being a loose cannon, so I wouldn't put it past him to slaughter his entire team and start new.

"Any witnesses to anything?"

"None."

"The explosives were on a remote? No tripwires?"

"Remote." His tone had a chill to it.

"And not one of your men watching the house saw anyone coming or going while the Army guys were in there?"

"No."

"Shit." I used the rag to clear my face. "I'll keep an ear to the ground and bring anything to you that I find."

"No," he cut me off, "I want you to bring me a head."

"Attached or severed?"

"Surprise me." He stood and tugged his jacket free from the chair. "Just bring me proof of who did this, or everyone is dead."

"Understood."

"I trust you, Eric. Don't let me down."

"Have I ever?" I shot back, and he raised an eyebrow at me as he tossed his half-smoked cigar into the corner of the room and left. His entourage of men who might not be here next week followed.

I moved back toward the fan and closed my eyes with a huff.

"What we got, Eric?" Alejandro asked as he came back inside. "What did the Big Boss man want?"

"A severed head."

———

I spent a good number of hours making sure I visited every piece of shit in the area where the Blackstone team had hit. I made sure my efforts were getting back to Castillo. I knew more than anything he needed to know that I had his back. He was, after all, my boss and someone I needed to remain in good graces if I ever wanted to get to the top of the Cartel organizations. Grunt work sucked, and normally I'd send my own dipshits to do it, but Castillo asked me personally, and I was determined to make sure he saw me doing it. I knew I needed to provide someone to take the blame, since no one had been seen entering or leaving that night.

And who better than the dumbest of them all.

I dragged one of his shirts through the dust and rubble from that night. I ripped the sleeve to add to the affect. His body jiggled when I used the end of a nail to tear his skin and rip his flesh open, then I used gauze to wrap it up. I rubbed some dirt around the edges of the bandage to make it look a few days old. Then I removed his nasty shoe and pressed it into the powder for a partial print and slipped it back on. I tossed his severed head into a box and then snapped some photos of my "findings."

I carried the box outside and wrapped it in a tarp in my trunk then headed to the meeting spot I was ordered to use once I found something.

Castillo met me at the steps of the place deep in the desert. His men scanned the horizon for any visitors.

"I hear you found my guy."

"I did." I popped my trunk, grabbed the box, and tossed the head on the ground.

"That was quick."

"You gave an order, and I'm good at what I do." He twisted his lips at my comment. I knew Castillo enjoyed a level of cockiness in his men. He didn't want a lap dog. He needed someone who could do a job and do it well. That was me.

"Who is it?"

"A local named Juan Diaz." I pulled out my phone and handed it to him so he could see some photos of what I found in the house. "I've worked with him a few times. Dumb as shit, stupid as shit, and now dead as shit." I smirked at my poetry. "The shoe and the cut on his arm are all consistent with the house. I looked around and found a small tunnel running from under the house to a road just southeast of the property. My guess, that's how he wasn't seen."

"And do you have a why for me?"

"He made a bad deal with some guys in El Salvador. When it went south, he used the only resource he had left, his cousin. His cousin lives in Washington and works near a military base. He's got connections. One thing led to another, and Juan flipped and now feeds them info." I took back my phone and replaced it with Juan's. "That's the number he used. I figured you might want it." I watched him scroll though how many times Juan had called it. "By saving the Army team, he was promised a life in Texas. He's to leave in four days. Well, was." I smirked darkly.

"Well done, Eric." He tucked the phone in his pocket. "I want to meet this cousin of his. Maybe we can encourage him to do work for us, too."

"He's already been contacted," I assured him. I'd actually sent men to kill him. I didn't need any loose ends, and I was tired of this shit and wanted to get back to moving my girls.

Castillo held out a hand, and one of his men handed him a thick envelope of cash.

"A thank you for your quick work." He handed it to me. "I'll be in touch."

"Anytime." I tossed the wad of cash on the passenger seat and started my car blasting the AC. I gave a nod before I sent a dust cloud into the air and headed back to the city.

SEVENTEEN

Cole had updated Frank on the situation when we arrived home. I knew there would be a lot of questions about how it all played out. The death of those girls weighed heavily on all of us. A strangeness was in the air. A tenseness I could feel. I looked around as I approached the house and spotted a woman putting travel bags in the back of a truck. There was a vibe about her, and I knew some shit must have happened. I gave her a glance as I passed her, but she didn't look up.

"I understand you had a rough trip." Dr. Roberts stopped me when I stepped inside.

"It could have gone better." I shrugged. I caught a glimpse of Keith and his son on the patio.

"Tonight's protocol will have to be a little different,

but I will ask you this." He studied my face. "How's your body from the blast?"

"Surprisingly all right, but ask me tomorrow." I gave him a small smile.

"And your mental state?"

I knew *fine* wouldn't be the correct answer, so I gave him the truth.

"I think I'm more curious about who the hell the guy was who warned us off. As for everything else, I'm okay. If that changes, you'll be the first to know."

"Good." He placed a hand on my shoulder. "I heard you impressed again on this mission. I'm glad you're back in one piece."

"Thanks."

A hot shower and some dry clothes made me feel like myself again. The house was quiet when I walked downstairs, and the whole intense vibe of the house messed with my head.

"I have a ring full of keys, but I can't open a single door," Olivia said again in a frustrated voice. "Come on, Aunt June. These will really help to sharpen your skills."

"I don't know, Liv." She huffed and sounded as drained as the rest of us.

"A piano," I called out.

"See! Sharp as a tack. Thank you, Ty!" She sighed with relief.

I went to the kitchen and ran into Mike as he popped a beer cap.

"Where is everyone? Something feels off."

"Yeah, we all feel it. Cole is dealing with Lexi, Keith's wife, who is now officially not living here." *Oh, shit, that woman out front.* "Yeah." He nodded. "So, things will be tense for a bit. John's talking to Paul. I'm not sure where everyone else is."

"Oh." I looked away and let my own pain seep in.

"Yeah, you know the story. John and Paul were like brothers. Now, whenever we come back from a mission, he fills Paul in." He plucked the beer cap off the counter and tucked it in his pocket. "Sounds odd, but don't worry. Doc Roberts is aware. Doc says Paul's picture, the one that hangs in our conference room, kind of keeps him with us." He sighed. "Everyone has their thing, I guess."

"True." My mouth went dry as I thought of Brown. "And Mark?" I tried to focus on something else.

"Ah, yes." He held up keys. "He wants you to meet him here." He handed me a piece of paper.

Mike slapped my shoulder as he headed toward the living room, and I turned on my heel and left to go find Mark.

The Creek Restaurant was on the outskirts of town. Country music played outside, and the inside sounded busy. I cringed at a woman who had on a pair of cow-print shoes. She grinned at me. *Nope.* I wondered why in hell Mark wanted to meet at a place like this.

"Ty Beckett?" A woman came over. "Your friend asked me to take you to him." She waved for me to follow. She took me around the back and up the side to where Mark sat.

"There you are, muffin. Have a seat." He kicked out the chair opposite, and I lowered into it. "He's had a hard day," he explained to the waitress, "so let's get him a beer and some nachos to share." She waited a beat then left. I tried to deal with my back to the exits. Already I felt uneasy.

"I didn't know we were on a date." I gritted my teeth and moved my chair on an angle.

"Well," he checked his phone, "the waitress has been making hungry eyes at me and you, and we are going home together, so I figured I'd keep up the charade. Besides, we're not the only ones on a date tonight." He nodded over my shoulder, and I turned and caught a glimpse of Ivy. Her back was to us, and she sat alone.

"Oh, shit," I muttered as I turned back to look at Mark. "Where's her date?"

"He's late, but we don't like him." He waited for the waitress to put my beer down. "Oh, speak of the devil." He looked at me. "He's arrived."

"This feels all wrong." I tried not to turn around.

"It's not wrong, it's our job. I'm tired from our mission, and Keith was next in line to go, but..." he made an annoyed face, "he has issues. Anyway, Quinn was ousted by this douche. He thought he was stalking her. Quinn apparently needs some work on his skills. So, I called you for company. Besides, Ivy likes you."

"You're no better than the wives." I chuckled a bit, pleased I was here.

"When you have Mia for a wife and Savi as a sister-in-law, you just learn to give in."

"Smart man." I glanced at the waitress, who wiped her hands on her shirt, and it got my mind going. "Is Ivy wearing a silk shirt?"

"Silk? You're asking me about the material of the shirt she's wearing? You mean like fabric?" His face dropped. "I mean, I can tell you if it's like a shirt, or a dress, or even a pantsuit."

I eyed him, and he rolled his eyes and nodded.

"Fine." He leaned to the side slightly. "It looks like polyester."

I smirked. She didn't wear silk.

"I'm glad we have satisfied your fabric fetish." Mark raised an eyebrow and shook his head when I didn't give him anything. We sat in silence and picked at the nachos. There was a table of six to my left and four to my right. My leg bounced under the table, as restless as the rest of me. I could hear a mix of voices—

"I got your six." His sensed my unease with my back to everyone. I gave a quick nod.

"You have to give me something, Mark." I twisted the bottle in my hand.

"He's touchy," he began to give me a little feedback, "but she doesn't lean into him. He's working for it, though."

Jesus, I felt twitchy.

"I can tell he just put his hand on her leg, and she laughed." He squinted. "Ugh. He's got this fucking thing where he twirls the front of his hair over and over with his finger. It's disconcerting."

I stilled, and Mark caught it. My blood froze as I got to my feet. Mark mirrored me.

"Beckett?" Mark slipped into Blackstone mode while I slipped into murder mode.

I spotted him, and every fiber in my body twisted into white hot rage. I didn't have to study his face because his body language told me exactly who he was. I plowed toward him with hate building inside me at every step. I could taste blood in my mouth. When I got close enough, I pulled back my arm and drove my fist as hard as I could into his face. He fell backward with his chair.

"Ty!" Ivy screamed as she jumped to her feet. I quickly tucked her body behind me. I wouldn't let Hill get anywhere near her. Mark was suddenly next to me on the phone while Hill rolled about on the floor with his hands to his nose. "Oh, my God." Ivy held tight to my arm as she looked down at him. "Carson, are you okay?"

"His name isn't Carson," I hissed and felt dangerously close to losing all self-control.

"What?"

"Stay the fuck away from her," I seethed and wanted to snap his neck right off. "The next time, I'll punch right through your skull." Mark gathered Ivy's things while Hill made eye contact with me, and for a split second, I saw his smile. It took everything in me not to kill him right there and then, but a cough made me look up, and I could see everyone's eyes on me. Some even had their phones out, and I knew it was time to leave.

"Mark?" Ivy began to step away, but I shot her a look and she stayed where she was.

"Let's go." Mark hurried us out the door. Once outside, I felt my head pound. All the images of Brown's head exploding and Hill's lies swirled about inside to the point of pain. I spun around. I needed to end this shit right now. Mark got in my face.

"Beckett, Beckett, listen to me. I got this guy. Remember I have your six." He held up his hands. "He's not going anywhere. I've got him," He repeated. "I need you to get Ivy home." I closed my eyes and tried to calm down. "Get her home, Ty."

"All right, all right." I held up my hands and turned and walked toward Ivy. She looked rattled.

"What the hell was that? Ty?" she asked once I got close enough.

"Come on." I put a hand against her lower back and gave her a nudge toward the car while I pressed the button to unlock the doors to the SUV. I opened hers and waited for her to get in.

"Can you fill me in why you attacked my date?"

"No." I couldn't. Not yet.

"Ty." I felt like an asshole but what had happened was a hit to an open wound, and there was no stopping what I might say next. "Hey." She reached out and placed her hands flat to my chest. I could see her study my face.

"Please, Ivy," I needed to get out of there, "get in."

Her hands fell away, and she slipped quietly into the front seat. With a quick look over my shoulder, I yanked my door open and got in beside her.

The dark night made the trees blur into different shades of black and gray as we drove. I scanned the mirrors and was on high alert. For what, I didn't know. All I knew was the battle inside.

My mind dipped to dangerous places and taunted me to lose my temper. Brown's look when the bullet drilled into his skull repeated over and over until I squeezed my eyes shut for a quick second. Then there was Ivy. How did he know her? How did he find me? What was I missing? Did I lose my touch because I was distracted by her?

The dash lit up, and I saw it was Cole. I grabbed the earpiece and popped it in.

"Beckett," I answered.

"We clear to talk?"

"Yes." I glanced at Ivy, who had her head turned to look out the side window.

"Are you good?" I hesitated, and he tried again. "Scale from one to ten?"

"Three." I wouldn't lie to Cole, but I wasn't about to apologize either. Ivy was at dinner with a stone-cold murderer. "I was following orders."

"Understood." Cole cleared his throat. "I see you're almost to the first checkpoint. After the last checkpoint, there's a road to your left. If you need a breather or need to hash some shit out, do it there. You'll be left alone. I'll get the guys to pull back to give you time."

"Copy that."

"Meet in my office at zero-eight-hundred."

"Roger." I tossed the earpiece in the cup holder as the call ended.

I could barely stand my own head by the time I turned left on the road after we got through the last checkpoint.

"Where are we going?" Ivy seemed to snap out of her own thoughts as she looked up at my left turn.

I didn't answer, and she got quiet again. I parked about a mile into the woods and turned off the engine. I jumped out of the driver's seat and into the cool air. I ripped off my hat and ran my hands through my hair.

Every breath I took felt like a noose tightening around my neck. I felt everything close in as I tried to control my breath.

"Ty?" I heard her door open.

"Get back in the truck, Ivy," I warned, but I heard her struggle to walk in her heels. I needed a moment to think, to breathe, to not snap and lose all self-control.

"No, I deserve some kind of explanation of what's going on here. I can see you're in pain, and it's obvious that..." I marched right up to her and backed her up until she was pressed against the hood of the truck. Her neck strained as she swallowed hard, but she lifted her chin and held her ground.

"The guy you've been seeing is the very one who..." The words stuck on my tongue. I couldn't say it. I didn't want to be pressed for more answers.

"Who what?"

"Did you kiss him?" She dropped her arms with an eye roll and moved away from me.

"You don't get to ask all the questions here." She whirled around. "You punched my date in the face! Why did you do it?"

"I can't—"

"Can't talk about it?" She cut me off, fuming mad now. "What? Were you jealous?"

"Yes!" I shouted louder. "And I don't know if it's because you've consumed my every thought since the moment I met you, but I'd do anything to get you out of here." I pointed at my head and squeezed my eyes shut.

"Then let's go, Ty." She waved a hand in front of her. "Let's get sex off the table, and then we'll know. It's nothing but pure, hot lust," she challenged.

My entire body twitched in her direction.

"I can't promise—"

"Then don't." She reached up and pulled her panties down from under her skirt and tossed them on the hood. "We both know we want it."

Fuck it.

In two strides, I pulled her to me, and our mouths connected. I started to unbutton her shirt but got impatient, so I yanked the rest, sending the small buttons to scatter around us. I reached down to lift her, and she wrapped her legs around my waist and kissed me again. I spun around and walked us the few steps to the truck and leaned her against the door and let her stand.

She smiled against my lips. "Concerned someone might see us?"

I dismissed her comment and removed her shirt. She unclasped the clip between her breasts and disconnected the contraption. They fell, heavy, and her nipples perked at the sudden chill. She had great boobs, like perfect come-grab-me-boobs. She wiggled free of her bra and slowly undid my belt and jeans to free me. She stood and admired what I brought to the party and licked her lips. I thumbed her nipple, trying to savor the moment the best I could, but Hill somehow beat down my barrier and reminded me that he was always on the edge of my thoughts.

"Just tell me," I couldn't take not knowing, "did he ever kiss you?"

"No." She shook her head and slipped her soft hand over my painful erection. "I wouldn't let him."

That was all I needed to hear. I lifted her again and leaned her against the door. I kissed along her neck, up to her ear, and nipped her earlobe. My hand palmed her plump breast, then I dove down and caught her nipple between my teeth. I drew it into my mouth and sucked as her legs squeezed me. She liked that. I gave the other one the same amount of attention and drew out a throaty moan. She pulled at the hem of my shirt, and I drew it over my head, so we were skin to skin. Nothing on but my jeans and her hiked up skirt. It was a major turn-on.

I squeezed her breasts together and licked between

them. Her skin was like silk. I liked silk. Her perfume flooded my nose, and I lost myself in her scent.

She grabbed my hair and pulled my head back then stared down at me. Her hooded eyes told me she was ready. Her arousal dampened my stomach. It was so fucking hot.

I circled my hips and lined up the tip so it rubbed her nub.

"I'm bare," I suddenly realized. I couldn't believe I didn't think about a condom. That was what this woman did to me.

"I get the shot," she whispered, "and I get checked after every partner."

"Same." I hesitated to see if she was okay with it.

"Ty?"

"Yeah?"

"Get in me." I didn't miss a beat and pushed in hard and slow. Each inch I gained inside her drove me wild with need. She let out a cry when I was fully in, but I pulled her down harder, wanting more of her. I leaned forward and licked the length of her neck, then I pulled back and drove back in. She shot up the side of the truck, and when she came back down, I met her with a flick of my hips.

"Oh, my God," she moaned and shook her head to send her hair all over my scorched skin. The soft coolness of it heightened my senses. It felt fucking amazing. She reached back and grabbed the bar on the roof to allow me a different angle. I continued to thrust, lick, and suck all over her body. I buried my face in her breasts and let out a primal groan. It had never been like this with Demi, or anyone. I had never been this lost and found at the same time.

"Don't come, Ivy." I took her harder, and she hung on, and all the while her legs trembled and squeezed my waist. "I knew you'd be good." I couldn't stop my words. "So good." Thrust, thrust. "The things I want to do to your body."

"Ty, I can't, I'm so close," she cried, and I pounded harder. "I'm…!" she screamed as she came, and I followed only seconds behind. The force that rocked through me was so intense that I nearly lost my footing. I wrapped my arms around her body and shook through the best orgasm I'd ever had. I felt like I was sixteen again and had just lost my virginity. I never thought I'd ever feel that good again. *Shit, was I wrong. This was way better.*

"I need more." I placed her on her feet and whirled her around. My balls begged to hear her scream again, and I nearly clawed at her to get into position.

"Are you serious?" She deliriously laughed over her shoulder. "I don't think I can stand at this point, especially in these heels."

"I've got you." Her hands flexed against the window, and I admired her slender back and neck. Her bikini lines were incredibly sexy, and I drew my fingertip along them, dipping down into her soaked opening. "Jesus, that's hot," I muttered. I loved me in her. My fingers teased her, and her hair tumbled down when her head dropped back as I grabbed a fistful as I slipped back in, never fully losing my erection. I gave her a little tug, and she stood straighter. I smirked at how responsive she was, even after having an orgasm.

"Mmm," I growled in her ear and massaged both of her breasts while I pushed deeper inside of her, "to think I waited this long to be in you." I felt the smile spread across her face as she started to rock her hips. "Do you want more?" She nodded with a huff, her hair wildly thrown across her face. I moved my hands to cover hers. "Lean forward." We leaned forward together until her hands were pressed hard against the glass. Then I pushed up, nearly lifting her off her feet.

"Oh!" She strained against my force. "That's so," she swallowed, "so good."

"I can't get deep enough," I hissed in her ear. "I want all of you. I want to consume you the way you do when you just so much as look at me." I nipped her shoulder.

This time she was vocal and let me know exactly how she liked it. Her screams were mixed with moans as she clawed at the window. I reached back for her hips, and we moved like a wave, in sync with one another. When I couldn't take it anymore, I let my hands wander over every part of her. Her curves were mouthwatering, and I planned to study them, so they were burned into my memory.

She reached back and cupped my balls, rolling them over the palm of her hand. I stilled, letting out a quick shot of air. She chuckled, knowing she had me.

"Mm, did I discover something you like?" She grinned and gave a gentle tug, and I nearly came.

"Ivy," I warned through a hungry moan.

"Don't you like?" she teased, knowing I fucking loved it.

"Do it again," I ordered as I inched my fingers to her greedy little nub, and in a matter of two circles, we were both coming again.

I pressed my forehead to her shoulder and let everything float away. I was free, light and weightless, as I lost myself inside her. Sounds and colors morphed into one and poured over me like warm water. She was a drug I wanted to feed on.

I drew in a deep, steady breath that coated my lungs with her sweet scent. My heart pounded into her back, and I loved how my big body swallowed hers. She was trapped between me and the door, nowhere to go.

"I can't feel my body." She granted me a delicious groan. I pulled her back to open the passenger door. She winced when I slid out and looked at me, confused, when I took her seat. "You've got to be kidding me." She laughed.

"No. Come here." I pulled her on top of me and fed myself back into her. "You said we need to get us out of our systems. That's what I'm trying to do."

"You're going to kill me with orgasms."

"Yeah." I grinned and took in her flushed, sleepy face. Though it was dark, we were more intimate in that position, and I half wondered if she'd look away. She didn't.

She kept her hooded, sexy eyes on me as she put her hands on the armrest and center console. To my surprise, she started to ride me. Her skin glistened in the low lighting of the dashboard. The little sounds she made and the way her stomach flexed with every rock nearly drove me insane. "You're so fucking sexy, Ivy." Her hands dragged down my front, and her nails caressed my pelvic bone.

"So are you." She leaned forward and licked my collarbone. "I've never had a three-orgasm night."

"Well, let's make sure that happens."

I rolled her hips and thrust up from the bottom, one hand clamped down on her shoulder and the other to her waist. She tipped her head back and fought for breath as she built and built.

"Yes, just like that." I coached her. "Feel me inside of you." Her breasts bounced wildly as the windows fogged, and my need for this woman consumed me even more than before.

She let out a delicious moan, then grabbed my hand on her hip as an anchor. "Give me more." She sent my mind wild, and I picked up the pace. "Yes, just like that!" she cried.

My muscles screamed at me, and my stomach coiled, both excited and anxious for what was about to happen. In and out I pumped, giving her everything I had, and then some. Every thrust felt better than the last. It was like I couldn't stop. My head fought to stay focused, and my hips had a mind of their own. I was like an animal on the hunt for her screams. In that moment, nothing mattered but her and me. She tipped her chin and closed her eyes, her mouth parted, and I felt my balls tug upward. I widened my legs and at the last moment switched angles.

"Ty!" she screamed as she threw herself at me. I wrapped my arms around her and thrust a few more times, then I let go.

Again, I was taken somewhere else. An unknown place of bliss that I was lost in. I came so hard I lost all my senses.

We lay tangled in each other, trying to catch our breath. I could have spent the night like that, but I knew we couldn't. Besides, our clothes were thrown about outside, and it would only be a matter of time before someone came to find us.

"Hey," I whispered, loving the way her skin felt on mine.

"Mm?" She sounded sleepy.

"We should get back." I rubbed her back, but she suddenly moved without warning.

"Yeah." She peeled off me, opened the door, and carefully slid off me. I moaned when I saw the mess on me. I wanted more, but I knew she needed to be able to walk. I joined her as she started to gather things. We dressed without a word, and I wondered what was going through her mind.

Once we were back to something resembling

presentable, we drove back and parked in Shadows' driveway. I glanced at her.

"Everything okay?"

"Yeah." She gave a smile. "You?"

"Yeah."

"Good." She paused, and I suddenly wanted to explain what had happened at the restaurant.

"Ivy, you should know." I hesitated, unsure how to explain Hill correctly.

"We're good, Ty. Now we know, and things can go back to normal. Lust is a real bitch sometimes." She opened her door and hopped out on wobbly legs. I turned off the truck and raced out to join her. "As for the rest of it," she said on her way to the door. "I need a shower and some rest before we can dive into Carson and all that. Tomorrow?"

"Yes. But, Ivy, wait." She paused. "Things are so much more complicated than I can explain in a few sentences."

"I, of all people, get that." There was an awkward stretch of silence, and just when I was about to try, she stepped back. "Goodnight, Ty."

EIGHTEEN

TY

"Hill had plans for Ivy, and I believe it was my fault this happened." I had spent the last forty minutes giving Cole, Daniel, and Frank the details of what went down the night before. Mark was also in the meeting but remained quiet for most of it.

"Meaning?"

"You know what happened just before we came home. You read my file." I glanced at Frank, who had arrived early that morning. "He knows I won't let Brown's murder go, not without a fight, and I won't. I don't know how he found me or why he chose Ivy." Mark huffed and made us look at him. "But he's sending me a message that he can meddle in my business."

"You've got something to say?" Cole questioned Mark.

"Only that if I was worried about Ty digging into a murder that could send me away for life, I'd go after his girl, too."

"We're not dating," I cut in.

"It may not be official, but hell, you two have more heat than an afternoon in a southern kitchen in the dead of summer."

"Even if that's true," Daniel spoke up, "that doesn't explain how Hill knew you two were together."

"Were you and Ivy out somewhere together?" Frank gave me a curious look.

"Shit." I closed my eyes as a thought slammed into me. "Cole, can you access the logbook for Camp Green?" He opened his laptop and started typing. "Nothing."

"His name doesn't come up?" I rubbed my face and thought for a moment. "Try Matthew Rivera." I waited, and a moment later he huffed.

"Matthew Rivera was logged in the same time we were there." He confirmed my thoughts.

"Fucking vultures," I hissed and slammed my fist into the steel table.

"Where is Hill now?" Cole looked at Mark.

"He wasn't the one who threw the punch, so I couldn't press charges against him. So, I peeled him off the floor, stuck him in a cab, and threatened him if he ever returned to Redstone." Mark shrugged. "Discreetly, of course."

"You let him go?" I couldn't help saying it even

though I knew he had to. Thoughts entered my head of how I could have left him at the airport in a wheelchair.

"He used a fake name to pick up a woman, but it's not a crime." Mark leaned forward. Frank made a sound as he looked at his phone, but when he didn't comment, Mark shrugged and went on. "Sorry, Ty. His background is squeaky clean, too. Not even a parking ticket." Mark made a zero shape with two fingers and then let his arm drop in defeat. "I got nothing."

"His brother is a JAG lawyer. He gets off on everything." I squeezed my eyes shut when I saw Brown's face again as the bullet plowed between his eyes. Frank quickly exited the room.

"Again, I'm sorry," Mark repeated and lowered his voice. "We totally get losing someone we shouldn't."

I thought my head was going to explode. First Hill and Brown, and now the thought of Hill and Ivy.

"Beckett," Cole used my last name, and I knew there was an order coming, "Doc Roberts is waiting for you."

Fuck.

I opened the door and flew out more murderous than I'd ever felt before. My blood boiled and my heart raced to catch up. Frank caught my eye from the hall, and his expression told me more shit was about to hit the fan.

"Hey, Ty." Doc Roberts read my mood like an open book. "Take a seat." I felt caged and wild. I was unsure what might come out, so I stood back up and grabbed the door handle.

"Do you need a moment to cool off?" He removed his

glasses. A moment wouldn't be nearly enough. "You need to be cleared, Ty." His voice changed to a firm, quiet tone. "If you aren't and they get the call, you'll be staying put."

That wasn't going to happen.

I stepped inside, closed the door, and took a seat across from him.

"I'll keep this short, but I need to know a few things." I nodded and leaned into my arms, my hands pressed hard against my thighs. I was incredibly jacked up, and I wasn't sure how I was going to do. I escaped into my Middle East mindset.

"Have you made any friends here?" he started.

"Everyone seems nice."

"Do you consider them friends?"

"I do." That was the truth.

"You seem to be adjusting well to this lifestyle. Do you miss being in Afghanistan?"

"Sometimes, yes."

"Why is that?" I fought Brown's image away.

"It was quiet. I had one mission. I was focused, no distractions." His head tilted slightly as he studied me.

"Yes, I would agree most soldiers who spent as much time over there as you did would probably have experienced that feeling. Life is simple. You had only two things to worry about. The mission and keeping alive."

"I miss my team," I confessed. "Moore should be arriving here soon. He'll be my number two." I figured he'd appreciate the offer of some information without me being pressed for it. I'd been through enough of these psych evals to know what would win me bonus points.

"I'm pleased to hear that. I'm sure you two will have a lot to catch up on."

I nodded.

"Tell me about the man who saved you at the house in Mexico." He changed the subject fast.

"I don't know. One moment I'm about to step into a room to clear it, and the next I'm jerked back out as a blast shot toward my face."

"Do you have any idea what he looked like?"

"Not really. The smoke was thick, and my eyes were watering. The ringing in my ears was so loud I could only read his lips, so I can't even describe his voice. His eyes were wide, though, like he was scared we were there. A panic, almost." I let my mind wander into that memory for a moment to try to pull anything that I could.

"Okay."

"He ran out a different way than we came in," I remembered, "like he knew the house."

"Like he had been there before?" He scribbled on his notepad.

"It would seem that way." I glanced at my watch and knew I had put in enough time here.

"What distractions do you have here?" he threw at me suddenly.

"Ivy," I blurted without even thinking.

"Oh?" He lifted a hand. "How does Dr. Ivy Knight distract you?"

"That was dirty, Doc."

"It was," he agreed, "but sometimes what's really bothering you is the one thing you don't want to admit."

"I'll take a pass on this topic."

"A pass?" He seemed amused.

"A female problem isn't going to make or break me in the field."

"Oh, Ty," he chuckled lightly, "I highly disagree." I stared at him the same way he stared at me. "All right, well, it must have been difficult to see your distraction on a date with the one man you want to bring to justice." A pain shot through my head, and I pushed the heel of my palm above my eye, hoping for some relief. "Have you had your CAT scan yet?"

"I have it at thirteen-hundred."

"If it comes back fine, I'll clear you to be back on duty." He leaned forward. "But, Ty, you need to find a way past your vendetta with Hill. Give whatever you have to our lawyers and let us deal with taking him down."

I didn't reply. I knew that would never happen. It would be lost in the hundreds of other cases just like Brown's. Afghanistan was a wild west for soldiers to lose their shit and kill freely. Hill wasn't the first to take advantage and kill one of our own. I owed it to Brown's family to make it right. I owed it to Brown.

"Hey, Ty," Mike stopped me in the hallway on my way out of Doc's office, "is this the guy who saved your ass?" I took the photo then handed it back quickly. I still burned with anger over Hill. I tried to swallow it, so I didn't take my rage out on my teammate.

"No."

"Are you sure?" I turned to look back at him.

"Yes. Why? Who's that?"

"One of our informants, Juan Diaz."

"That's not him."

"Interesting." He sounded puzzled.

"Why?"

"Because Frank just told me he was killed because he saved you from being blown to bits in that house."

My head shot up, and I rubbed it as it pounded. "It wasn't him."

"Copy that." Mike turned on his heel and left without another word.

When I turned back around, I came face to face with the mini drill sergeant. She stared up at me with squinted dark eyes as though she wanted to read my mind.

"Hi, Olivia." I went for a smile, but it didn't quite live up to her expectations, and it showed. She was a great kid, but I wasn't fit to be around anyone right now.

"Whenever my dad's face looks like that, he has a place he goes." She sounded so grown up.

"Show me." Maybe the kid had something here. I was curious. She glanced down at her sneakers. "Just let me grab my boots."

She led the way at a good clip along a path that wound up the side of the mountain and then continued into the woods for another half mile or so until we came to a clearing. She stopped.

"Grandpa said the first time Zack did it, it scared the shit out of him so badly he couldn't think straight for three days." I side-eyed her at her language, and she shrugged. "I was simply quoting." I examined the steel post in the ground and the cable attached to it. The platform near the mountain's edge had a sign above it. *A man is determined not by his strength but by his ability to control his strength. – Edison Logan*

"There's a fast rope in the middle. There's two, actually, in case they want to compete against each other."

"It's impressive." I felt my energy surge. I lived for this kind of stuff.

"It's nuts, actually." She shook her head. "Mom hates when Dad does it. She won't even speak to him at dinner." She chuckled. "But the next morning they're always fine, so I guess she gets over it." She made a face, and I forced my smirk away. "Normally, Uncle John is here three times a week. Uncle Mike said he had a bad rappel one time and never got over it. I think he trains so he can be ready if it ever happens again."

"Makes sense." I agreed with John's reasoning. You could shy away from the things that scarred or scared you, or you could face them head on until they didn't anymore.

"Can I ask you something?"

"Sure." I peered over the ledge and saw I was a good sixty-plus feet up.

"Are you as old as my dad?" That was an odd question.

"You read my file." I smirked, curious to know where this was going. "I believe I am ten or so years younger."

"Dad only lets me see some of it." She scoffed. "So just around thirty?"

"Yes." I looked over at her. "Why?"

"Well, I'm ten, so I was just wondering when you're going to marry Dr. Knight."

What?

"Knight and I aren't dating."

"Oh, okay." Her tone was a bit upbeat.

"And where is all this coming from?"

"Well, Milly, my best friend from riding," she filled in some backstory for me, "said her dad is looking to date. Her parents split when she was born. And I thought since Dr. Knight is so pretty, she might like to meet him." She went back to looking out over the lake below us.

My head hurt with what she said, and it was too soon and too raw for me to even think about that topic right now.

I spotted powder and rubbed it into my hands, getting rid of any sweat.

"You're going now?" Her eyes widened.

"You brought me here, didn't you."

"Yeah, but I should let dad or grandpa know. I mean what if something happens?"

"Then I better be careful, hadn't I?" I handed her my

phone and pulled on the gloves that were hanging on the hook and stepped out onto the ledge, grabbing the rope.

"Ty," she seemed nervous as I hooked a weight belt to my waist. I not only wanted to make it harder, but I wanted it to drop if I needed to. It would break the surface of the water before me.

"I'll be right back." I eased over the edge and then let gravity drive me downward. I repelled down quickly to the water, but before my feet even touched the surface, I squeezed my boots to stop the descent and used all my upper strength to climb right back up the rope. Just before I got to the top, I did it again. I did it five more times until my muscles screamed for a break. Physical activity was the only way I could work out the shit in my head. Though it wasn't a permeant fix, it helped.

"That was crazy!" Olivia beamed, holding up my phone. She had recorded me, apparently. "This should be on the Army website."

"I appreciate the love, but I don't do websites." I tucked the gloves away and pointed for us to leave.

"Want to do the obstacle course we have here?"

"Another time. I have a doctor's appointment I can't miss."

"Oh, yes," she checked her watch, "your CAT is soon." I shook my head at her. "I told ya, Ty, I'll run this place someday." She gave me an impish grin.

"That, I don't, doubt."

Later that evening, Daniel and Sue wanted everyone in the house to join them at Zack's, so I sat at the table and listened to conversations that were in full swing. Dinner had been served and cleared, and now we were enjoying drinks as we discussed the outdoor pool Daniel wanted to build at Shadows.

"What's wrong with the lake, Grandpa?" Olivia's brow furrowed momentarily as she looked up at her grandfather. She'd beamed at him all through the meal. I could tell he was her idol.

"Well, sweetie, I think a pool would be useful for training. The guys could use it for diving and exercises that keep them underwater for long periods of time." He glanced at me. "Ty, I know you've spent a lot of time using water as a tool to hide. Perhaps I could pick your brain on that sometime."

"Of course." I wasn't up for much conversation. I'd wanted to skip out altogether, but I knew Dr. Roberts had his eye on me. Ivy was quiet tonight as well, I noticed. I knew I owed her an explanation, and I was a dick for not just spitting it out. My phone buzzed and pulled me from my thoughts.

> Moore: Just heard from Dustin. Hill never made it back to Washington. Rivera has been spending time with his brother.

I saw red with the idea of Hill still being in Montana. I rubbed my face, feeling my temper rise to the surface.

"Your CAT was clear." Cole leaned in next to me.

"You're officially back on call." I nodded, pleased at some fucking good news for once.

"Dad," Olivia beamed, "you should have seen Ty on the fast rope today." The entire table looked at me.

"What's a fast rope?" Ivy looked around like she'd missed something.

"You know how we repel down from the chopper?" She nodded at Mike as he explained. "Well, we have two practice ropes that hang sixty-two feet down from a cable across the lake."

"I hate those things," Mark cut in with a shake of his head. "I don't mind heights, but there's one spot in the rope that when you zip by it, it wiggles way below, and one wrong move…" He let out a huff. "Scares the shit right out of me. It's a damn long way down."

"I can safely say I don't miss those," Zack, who had been circling the table, chimed in.

"He went up and down like six times, Grandpa Zack," Olivia continued. "Zipped down, stopped right above the top of the water, and then only used his arms to pull himself back up. It was totally cool."

Though I appreciated her compliment, I wasn't in the mood for attention.

"Did you wear the belt?" Sue looked concerned.

"I did." I paused then felt like I should explain myself. "We used to train like that back in Afghanistan. It was nothing I couldn't handle."

"I took a video! Can you show them, Ty?"

"I don't think they need—"

"I'd like to see it," Ivy interrupted me. I cleared my throat with discomfort as I brought the video up and handed her my phone.

"Jesus," Ivy hissed, "that makes my knees go weak." She continued to watch, and I looked around at the people coming and going. It was quieter than before but still busy. "That's impressive." She handed me back my phone. "I'm glad I wasn't there."

"Why?"

"If something happened…" She paused. "What if you fell?"

"Then you fall." I shrugged as she looked at me. Even as I said it, I knew I sounded like an ass. I hated that I was shutting down inside. Daniel and Sue soon left with the younger kids, along with Abigail and Doc Roberts. We were still spread out along the table, and a few locals came by to talk to the wives and Keith.

"Doctor Ivy," Olivia moved next to her, "I have an important question to ask you."

"Oh?" Ivy turned to face her. "What's that?"

"Remember my friend Milly who you met the other day when you and Mom picked me up at that birthday party?"

"I do."

Really? This is happening now?

"Well, her father got divorced, and Milly and I thought since you're so pretty and you're not dating Ty like I thought," my gaze flipped up to meet Ivy's, "that maybe you could date him?"

"Oh," her tone went up, "ah, well, that's a very sweet offer, but I've never met the man, and I'm a bit scarred from my last blind date." She chuckled uncomfortably.

"He's really nice, though." She leaned into Ivy. "He's cute, but not like…" She looked at me, and I raised an eyebrow. "Just take this. It's got his number on it." She handed her a note, and Ivy nodded.

"Thanks for thinking of me." Ivy smiled and popped the paper into her purse.

"Olivia, what are you doing?" Savannah called.

"Nothing, Mom." She went back to sit next to her mother while I spun my beer glass between my fingers.

"Time." Mike grinned as he suddenly hit the table in front of John. Ivy jumped at him.

"Three men came in. Two are sitting at the bar, and the other," John thought for a moment, "went back to his car. Where a girl is waiting."

Moore and I used to do this all the time.

"He went to the bathroom," I cut in and took a sip of my beer.

"What did you see?" John seemed impressed.

"Three came in, two stayed at the bar the third started to head toward the car but spotted Ivy on his way out and circled back. He then went to his car where he's now reading something on his phone."

"Okay," Mike started, but John held up a hand.

"What else?" He looked at me.

I kept my gaze on my glass as I envisioned the entire place like a movie playing out in front of me.

"There are seven cars in the lot. Two older couples are occupying the booths in the back. They keep the younger teens up front, I'm sure for Zack to keep a visual on. There's a table of five guys, early twenties, who have had their attention tuned in to our table a little more than necessary."

"I noticed that, too," Cole grunted.

"The staff have changed their cashier twice since we arrived, took her out, then later put her back in. I say her employment might be short-lived. There're two exits, one at my three o'clock and another my seven."

"Holy shit. How do you do that?" Ivy stared at me.

"They said you were observant," John smiled, "but shit, I'm impressed."

"Is it exhausting?" Ivy probed.

"It's kept me alive."

"That didn't answer my question," she shot back, and for a moment I forgot who I was answering. Her tone had a bit of an edge to it, and I could tell her annoyance with my lack of communication still simmered on the surface.

Mike and John sat still and silent as they tried to hide their amusement.

"Yes, it can be." I took a deep breath and tried not to show the heaviness I carried inside. I didn't want her to see it. I knew she's taken it on. "But I can't turn it off even if I wanted to."

"Thank you." She held my gaze for a beat. "I appreciate the answer."

I felt the sting of her jab; it wasn't subtle.

Zack came to the table to wish us a good night. Everyone headed back to the SUVs, and I felt my phone buzz again.

"Go ahead. I'll be right there." I waved them off and glanced down.

Moore: Murry says he's got news about the day Brown was killed. I'll be in touch.

I squeezed my eyes shut and hoped to hell that my old friend Murry had something we could use against Hill.

Ty: Copy that.

Once outside, I found Ivy had waited for me.

"I'm not supposed to stray far from you." She shrugged.

"Right." I shook my head and mentally kicked myself for letting that detail slip.

"Hey, baby, wanna check out my back seat?" One of the guys who'd been inside earlier laughed with his buddies.

"Hey," she pulled my attention to her, "are you okay? You seem like you're about to snap."

"I'm fi—"

"Why don't you walk that fine ass over this way?" I swung my head in his direction and saw red. Ivy stepped in front of me and grabbed my arms to stop me.

"Ty, don't. They're just drunk."

"You got something to say, man?" He egged me on, and I heard Cole's voice call out for the rest of the team. "Girl, come home with me, and I'll show you the night of your dreams."

"Hey, hey, hey," Ivy pressed her hands to my vibrating chest, "Ty, look at me, please." It took a huge effort to tear my gaze from his to hers. "They're looking for a fight, you said it yourself, you saw them watching us in the restaurant. They're drunk and looking for something to prove."

"All good, Beckett?" Cole called.

I wanted to hurt them, feel my knuckles break their bones. The darkness that Hill brought out in me was wild —untamable, even—so it took a lot to pull back.

"Yeah." I called, and Ivy sighed with relief. Cole and the guys backed off and headed for the SUVs. I could hear the catcalls and jibes of the men as we walked away from the fight.

"Come on." I pulled her close and put my arm around her shoulder as we walked to join the others. My hand slid down over the bare skin on her back, and as we neared the side of the SUV, images of her pressed against it flooded my head. Cole stopped to help Catalina with something, so I took that moment to pull Ivy against me as I leaned against the car. It felt good but only increased the ache between my legs. I leaned down and brushed my lips around the shell of her ear.

"Lust is a bitch." I repeated the words she'd used on me.

"So's not getting answers," she shot back and tried to move away. I locked my grip on her hips.

"I'm in a very dark place," I admitted, selfishly wanting her body. "I made you a promise, and I intend to keep it. I just need time."

"There you go," Cole said to someone, and I quickly pressed Ivy away before he saw us and opened the back door for her.

"Thanks." She took a seat in the back, and I followed. Once settled, I rested my hand on her thigh. She didn't respond but didn't move it either.

We had just pulled up to the house when I felt my phone buzz again. I waited until I was inside the door then glanced at it.

> Moore: I have news. I'll call you later. But the son of a bitch has people watching you.

NINETEEN

ERIC

I stood on my patio and looked out over the city below. I had orders from Castillo that there was another shipment of girls on the way. I would need to contact Chili. He was the only one I sold to.

"Eric!" Alejandro hurried through the door and handed me a letter. I didn't have to see who it was from. I could tell by his pale face and urgency it was from the boss Castillo himself.

I turned over the sealed envelope and slid the card partway out.

"All good, boss?" He struggled to catch his breath.

"Have the car ready. I need to change." I handed him the card and raced inside.

The Castillos' summer house was a three-hour drive,

just enough time to figure out what to do if something was wrong. I had two brothers who worked his security team, and they owed me. They once had a sister in trouble, and I was able to get her out of the country. She now lived in Belize. It wasn't the best situation, but it was better than being married and beaten up by Castillo's ruthless cousin. They never traced it back to me because I was that good at making people disappear.

"Any idea why he's asking for you?" Alejandro scanned our surroundings. "Why he's made it personal by having you come to his home?"

"No." I really didn't, and it made me wonder if I should have gone to church first. I glanced at my watch and ran my finger around the band as I read the time.

We pulled off the road and stopped at a set of obnoxious gates, well-guarded and well-armed. I rolled down the back window and handed a guard the card that Castillo had sent to me.

"ID."

I handed him my ID and my weapon, knowing that was next. He studied the picture and looked at me. I removed my glasses and acted like he wasted my time.

"Can we pass?" I gnawed my toothpick.

"Go," he ordered, and I plucked my ID from his fingers and pointed at my gun.

"I want that back when I leave."

"Go." He hit the butt of the car as Filippo drove through the gates.

"Keep your eyes forward," I warned him. "If you look nervous, you'll make them nervous."

"Yes, boss." He tried to listen, but I knew he was scared shitless by the way he kept using his shirt to dry his forehead.

"Park over there." I pointed to the stairs and motioned for Alejandro to step out first. "Stay here, keep the car running, and don't say shit to anyone." Filippo nodded a bunch of times as I slipped out, and I threw a curse at the heat that beat down on my head.

"Arms up." Another guard pointed his weapon in my face while his buddy patted me down and then did the same to Alejandro. "They're clean."

Castillo stood at the top of the stairs and watched as we climbed toward him.

"Welcome, Eric. Come. I have someone I'd like you to meet. But you," he looked at Alejandro, "you need to stay here." I nodded for him to listen.

Once inside, I felt better in his central air. Christ, I missed air conditioners. I took note of the cameras pointed at me and how many armed guards there were in each room. I knew I had Castillo's trust, but that didn't mean I trusted him. Martín Castillo had good reason to be paranoid. Our business was always in the limelight, especially with Americans.

"Drink?" he asked. I nodded, and he snapped his fingers at a woman. Normally, I would decline liquor, but I needed to act like I was comfortable with him. The fact that I wondered why in the hell I had been suddenly summoned to his place, in the middle of the week, had me on edge, as it was unusual that he hadn't just sent word through his normal channels.

The woman came back with a cold Coca-Cola, and my mouth nearly watered at the sight of it.

"I thought you'd appreciate a little taste from home." He waved off the woman, and then one of his guards closed the door and left me alone with Castillo.

"I have something very sensitive that I need your help with."

"I'm listening." I took a sip of the soda and let the bubbles linger on my tongue to ease my nerves.

"You've proven you're trustworthy. My men report that you do an excellent job with the women." I nodded at one of the brothers, who gave me a quick look. *Nice to know I'm being watched, guys.* I would address that later. "And the way you handled the situation before speaks well of your work ethic."

"Was there any doubt?" I again used my cockiness to entertain him.

"You amuse me, Eric. Not a lot of men would be so," he paused while he thought of the right word, "comfortable with someone in my position."

"When you've got nothing to hide, and you know where your loyalty lies, it's easy to be comfortable," I assured him. I wanted to ease any fear he might have about me. My future depended on him, and I needed him to know I was reliable. "What is it you need help with?"

He fiddled with the cigar in his hand as he watched

me from across the room. He suddenly leaned forward, pressed a button on the table, and a door opened behind him. A strange clicking noise could be heard. It became louder and louder. I looked at him while he watched my reaction. An elderly lady entered the room. She held a black cane, and I saw the darkest eyes I'd ever seen on a person. Her stark white skin looked like it had never seen the light of day. My gaze dropped to her bony ankles, which were fastened with cuffs and a thick chain.

Who the hell was this?

"Eric Noah, meet Rosa Coppola."

What?

"As in the Coppola syndicate in Rome?"

Holy shit.

"Well, what *used* to be a syndicate. Things have changed now." He looked at the old lady, and she met his eyes for a moment, her hatred burned clear, but then she dropped her eyes and looked away as she muttered something in Italian.

"Okay." I waited for him to go on. "Why is she here?"

"She's here to pay off a debt."

"A debt," I repeated as I scrambled to follow.

"All right," he clapped his hands, "go away." He waved her off, and she glared at me and slowly walked out of the room and the door slammed shut.

Jesus, she was creepy.

"Now to business." He leaned toward me. "I've got some special girls coming over, and I need this to go very smoothly. No mess ups, you understand." He looked directly in my eyes. His eyes were cold and sent a shiver down my spine.

"All right." I shook it off. Why was I here? "So, why this special visit?" I gave him my own cold stare to gain some ground.

"This is not like any other drop. This is her drop, her payment for sins she brought on me." He pointed to the door where Lucifer's wife had emerged. "I need someone I can trust to handle this. It must go perfectly."

I shook my head, trying to process it all.

"Can you handle this, Eric?" I looked up at him, and his eyes now sparkled with excitement. "Because I'm about to become the most wanted Cartel member who's ever lived when I pull this off." He leaned back and laughed so hard he nearly hacked up a lung.

He had me at most wanted.

A slow smile spread across my lips as I turned to him, and I happily joined him in his laughter. I perfectly matched his ruthless dark side.

"Fuck yeah, I'm in."

On the drive home, I sat in silence and tuned out Alejandro's need to chat. He wasn't sure what had happened back at that house, but I knew he wanted to know. When we grew closer to Rosarito, I leaned forward.

"Take me to church."

"Sure thing, boss." Filippo quickly turned and headed in that direction. When we stopped, I waited for Alejandro to step out first, then he waited for me to exit.

"We'll park across the street."

"Good." I walked to the door, dropped the wad of cash from my last job in the donation box at the entrance, and disappeared into the chapel. I needed to pray.

TWENTY

IVY

The mood in the house was strange that evening, almost dark. I knew Frank had held a meeting earlier that day about the girls who were murdered in Mexico. He had information from one of his informants on what went down. The Cartel were ruthless, and the more I heard about what the guys dealt with, the more I was nervous about the idea of them leaving again. I had no idea when their next mission would be, and the unknown played on me. I just couldn't get how they did it.

Savannah assured me that the guys were carrying a lot and that on days like that everyone just laid low and processed. I guessed it made sense. The house that seemed to be so upbeat and free had a different side to it. Days of down and outs.

I hadn't seen Ty all day. I knew he was struggling, and the *fixer* in me wanted to help. I also wanted answers and hated that I hadn't gotten any yet. The sex had been great, and even last night had its moments. I knew if we'd been alone, I probably wouldn't have been able to stop myself.

Ty and I had a strong pull for one another; there was no dismissing that. But now my mind needed satisfaction as well.

I sank myself into my notes but soon found I couldn't focus for long, so I got up.

"Hey," I whispered softly to my uncle, whose gaze stared out the window over the top of his laptop. He was deep in thought. "Do you mind if I come in?"

"Of course." He removed his glasses and closed his laptop. "What's on your mind?"

"I'm feeling badly for Keith." I sat on the couch and picked at the corner of the pillow. "He took the kids for the weekend to let them know about their mother."

"Yes, that won't be an easy time for any of them." He glanced at his phone then slowly turned it over.

"Is everything okay?" I nodded at it.

"Yes," he smiled, but it didn't reach his eyes, "just waiting on a call."

"Shouldn't it be turned upward, then?"

"Have you spoken to Ty since last night?" He caught me off guard.

"No, I haven't seen him today at all."

"He's in a very dark place, Ivy. I urge you to tread lightly."

"Meaning?" I waited for him to go on.

"Meaning be careful with him. He's holding a very tight rein on a lot of anger, and though I believe he's fit to continue in the field, I sincerely believe he's not in the right frame of mind for anything else." He gave me a strange look.

"Uncle Reid, if you have something to say, say it."

"Dating someone in this house isn't easy."

What the hell does my uncle know about Ty and me?

"You should know." I raised my chin, and he shifted in his seat. "Look," I took a breath and tried to lower my defenses, "I know you're only looking out for me. You're basically my father, and I know I've got a lot going on right now personally, too." He nodded at that. "But Ty and I are just blowing off some steam together. I'm not looking for marriage. I'm looking for a friggin' distraction so I can take a breath without shaking as I exhale."

"Are you sleeping?"

"With him?" I blurted and then wished I hadn't.

"That was not at all what I meant, Ivy." He shook his head. "I meant through the night."

"Mostly," I lied, and he narrowed his gaze on me. "A few hours here and there. I'm functioning, so I'll take that as a win."

"Maybe it's time to take something for that."

"If the shoe was on the other foot, would you?"

"Okay." He held his hands up, palms out. He still seemed distracted, as though his mind wasn't at all on what we were discussing.

"Uncle, is there something bothering you?" I studied his face.

His phone vibrated, and he narrowed his eyes to focus on the screen.

"Sorry, Ivy, but I need to take this." He rushed out of the room, leaving me to wonder what in the world he was so worried about.

The homes on the property that housed the Blackstone men and their families seemed quiet and still. It was as though we were all waiting for a storm to hit. Even Scoot seemed uninterested in having a chat that evening. He just flopped down on my bed and glared at me when I turned on the TV.

I heard low music playing. I got up and popped my head outside hopefully. Yes, Ty's bedroom door was partly open. Maybe there was life in this house today after all.

I gave a light knock, but he didn't answer, so I pushed the big wooden door open and spotted him on the couch, nursing a drink in the dark. The TV flickered and provided the only light in the room. *Howling at the Moon* by D Fine Us flowed softly from the speakers.

"Are you okay?" I whispered, breaking the silence between us. His gaze didn't leave the screen, and I guessed the events over the past few days played havoc with his head. "Want to talk about it?" Nothing. I twisted around the bottle on the table next to him to read the label, but it was written in a different language. "What can I do to help?" I offered.

He smirked darkly behind the rim of the glass and

swallowed back the last of it. Just that look alone made my skin heat and my mouth run dry. *Focus.*

"Okay," I nodded, "I'll leave you be, then." We needed to talk, but this wasn't the time. I turned to leave, but his leg lifted, and his foot landed heavily on the table, blocking my path.

"You want to help?" His tone was almost eerie. I nodded, unsure where he was mentally.

He leaned over and dropped his glass on the table, and he cupped the back of my calf. Slowly, he slid his fingers upward, beneath my skirt. They found their way around my thigh to stroke my drenched panties. I felt the fabric press into my hip as they ripped. He did the same to the other side then tossed the scrap of fabric next to his glass.

His fingers returned while his gaze remained locked on mine. He looked haunted and tortured, and I wished I could say something to make that expression go away, but I knew it wasn't as easy as that. Darkness fills the spots that light couldn't reach. The scars inside us created pockets of pain that lay beneath, way beyond our ability to heal with words alone.

He reached down and nudged the pad of his finger inside me. My mouth parted and my chest heaved, outing my desire for him.

"Ty, talk—"

"Spread your legs more." Before I could think, he leaned forward and licked with a hungry tongue. The moment he tasted me, he growled and hiked my leg up so he could have me at a better angle. I was helpless to deny him anything at that point.

"Jesus, Ty." I steadied myself on his shoulders as he chose a pace that had my eyes rolling back in my head. "That feels amazing." I couldn't help but rock my hips to his rhythm. My skin grew hot, my head dazed, and my stomach twisted into a delicious knot. My moans filled the room, and when I found somewhere to put my other foot, I pressed against him harder as I fisted his hair. He was relentless and kept switching things up, never allowing me to gain any control. It was incredibly erotic and completely overpowered any thoughts I might have had in my head.

"Come on my tongue," he commanded. "Let me taste you as you lose control."

"I'm so close," I cried. "Harder." I needed more of him. I teetered on the brink of bliss. "Yes," I moaned as his tongue flicked and sucked on all the right spots. "Yes, Ty, yes!" I was so close I could taste it. I folded inward, ready to explode outward. I tightened and expanded at the same time. My skin went hot then cold, then hot again. I wasn't sure I could stand it when the climax hit. *Here I go.* I raced toward the edge, wings expanded, ready to take that leap off the cliff.

Suddenly, a buzz. He stilled, pulled away, as I cried out in shock and frustration.

"I need to take this." He held up his phone, and I blinked, confused, hanging over the sweet ledge of desire, watching my bliss fizzle out below me.

"Seriously?" I shook my head as a mixture of emotion came at me. I was only trying to help him. *Was, I though?* I was the one who'd been on the receiving end of the pleasure.

"I have to." He pushed to his feet, and I lowered my leg and pulled my skirt back in place as he left the room. I covered my face and took a long breath. What was I doing? Friends with benefits should come with rules, like never leave the other hanging on to a climax.

I tossed and turned all night. My skin was on fire, and the memories of Ty's tongue between my legs played behind my eyelids every time I closed them.

"Let me taste you as you lose control."

If I thought I was a pent-up mess before we had sex, I was incredibly wrong. I imagined it was what junkies felt like when they could only make a skinny line from the dust left in the bottom of their baggie. So close to the real hit, but it just didn't cut it. It only made it worse.

I tossed the sheets off, flung open the closet door, and dug around in my suitcase. Once my fingers felt my silicone friend, I slipped in the bathroom and got reacquainted.

Next morning, my run started out in the dark but ended with the sunrise. I peeled my jacket off my sweaty skin and wrapped it around my waist as I jogged down the hill to the patch of tarmac near the building that housed Shadows' helicopter. Sometimes I forgot that I lived on a special ops base. The massive house and lake hugged by the mountains seemed to draw your attention away from the everything else this place offered. I slipped inside the building and let my eyes adjust to the change in light. The massive beast in front of me had blades that spread like a hawk above me. I moved closer. The guns on the side sent a shiver down my back as I reached up and touched the cool steel. The inside was open, and I wondered how many times this chopper was under fire and how many soldiers' lives it had saved. How many times it had helped them escape in the nick of time as they were swallowed up in its belly, safe for at least that moment.

"Have you been inside one of these before?" Mark asked from behind me, nearly making me jump out of my skin.

"No." I held my chest to keep my heart in place. "Sorry. There's still so many places I haven't explored here yet."

"Don't be sorry." He rubbed the side with a big soft rag. "I'm just glad it's you who's exploring and not one of my rugrats again." He smiled. "They're like stray cats in an open field. Impossible to control."

"They're pretty great." I smiled back. "It'll be interesting to see what they do for a living after growing up in a place like this."

"Fingers crossed." He patted the word *Army* across his chest. "You want to hop in?" He motioned toward the chopper. I nodded and climbed in then stood where he pointed. I pressed my back into the wall.

"Aren't you scared of falling out?" I looked over the

edge and thought about how it might feel up off the ground as it hovered over a gunfight.

"Nah." He reached up and grabbed a strap. "We wear these, but you get used to holding on."

"I can't do heights very well." I shook my head and looked around. "God, the things you guys must see."

"It's not always pretty, but we don't focus on those parts." He pointed to the wall behind the pilot's seat. "We focus on these." He tapped some scratch marks in the steel. "This here is how many lives we saved over the years. This was my grandfather's team. My father's team, and ours." He smiled warmly as his thumb rubbed over the grooves.

"Your father's?" I stopped and thought about how I wasn't sure how his story connected.

"My family is confusing, but the best parts of it is that Abby was Cole's nanny. She adopted me, and I lived with her and Cole's family. To me, Abby and Sue are both my mothers, Daniel is my father, and Cole is my brother." A warm smile spread over his lips for a moment, like he was remembering some good.

"Family is what you make it." I wanted him to know I understood. My uncle was basically my father.

He suddenly stopped and ran his finger over the etched in dates. "You know what?"

"Mm?"

"We never added a date for Ty's team." He reached back and pulled a knife from his pocket. "Why don't you do the honors and scratch in the year."

"Me?"

"Yeah, why not? It's good luck when a lady does it." He winked playfully and pulled out his phone. "Ty can add the team's name later."

"Okay." I slowly moved up next to him, then on tiptoe I tentatively pressed the blade against the steel. I gained confidence, and clearly as I could, I scratched in the year with the point of the knife. I leaned forward, closed my eyes, and gently blew the flakes away. "Be safe out there," I whispered without thinking, then stepped back to rest on my heels.

"If that isn't luck, I don't know what is." Mark beamed with his phone pointed at me. "Thanks, Ivy. We're a superstitious bunch, so this will help."

I nodded then climbed down from the chopper. As I stood next to the huge machine, I pressed my whole hand against its side for a moment.

"Can I ask you something?"

"Sure." He came to stand beside me.

"At the risk of overstepping, I'm confused on something. Where is Lexi now?"

"Here." He handed me a dime. "I just hired you to listen to me. So now you can't repeat anything to anyone."

"I would never," I promised.

"Superstitious, remember?" He held out the dime, and I took it.

"The story we tell is if you leave, you're gone. No second chances or protection. That's more for the clients we bring back here to help. Some can be real assholes, and we almost hope they do leave." He shook his head like he wished he hadn't said that part. "But with the wives, it's different. Cole even said it to Savannah when she first arrived, but I can tell you he would have tied her up and stuck her in the basement if she wanted to leave. He was in love with her before he even met her." He waved his hand. "That's a long story. Anyway, as for Lexi, Cole gave her the whole shebang in her exit meeting. She accepted everything. She signed a lot of paperwork and was escorted to her cousin's house in Nova Scotia, Canada. She thinks she's free of us, no second chances, no protection. But, between you and me, that's not the case. She's family and will never really be cut loose. We have and always will have someone watching over her."

"Did she want to go to Canada?"

"Lexi is a lot of things, but she understood what it meant to leave."

"How is she now?"

"Really good. She got her old job back at a local café. She even applied to one of the universities up there, St. Mary's or something like that."

"Wow." I nodded, impressed at her ability to adjust so well. "That didn't take long."

"Nope, but that's Lexi. I wouldn't be shocked if she had it all lined up before she decided to leave Keith and their kids."

"Really?"

"Yeah." He turned and picked up a piece of metal and fitted it into a hole in the chopper. "Between us, I never totally trusted her. I wanted to, but she never fit the mold the other wives did. When you marry us, you marry all of us." He smirked. "Yeah, no, I just heard how that came out." He scrunched up his face. "I just mean you're choosing more than just marriage. It's a whole way of life. Yes, you have your husband, but you also gain a tight-knit family where we all look out for one another. Your entire life becomes part of the whole, and even your job has to be here. So far, that's worked for everyone but her."

"There's normally always one that doesn't work in most things."

"Yeah," his arms dropped, "I get that it isn't for everyone. I just hate that it destroyed my best friend's heart." I nodded. What he said was exactly what had happened.

"Well," I tried to sound upbeat, "at least he has an incredible family to help him get through it."

"That he does." He smiled at me. "So?"

"So?"

"So, what about you Doc? What do you think of living here?" I studied him a moment and handed back the dime. He lifted an eyebrow.

"I'm using it as a loan. I'll square up back at the house." I cleared my mind and went with the truth since he was so honest with me. "I love it here. I never thought I could get the city out of me, but honestly, I haven't thought about it once. Redstone is gorgeous, the property is endless, everyone is so kind and loving." I rubbed my face. "I feel safe here, given what happened back..." I stopped the next word that sat on my tongue, and my eyes shot to him.

"What happened back where?" His expression changed.

"I just mean, it's a nice change from my old life." I forced a smile and looked around.

"You know, Ivy, all the wives have been through something. Shit, we're all victims of something—"

"Yeah, no, I know." I wrapped my arms around myself. "They've mentioned that before."

"Does Ty know whatever it is you're holding inside?"

"Ty?" I shook my head. "Why would he?"

"No one plows another man's face like he did without feelings behind it."

The conversation had gotten away from me, so I needed to change direction quickly.

"Yeah, what the hell was that all about? Because I haven't gotten anything out of Ty."

"Your loan just ran out." He smiled.

"Mark, I would never pry, but it did involve me."

He squeezed his eyes shut and cursed while he thought for a moment. "You're right, it did, but it's Ty shit to share, Ivy."

"Fine." I backed off.

"But I will say it's bigger than just a jealous punch. There's some real ugly around that topic."

"Now that, I understand." I nodded, backing up. "Thanks, Mark."

"Any time, Ivy."

I walked the rest of the way back to the house. I needed to buy time for my head to digest everything Mark shared with me.

"Ivy!" Easton raced up the hill and tossed his little Logan arms around my waist. "I was looking for you."

"You were? Well, now you found me."

"Up?" He gave me those big eyes, and I couldn't resist. "Spin me like you did before."

"Oh, you want the airplane?" He nodded, and I leaned down so he could get on my back.

"Ready for take-off, captain!" he shouted. I held out my arms and raced down the hill, making airplane noises, and when we got to flat ground, I spun him around, and all I could hear was his laughter.

"Hang on, captain, one of the wings broke! Mayday, mayday!" I acted like I had a radio.

"Quick, call Blackstone! Daddy will save us!" He giggled with pride. The wind and colors whipped around us, and I felt for just a moment that I was in his head inside his imaginary world with him.

"Ivy." Frank's voice pulled me from our fun, and I slowly stopped spinning as I saw his dark expression. Little did I know the spins were only the start of what was to come.

———

The next twelve hours were exhausting. I searched every face that crossed my path. The plane ride was a blur. I sat between my uncle and Frank, and though I appreciated the first-class ticket, I could have been stuck in the back of the plane by the restrooms for all I cared. I had no idea what I would walk into when I landed in Washington. I just knew I needed to see things myself.

"Are you sure?" Frank looked over my head at my uncle then back at me.

"It's my home." I swallowed the lump in my throat and pressed my hands flat to my thighs as I looked up at my townhouse from the street.

"Ivy."

"I know my limits, Uncle Reid," I tossed over my shoulder as I climbed the steps to the one place that used to provide such protection for me. My fingers pulled up the police tape so I could duck underneath. A few police officers gave me a nod as I took in my battered home.

I knew I'd left my place basically stripped of my things. I'd even arranged for a friend from Barbados who needed a place while she got settled in her new job to stay here. We thought it might be good for someone to be here, at least for a few weeks, to make it look like the place was occupied. The few pieces of furniture I'd left for her and some of her own things were strewn about.

"Is Kylee all right?" I wouldn't forgive myself if she got hurt.

"He was long gone before Kylee got here. She called

the police, and they passed the information on to me. She's at a hotel tonight."

"I'll call her later." I was relieved she was okay.

"We think he came in through the kitchen window." Frank walked by me, and I followed him down the narrow hall to my sweet little farmhouse-themed kitchen. I remembered how much fun I'd had choosing decorations to make it homey.

The window was smashed, and dirt smudged the edges of the sill. I leaned down and picked up the broken jar that had held my basil. I could smell the aroma of it as I scooped up the poor plant and held it gently in my hand. It roots were still intact. The water system that I had bought online seemed to have worked, and I was happy my friend continued to fill it with water. I tucked it and the rest of its soil into a new container and held on to it like an anchor.

"He dug through that." He pointed to my mail that was scattered over the table and on the floor around it. We hadn't wanted to cancel my mail right away either. Kylee emptied the box each day and brought it inside to make it look like I was still there. Though she knew the danger of staying here from the little I could share, she was trained in jujitsu and felt confident she could handle things. "Whoever it was opened a few things. We'll try to get some prints to compare later. It'll take a bit of time."

"What else?" I whispered.

"He listened to your messages." He pointed to the recorder that had been planted the morning before I left.

The blinking light from the message my friend had left was now gone. We had purposely set it up that way to see if anyone would check it.

"We're hoping he took the bait. From here, we think he sat on your couch." He pointed at some mail strewn on the floor near the couch. Then he moved to the stairs that led to my bathroom and bedroom. I suddenly felt sick and willed my feet to follow.

Frank cleared his throat as we entered my destroyed bathroom. "Do you see anything missing? I know most of your stuff is gone, but still." I looked around and noticed a couple of my old perfumes I'd left on the shelf were missing.

"Nothing worth mentioning."

"No, it is worth mentioning." Frank bent down. "Ivy, we need to know where his head's at. Is he simply hunting you down to silence you? Or," his face slipped, "is it more than that?"

My stomach twisted into a knot, and I felt tears prickle the back of my eyes.

"My Coco Chanel and coconut body spray appear to be missing. Those other things are my friend's, so I couldn't tell you if anything of hers is gone."

"Okay, we can check that." He nodded at the detective who was shadowing us. I turned around and headed for my bedroom. "I'll have her do a walkthrough myself. She was quick to let us know about the break-in. I have her staying at the Marriott." I nodded, glad he repeated himself so I could take it all in.

"Perhaps," my uncle stepped in front of me and placed a hand on my shoulder, "we could maybe skip your bedroom."

"I flew across country to face this, Uncle Reid. I appreciate you wanting to protect me, but please let me do this." He waited a beat then stepped out of my way with a shake of his head. I braced myself and stepped inside to take in the scene.

The blankets had been shoved aside, and there was a yellow forensics number next to something I couldn't quite make out. I closed my eyes and pushed the nasty thoughts away. One of my old red silk blouses was crumbled on the floor and looked like parts of it were stuck together as if it had been used to…my stomach rolled. Careful not to step on it, I moved closer and then felt the spins return as I read what was written on the vanity mirror. In black Sharpie were the words, *"I'm trained. I hunt. I'll find you."*

I caught my uncle's reflection in the mirror as he reached out to take my shoulders, but then he stopped himself.

"Does this mean I don't need to testify?" I tried to speak clearly, but my voice betrayed my frayed nerves.

"Actually," Frank spoke up, "it means the opposite. We need you now more than ever."

"I tried to talk to the judge," my uncle said, "but he wants to use this case to drive home that a sol—"

"I got it." I cut him off. I didn't want to hear the rest. "When?"

"Well," Frank let out a sigh, "I'm not sure. This changes things. It'll push it back some."

"I suspect it does." I eyed my closet and the few things I'd left behind for Kylee, now tossed on the floor. "I don't suppose Kylee will want to stay here now." I put a hand to my stomach and prayed I wouldn't bring up anything left inside it. "I think I've seen enough."

"Okay." My uncle carefully took my arm. "I think you have, too."

I walked with him down the stairs and avoided all the sympathetic faces that looked my way.

I looked at the table that ran along the wall and snatched up the little sailboat my mom had given me when I first moved in. I couldn't believe I'd left it. It had a polished granite bottom and a carved wooden sail glued to the top. I stroked the grain of the wood. It was lovely.

We headed down the stairs to where the car was waiting. My uncle reached to open the door for me.

"Dr. Knight?" a woman called. I turned to see who it was. She had a weathered face that had seen some better days. "Dr. Ivy Knight?"

"Yes." I didn't see the slap coming I just felt it impact my cheek and send me hard against my uncle. My ears rang, and my eyes watered as I blinked back the pain.

"You saw all the signs!" she screamed as the officers grabbed her. "You knew what was going to happen, and you did nothing! You should be stripped of your license."

My uncle slammed the car door on her screams as I put a hand to my face in shock.

TWENTY-ONE

There was a massive weather system warning for high winds and torrential downpours for the town of Redstone. Thunderstorms were a direct threat to loss of power, and the city's dispatch center had already put the word out for supplies. We were called in by the mayor to help the city prepare for the storm. We'd started at zero-four-hundred, and only now, hours later, we'd managed a moment to stop, eat, and refuel. The air was heavy and thick, and my skin felt damp and sticky. The low-pressure system didn't help my head, and a small part of me worried if my headaches would ever go away.

"You can feel the change in the air." Mike swallowed back some water. "I have a feeling this'll be a bad one."

"Me too." It was true; I felt it in my gut. The storm

clouds off in the distance were black as night and had a weird look to them.

"Anyone hear from Doc yet?" Mark looked at Cole. "Shouldn't their flight be landing soon?"

"Yeah," Cole checked his watch, "they land in twenty."

"Where was Doc?" I took a handful of raspberries from a bowl and made a face at how tart they were.

"Handling some business back in Washington. He took Ivy along." That caught my attention. I hadn't seen her since the night in my room when Moore called. I'd taken my news directly to Cole, who had Hill's photo sent to the local police. Though he hadn't broken any laws, he was dangerously close to discovering the safehouse. The fact that he was still enlisted in the Army meant he should have been back at his own base, not ours. Cole glanced at Daniel, and they seemed to speak without speaking. I didn't pry. If they wanted me to know what was up with Doc, they'd tell me.

My mind drifted back to Ivy, and I knew I needed to do some damage control with her. Things weren't right in my head, but she didn't deserve to be treated that way. It was the main reason I didn't date. I didn't *boyfriend* well. I had a habit of shutting down and letting people in and out of my life at times. But it was a bad habit, and as a male, I knew it wasn't going to be easy for me. We weren't a couple. We were both trying to get the physical attraction out of the way so we could just be around one another and be friends. That proved to be harder than we both expected.

"Feel that?" John held his hand up. "Rain's here." Tiny drops cooled my skin, and in a matter of seconds, it switched to a downpour.

We hurried to tuck our food away and headed for home.

The rain pounded the windshield as we zigzagged through the mountain roads. Lightning streaked the sky, and thunder shook the SUV as we stopped at checkpoint one.

"Colonel Logan," the MP squinted to see inside the car, "glad to see you made it up the road all right. They say the other side's completely washed out."

"Did Dr. Roberts and Dr. Knight make it back?" Cole asked.

"Yes, sir, they came in," he leaned back inside his little building and looked at his logbook, "a little after nine-teen-hundred."

"Very good." Cole rolled his window up, and we carried on.

"Any idea if Frank is with them?" Cole asked his father quietly.

"No, the altercation at the end of the visit made him decide to stay there."

Altercation? I wondered what that was about, but my training prevented me from asking.

Once inside the garage, we stripped off our gear and

headed inside for a hot shower and some much-needed food.

Abigail and Savannah had outdone themselves with three different types of chili. The fresh rolls melted in my mouth, and after two helpings, I felt the warmth spread from the inside out.

"Quinn and Davie are here. They helped bring the rest of the food down to the mud hall for the shift change," Savannah informed Cole, who smiled at her. "You know I hate them out there in this weather." He leaned over and kissed her, then gave her a reassuring pat.

"How was your trip to Washington?" June asked Dr. Roberts, who looked like he had been through hell and back. He pulled out his chair, placed his napkin on his lap, then removed his glasses and rubbed the red spots they'd left on his nose.

"That bad, huh?" June reached over and patted his hand as she gave Cole a strange look.

"Where's Ivy?" I leaned back in my chair to see the kitchen was empty.

"She decided to skip dinner this evening." Dr. Roberts forced a smile at me. "She's a bit tired from our trip." I nodded and went back to my meal.

"Can I get her anything?" Savannah whispered, but I read her lips.

"She won't eat. I tried."

I closed my eyes and hoped to hell this wasn't my doing. Guilt hit my chest hard. I knew even if it wasn't my fault, I needed to fix my part in whatever was going on.

"I need to make a few calls. Thank you for that delicious meal. I feel much better." I removed my dishes and headed for the kitchen to load them in the dishwasher. Once I was finished, I headed up the stairs and down the hall. I knocked quietly on her door.

"Ivy?" I called. "Can we talk?"

Nothing.

I tried the handle, and the door opened.

She stood with her back to me as she looked out the window. She wore a pink silk robe that stopped mid-thigh. Lord, the woman could bring me to my knees without even trying. Her wavy hair was loose around her shoulders, and it was obvious she wasn't expecting company tonight. The fireplace snapped and popped as the strong winds nailed the window with rain pellets.

"Hey," I whispered and closed the door behind me, "I know I've been a mess lately, and you were in the crossfire." I let my mouth run. "I want to talk to you about the guy you were dating and my part in that, but most of all I just wanted to say I'm sorry. You're the last person I'd want to upset."

She stood perfectly still. I wished she'd turn so I could read her face.

"I suck at this stuff," I tried again, "but you get me to this point where even if someone glances at you, I want to hurt them. I get how it sounds, but..." She moved her hands to cover her mouth, and suddenly something strange passed through me.

"Ivy," my tone hardened, "turn around and look at me." Her arms fell to her sides and her shoulders tensed. "Turn." Slowly, she turned her body, but her hair blocked part of her face. I stepped closer to get a good look at her. She reached up a hand to stop me.

"Ty," she sobbed, and I felt my stomach sink, "you should go."

"No." I grabbed her hand as I slowly moved close. "What happened?" I brushed her hair back from her face and saw that her cheeks were wet with tears. One cheek was slightly swollen. "Ivy, what the hell happened?"

"He," her entire body shook, "he…"

"He who?"

"Ty, he was in my house." She grabbed my arms as if to anchor herself, but I pulled her in, holding her tight as she sobbed. I wanted to press for answers, I wanted to know who I would have to kill, but right now she needed me. "I can't do this Ty." She shook her head. "I'm not this person." I wasn't sure what she meant, so I kept my arms around her. "I…he was in my bed." I froze and pushed back the urge to call Frank and get some damn answers. "I haven't slept in weeks. I was holding it together, but now I feel like I'm becoming unhinged. I hate feeling like this, exposed and vulnerable."

"I won't let anything happen to you," I promised and kissed her head to seal my words.

"I won't be your problem." Her words shook as they

came out. She suddenly pulled away and dried her cheeks, taking a deep breath.

"You're not a *problem*, Ivy." I watched her try to pull herself together. She lifted her chin, but I stood my ground. "You forget what I do for a living, sweetheart. I'll outlast your stubbornness."

"I'm so tired," she confessed and dropped her guard. "I just want to close my eyes and not be scared."

I walked over to her massive bed and pulled back the blankets. I waited for her to think about it for a moment, then she slipped her robe off and draped it at the end of the bed. She sat then swung her legs around, lay on her side with her legs pulled up, and settled in. I reached back, pulled my shirt off, undid my belt, kicked off my shoes and stripped down to my boxers.

"What are you doing?"

"You need sleep, so I'm helping with that." I swung my leg over hers and spooned her sexy body. I pulled the blankets over the two of us and clicked off the light.

"Don't talk, just sleep." I ordered.

The wind howled at the hidden moon, and the lightening fought with the thunder. All the while, the rain beat the windows in one wicked battle of who was the strongest. After a few moments, Ivy rolled onto her back as a crack of thunder hit close by, and her breathing gave a little hitch. I reached over and rested my hand on her cool thigh. The room lit up, and her hand slid over mine.

"I'm so scared," she whispered, and I could tell she was barely hanging on.

"Come here, baby." I pulled her back against my chest and curled once again around her body. My arm slipped under her pillow while she pulled my other hand to cup her breast. "I got you." I kissed her neck. "Nothing's getting through me." She nodded and held my arm. If time could have stopped just then and I could have lived in that moment for the rest of my life, I would have welcomed it.

The position of my head was such that I could see her eyes were open. She stared at the flickering flames, and I wondered what was going through her head.

"Who hit you?" I asked softly. "Was it *him*?" *Him* had no name, but I needed to piece her story together.

"No." She sniffed.

"Is the person somehow connected to *him*?"

"Yes."

"I hate half stories." I closed my eyes and wanted to scream.

"I hate them, too." A tear hit my arm, and I tried not to push.

She lifted my arm and rolled to face me. Her bare leg slipped between mine, and her gorgeous breasts nearly spilled out of her teddy as they pressed into my chest. I brushed her hair away from her face and caught a tear as it escaped from under her lashes.

Her finger traced down my chain to my dog tags, and she lip read the scrap of metal I wore around my neck so they could identify me when I died. Sounded bleak, but it was reality, and up until that moment they'd been my good luck charms.

"Thank you for staying with me."

I lifted her chin to look at me. "You're welcome." I took in her beauty; how could I not? Ivy was everything I didn't know I wanted. Whether this thing between us would fizzle out or not, I wanted to be here in bed with her. She moved her gaze to my lips then back up to my eyes. I inched my hand up from her hip under her teddy to feel her lacy panties underneath. *Seriously?* I wanted to cry at how sexy they felt. She tugged on my tags, and I rolled into her, thrusting a hand into her hair. My thumb brushed softly against her pink cheek.

"I thought I'd seen just about every level of cruelty this world has to offer, but I was wrong." I kept my voice soft, and she searched my face for something. "How could anyone hurt someone like you?" I stared down at her, and she shook her head.

"It's why I came here," she huffed through her shaky breath, "and now…"

"Now look," I brushed her cheek, "you're on a mountain surrounded by hundreds of armed soldiers, in a safehouse, in a ridiculously sexy nighty, next to man who won't let you ten feet from his sight." I smirked, and she rolled her eyes, but a smile broke free.

"My very own alpha wolf," she teased. I could see her fear. It was just below the surface, waiting for the right moment to attack again, and I respected her effort to control it.

"Mmhm," I grunted, "and I protect my own." I leaned down and gave her a soft kiss. I pulled back then just slightly, unsure of her reaction. I didn't want to bring sex into play. I wanted her to see it was more than that. That I'd heard her cry for help and understood it. That I was here for her and wanted nothing else in return. "You should get some sleep."

She studied my face for a moment, and I saw acceptance in her eyes.

"Goodnight, Ty." She leaned up and kissed me back.

"Night." I caught her lips again and kissed gently for a moment longer. She tasted so good. Her tongue touched mine. My body ached for her, and I wanted to sink myself deep inside, if only for a moment. *No.* Somehow, I found the will to pull away. It didn't help that her breasts spilled from that damn teddy. "Roll over." I ordered, and she did. I tucked her back to my front again, and I held her close to my chest. "Go to sleep." I tucked my nose into her hair and allowed myself to relax. The last thing I remembered was the sound of her even breathing while the rain and winds fought the good fight outside the window.

My mouth was dry as cotton when I woke with a start from my own hell. Brown's face fizzled away as I took in my surroundings. The fire was still going and provided enough light for me to see that Ivy was next to me, her body turned toward mine.

I clicked on the small light on my side of the bed, but nothing happened. The power must have gone out. The generators only covered the important places of the house, and Ivy's room wasn't one of them. I licked around the inside of my mouth and knew I needed water. Careful not to wake her, I slipped out of bed, pulled on my jeans, and carefully felt my way to the kitchen. The storm provided just enough light for me to grab two water bottles out of the fridge.

"How's Ivy?" Dr. Roberts nearly got a kick to the chest when he spoke. He sat at the island in the dark. I guessed they only used the generators when it was most important.

"Rattled." I moved toward him. He wore a robe and had a novel in front of him. "Everything okay, Doc?"

"I wish it was." He clicked off the little booklight he'd used to read on the counter next to him.

"Want to talk about it?"

"Unfortunately, I can't." He cleared his throat. "Job hazard." He shrugged. "Though I do appreciate the ear."

I turned to leave but stopped myself. "This thing that's going on with Ivy, is it something I should know about?"

"You?" He seemed to struggle to follow my train of thought.

"Cole asked me to watch over her when we're out in public. So, if there's someone in particular I should be watching out for, it would be helpful to know who that might be."

"Logical question." He nodded. "Though I'm bound by law not to discuss it, I will share this. Ivy is caught in between the law and a very dangerous person."

"The same man who went to her house?" He raised an

eyebrow. "She was panicking and talking in half sentences. Don't worry. I just know someone was in her house, and I know someone else hit her across the cheek. She's obviously terrified, and I just feel…"

"Helpless?" He half smiled. "Welcome to my night," he admitted.

"Is this dangerous person in custody?"

"No." He pulled his glasses off. "And I fear things might get a tad worse before they get better. So, let's make sure we're on high alert. If *your* enemy could get to Ivy, so can *hers*."

A deep cold spread through me at that thought. It was true Hill found her. Who knew what this other guy could do.

"I'm going to assume that he's military?" He held my gaze, and I read him loud and clear.

"Copy that."

"Ty?" He studied me for a moment. "Is Ivy a distraction for you, still?"

"Not a bad one."

"Good." He tapped his knee. "She's strong, but this might cripple her. I'm glad she can open up to you."

"Yeah, me too." I held up a water bottle as a wave and hurried back upstairs. I was pleased for Doc's insight, and I was happy he could see I only wanted to protect her.

I slipped back into the room quietly until my hip bumped the dresser and Ivy shot straight up in bed. She reached over and grabbed something from the table.

"Ty?" I heard the blankets move as she called out. "Ty?"

"It's me." I crossed the room and sat on the side of the bed. "I just got us some water."

"Okay." I heard the fear in her voice even though I couldn't see her face clearly in the dark.

"No need for these." I carefully removed the scissors from her hand, glad they'd glinted in the lightning as she held them up. "Thirsty?" She shook her head. "It's early, so back to bed you go." She stilled, and I brushed the hair off her shoulder. "I'm not going anywhere."

I climbed in next to her, and she rested her hand on my chest. Her fingers tangled in my chain, and she let out a sigh. I was thankful for the gas fireplace, and I didn't have to worry about more firewood. The storm cooled the house down, and there was a small nip in the air. I was more than ready for fall to come.

"At the end, in Afghanistan, everyone was pulling out." I lowered my voice. "Two special ops teams were called to stay and take on one last mission." I ran my fingertips up and down her arm. "At one point, when we were under attack, our teams got split up. Two of my men were with Captain Flex, and I had three of his. One of them had no respect for how I ran my unit. We'd bumped heads many times in the field. It was the last day, and we'd made it to our checkpoint. We were waiting for our chopper to get out." I took a sip of my water.

"Brown, one of my brothers, one of my oldest friends,

had been struggling mentally, and I wished I'd sent him back home. Damn, I should never have taken him on that last mission. It's hard to break up a team, though. You know?" She rubbed my chest gently but didn't speak. "One of Flex's guys knew he was losing it but still gave him a hard time through the whole damn mission. Anyway, to make a long story short, he went into a house and held a family at gunpoint." She flinched, and her hand rubbed my chest again.

"I got to Brown, and I was able to get him to focus on me. I was making progress. He wasn't a threat to the family at that point, but the asshole showed up. Instead of taking my order to leave, he shot Brown right between the eyes." Ivy pushed up and leaned on her elbow to look at me in horror. "We were ten minutes away from going home, and he was murdered by someone under my command."

"Oh, Ty," she shook her head, "I'm so sorry to hear that."

"Yeah, I couldn't believe it. I was in shock, too. Apparently, he tossed his gun, told the others it was a local who took him out, and because the Taliban arrived just then, I couldn't gather any evidence or even get Brown's body out. I had to leave him there. It's just my word against his now." I cleared my throat. "I saw him toss it, too. I just didn't register what was happening in the moment."

"That guy needs some major psychological help."

"Yeah, or something." I put my face close to hers so I

could see her eyes. "His name is Hill, but you know him by Carson."

Her brows pinched in confusion, then her eyes widened, and she moved to her knees. Her hands covered her mouth as she let out a gasp. "What the hell?"

"He killed one of my men, one of my buddies, and then he went after you." I tucked a hand behind my head. "Now you know why I punched him."

"Jesus, Ty," she dropped her hands, "if I had known that, I would've helped you take him out."

"His time is coming," I promised her.

"But why me? He doesn't even know me."

"Because I had my hands on you at Camp Green. One of his friends was visiting when we were there and must have told Hill. Doesn't take much to Google a photo, name, or anything anymore, especially when you have access at a base." Her face fell, and I cursed as I realized what I'd said and what it could mean.

"So, it's that easy to find me?"

"Not with me around." I threaded my fingers through hers.

"I'm sorry, Ty. I honestly had no idea who he was."

"I know that. You couldn't have," I assured her, "but it stung like a bitch seeing him with you."

"I'm serious when I said nothing happened."

"I know." I pulled her back down to snuggle in. "It's over with now." That was a lie, but she didn't need to carry anything else. I'd deal with Hill myself.

Morning came all too early. The alarm on my phone

screamed at me, but the half-naked woman draped over my chest made it nearly impossible to get up.

I ran my hand down her back and cupped her butt, which in turn granted me a sleepy moan.

"I need to go," I muttered and was pleased to see the storm was tapering off.

"'Kay." She didn't move.

"You're not making this easy." I chuckled and tucked her harder into my side.

"Mm," she moaned again.

"I have to train in slippery wet terrain today, ten miles up the side of a mountain and then back down again. So, you can see my problem right now. How hard this is."

She chuckled and slid her hand over my stomach then wrapped it around my erection. "You're hard." She leaned her head back to see me, and her eyes told me she was up to no good.

A knock at the door made us both go still.

"Ivy, it's Savi. Are you in there?"

Ivy sat up and reached for her robe. She hopped off the bed then glanced at me before she opened the door.

"Morning." Savannah handed her something. "We heard you didn't have a great day yesterday, so Sloane and I are taking you to town for a little girl time."

What? No, she shouldn't be leaving the house.

"I've got a mountain of paperwork, and I really should stay—"

"Doc Roberts cleared your schedule, and Cole has the guys training today. Plus, they'll be joining us for dinner in town because it's a tradition to watch the first preseason game at Zack's."

"Okay, sure." She hesitated. "You know what? That sounds like fun. I could use a little girl time."

"Great. Meet us downstairs in twenty."

"Will do." She closed the door and gave me a small smile. "I guess it's girls' day." Her face slipped a little, and I could see her nerves were getting the best of her. "It'll be okay," she said to herself.

"Did Cole give you a phone?" I asked because all team members were given special phones to use that couldn't be tracked by anyone else but those at the house. I wasn't sure if that extended to her.

"Yes." She pointed to her purse.

"May I?" I hated to touch a woman's purse without permission. It was like going to a tarot card reader. I might not believe in it, but I sure as hell don't fuck with it.

"Yeah." She headed into the bathroom, and a moment later I heard the water running. I programed my number into her phone so she could call me. I grabbed my clothes and pulled on my pants. As she walked by a few seconds later, I snagged her arm and tugged her to me.

"You have my number now. If you need me, call." I tucked her hair behind her ear.

"Thank you," she tried to smile again, "for last night too."

"Of course." I leaned down and kissed her lips. "I guess I'll see you in town tonight."

"Yeah." She stepped back as I gathered my things, and I gave her one last glance as I left her room.

"Hey, there." Mark was suddenly in front of me with a shit eating grin. "Looks like someone had a fun night."

"Ah, fuck," I muttered, as he chuckled down the hallway.

"I hope you enjoyed your night because today is gonna be a bitch in this mud."

He wasn't lying.

We spent the morning in the lake, mid-day in the mud, and then the afternoon on the cliff. The storm that had left in the morning had returned with a vengeance.

The six of us stood bent at the waist, butts against the side of a rock wall, under a waterfall as we held a thirty-pound log across our shoulders. Our arms were linked as we fought against the power of the water that poured on top of us. It was definitely a test of strength, will, and determination. Daniel stood under an umbrella with a stopwatch, while Dell, a Dusk teammate, stood watch in case we needed a medic.

"Fucking leg cramp." John cursed and shifted to get a better footing.

When your muscles were pushed past their limit, it forced you to dig deep and wrestle with the mental demons that tried to take you down. I knew why Cole chose that drill. He knew we were dealing with a lot of shit, and he had to know our heads would be sharp for the next mission. Though therapy worked wonders, we needed mental endurance as well as physical.

"And up!" Daniel yelled, and we lifted the log over our heads in a power struggle with the water. "And drop!" In unison, we dropped the log and rushed out of the waterfall.

My head dropped back, and I let the rain pelt my face, then walked in a circle on rubber legs.

"Forty-six minutes," Daniel called out with a grin. "Grab your shit. We're finished for the day."

Cole tossed me a protein pouch, and I sucked back the gel. I needed it. I kept moving even as I swallowed so my body didn't lock up.

"I think I saw Jesus at one point." Mark leaned back and groaned as he wiped the rain from his eyes. "Fuck you, Cole." Cole chuckled and beamed at me, as I joined him in a laugh.

"Great time." Dell smacked Mike on the shoulder. Mike rubbed his fingers together to try to get some feeling back in his hands.

"Yeah, not bad, boys." Mike gave up and put a hand above his eyes to shield them from the relentless rain as he looked up at Cole.

"Are we meeting everyone in town?"

"We are." Cole grabbed his pack. "Let's get cleaned up, boys, so we can head to town."

We walked down the path, and Mike came up next to me as we got to the clearing.

"Hey," he waved me in a different direction, "got a minute?"

"Sure."

We walked together toward the building we used to tack up before our missions. He typed in the password, the door clicked open, and we stepped inside. I dropped my rucksack in the corner and turned to see him looking out the door. I wiped the water off my face with a rag, thankful to be out of the rain.

"Okay," he rested his hands on his hips, "so, one thing we're taught in the military is it's black or white, right? There's no stepping into the gray. We do our job by the book, and if something happens, we know we'll face a mountain of paperwork, interviews, and a lot of shit. No one wants that, so we hope we never waver from the line."

"Correct." I nodded, beyond curious to see where this was going.

"But when we're here," he waved a hand, "we're not under the same rules as before. We're under Frank's command. He turns his head, from time to time, so we're able to tilt the scale when there's a need." He paused. "I don't know much about what happened to you in Afghanistan, Ty, but I do know something about a brother who's in a struggle to right a wrong."

"I'm listening."

"So, I've got a guy." I grinned at that, and he saw the humor and grinned back then went on. "Yeah, so, I got a guy—a friend, really—who can track down people, dig up info, or even make someone disappear in the right circumstance. He's good people. He just got handed a different direction in life, and because of his past, he took it."

Interesting. I thought for a moment and saw Mike shift as he eyeballed my reaction. I could tell it took a lot for him to tell me about this guy. He didn't know me all that well. Being brothers in arms meant a lot, and I appreciated his candor.

"And you trust him?"

"I do. Always have. He's helped a few of us out before. Sometimes you just need to step into the gray to make things right, and this guy knows all about that."

"Okay." I chewed my cheek as I thought, and he sensed my hesitation.

"Savannah knows him and knows his wife too. If you have any concerns, you can talk to her. You know she'll give it to you straight." We both grinned at that. It was a true statement if there ever was one.

"And what would this guy want in return?"

"He's not like that." He shook his head. "If things didn't turn south for him, he'd be here as one of us. I'm sure of it."

"What's his name?"

"Trigger." He rubbed his head. "He's the Pres of the Devil's Reach MC in Cali."

"Motorcycle gang?" I narrowed my eyes at him.

"Yeah, he prefers club, but one hundred percent."

Really? So, that's what the wives were talking about!

"You do have some impressive hookups."

"You need to in this line of work." He checked his watch.

"I'm starting to see that." I grabbed my rucksack, as

we had to get going if we were to be ready in time. "Thanks, Mike. I'll see what I can do first, but I'll let you know if I need to go there."

"Anytime." We stepped out into the rain and raced toward the house.

TWENTY-TWO

IVY

"Savi?" I heard Sloane's voice. It sounded almost dreamy.

"Mm," she moaned back softly.

"If I ever question girls' day out, remind me of this moment right here where mud smothered areas I didn't even know I had." Both Savi and Sloane chuckled in agreement.

"I promise." She sighed in happiness. "Speaking of smothered areas…"

"Smooth, Savi." Sloane laughed harder.

"How's it going with Ty?" Savi went on.

I sank farther into the mud and breathed deeply. The scent of fresh roses found my nostrils. Little wisps of cool mist puffed across my face and kept my skin from completely hardening. I opened my eyes and lifted my cucumber slice for just a second to look out the floor-to-ceiling window. The panoramic view of the gorgeous trees and flowers was intoxicating. We were nestled in this little piece of heaven outside of town. They had just the right level of soft music and bird sounds to give me the white noise I needed to turn off my head. I was completely relaxed for the first time in ages.

"Ivy?" she said again. "You asleep?"

"If you were to ask me yesterday," I let out a soft sigh, "I'd have said we attempted to hash out our attraction for each other, but it wasn't enough." I sighed again, only heavier as I thought how much more I now wanted Ty physically.

"And now?" she pressed.

"Now…" I paused, trying to understand just what we actually were to each other. "I just don't know."

"He spent the night with you, didn't he?" I lifted my cucumber and peered at her. She shrugged like she knew I was looking at her. "I baited Mark with cookies, and he spilled what he knew. To be fair, I thought he was keeping a secret about Olivia, so I truly wasn't trying to dig about you two."

"I see." I dropped the cool slice back in place and chuckled. Mark really was everywhere. "He came to my room to apologize for being so distant after the Carson thing." I kept the details to a need-to-know basis for Ty's privacy. "He saw I was upset and ended up spending the night with me."

"Really?" Sloane jumped in.

"Yes. He was a total gentleman, though, and a few times there he could have made something happen, but he stopped it. He wanted to prove he was there for the right reasons."

"Wow, he really is one of the good ones, hey, Savi?" Sloane seemed impressed.

"I had a really good feeling on Ty when I read his file. Now, hearing this," Savi sat up as the timer went off, "and from what I'd heard about him in the field, I'm really liking this guy."

"So, what now?" We peeled ourselves out of our mud cocoons.

"I don't know." I stepped into the warm pool where we were to scrub ourselves clean. "I have no idea if last night changed our status of what we are to each other or not. Was he just being kind because he knew I needed someone to hold me last night?"

"Can I give my two cents?" Savi leaned her head back into the water to get the mud out.

"I welcome it."

"We're surrounded by amazing men, and each one of them is willing to push aside all they carry from their job to make sure we're okay. They don't expect sex afterward. They expect us to lean on them the way they lean on us. Ty seems to fit that mold. Last night, he was there for you. Simple as that. Just be yourself and see how he reacts."

"I can do that." I liked the idea of just being myself and seeing where it took me.

Victor had hands like a Greek god. The way he pressed his thumbs into my lower back nearly made me in a puddle of goo. The room was round, and our beds were angled so our heads were in the center and our bodies were pointed out like the petals on a daisy. I thought after our facials and mud bath, things couldn't get better until we reached this room.

"Don't tell my husband this, but I'd leave him just so I could date your hands, Farley." Savi moaned, and Farley chuckled in his Bajan accent.

"You say that every time, Mrs. Logan, but yet, you wear the ring." He played along. "A man's heart can only take so much."

"So many men, and just one of me." She chuckled, and Sloane rolled to face me.

"While Savannah plots her divorce," she playfully rolled her eyes, "can I ask you something?

"Of course." I tried to pull my mind from Victor's hands.

"How are you holding up, Ivy?" I gave her a 'what do you mean' look. "Doc came home carrying all kinds of heavy. You skipped out on dinner, and Ty bolted to your room the moment he could. I know you're the therapist, and I'm sure Doc is a sound ear for you, but friend to friend, I just want to check in because I know what it's like to fear for your life."

Oh.

"Relax, beautiful queen." Victor pressed his hands

into my shoulders, and the tension her question brought floated away. "Yes, just like that."

Sloane hid her smile at his choice of words, and I closed my eyes. "Beautiful queen" was never something I'd have thought anyone would call me.

Sloane had to turn her grin away as he began to coach me through the rest of the massage. I was nearly in tears trying to hold it together myself.

By time Sloane and I were finished and moved to the lounge for a glass of cucumber water, I felt like a whole new person. My hair was cut and colored. My mani and pedi were gorgeous, my skin glowed, and my muscles had been caressed and cared for by dear, sweet Victor. He was now my new love. Savi had already left the lounge and gone to change. Sloane and I somehow got ourselves to the change room and managed to get our lockers opened.

"I'm going to go deal with the front desk. I'll meet you two out front." Savi waved as she dashed out the door, leaving Sloane and me to dress.

I reached into the locker and pulled out my dress. I should have known better and worn jeans on a day like today. Though the rain looked like it was tapering off when we left, it had come back tenfold to prove it wasn't going anywhere any time soon. I should have listened to Keith's warning to bring warm clothes. But I seriously hated any kind of jeans or pants. I tugged on the dress and was glad I'd at least brought a sweater.

"We've had a few women come through the house for multiple reasons." Sloane slipped her shirt over her head.

"Savi was always her kind self. She entertained and so on. Then you showed up, and she saw you."

"Saw me?" I didn't follow.

"Yeah. You fit in without even trying. Like you are a part of the family already."

"That's nice." I threaded the belt around my waist.

"The guys love Ty. He is one of the best hires we've had in a long time. There's no doubt in anyone's mind he'll make a great team leader."

"I bet he'd like to hear that."

"But that's why Savi is acting the way she is right now," she stopped to looked at me, "playing matchmaker with you two. Ty isn't leaving, but you might be."

"I don't know what will happen after..." I stopped myself.

"She doesn't want you to leave." She continued to dress. "None of us want you to, to be honest."

"I really like it here, but I do have a life back in Washington." I pulled out my sweater and umbrella.

"Look," Sloane closed her locker, "I can help you."

"With?"

"With whatever it is that's going on."

"I can't legally talk about it."

"Right. But you could if I was your lawyer."

"Frank got me representation."

"Fire him. I'll work my ass off on your case, and you'll have someone who you'll know is really going to go to bat for you."

I bit my lip and thought about it for a moment. I

really would love to have someone here I could talk to about it besides my uncle. He worried too much as it was.

"Look, Ivy, I had a client come after me because of a verdict he didn't like." Sloane looked at me as she spoke. "They attacked me in my own home and tried to kidnap me." She swallowed, and her eyes went glossy. "I know how helpless one can feel and how much damage that feeling can bring a person, even if you think you have everything under control." I felt my own eyes water.

"It was scary, and there's still days I struggle with feeling safe in my own skin, but I let people in, and I'm getting through it. I know you have Frank and Doc on your side, but having another woman in your corner is another level of strength to have. Let me help you, Ivy."

I brushed a tear away and let out a long breath.

"Ready?" Savi called from the doorway.

"Okay," I nodded at Sloane, "I'd like that a lot." She pulled me in and hugged me.

"Let's chat tomorrow, but tonight we have fun."

"Lord, I feel like I'm waiting on Mark," Savi huffed, and we both laughed as we headed for the door.

Quinn and Dell drove us to Zack's, where the guys were already into their first pitcher of beer.

"Well, now," Cole stood and greeted Savi with a kiss, "look at you three."

"Hello, my other half." John handed Sloane a drink. "How was your day?"

"Just like heaven." I smiled as Ty pulled out the seat next to him. "Thank you."

"Jesus," he huffed from behind me, and I looked at him over my shoulder. "Nothing." He huffed again as he took the seat next to me. I caught Savi's grin and brow wiggle.

"How was your day?" I looked around at the guys.

"Cole tried to kill us today." Mark dripped with sarcasm from across the table. "Apparently, because it was raining."

"Oh, so, you had a good day, then?" I smirked, and he rolled his eyes and looked at the television with a disgusted grunt.

"You know what football season means?" Mark directed his comment to the table.

"It's only a few months away from hockey season?" I answered.

His face morphed into a smile as he hit John's shoulder. "God bless Frank. He sent us a hockey chick!"

Ty laughed quietly as the rest of the table broke out in banter.

"Ivy had Victor today, didn't you, *beautiful queen?*" Savi snorted with laughter as Catalina held a hand to her chest dramatically.

"Victor's hands are magical," I breathed, and Sloane laughed as John stared her down.

"The best were his little words of encouragement while he caressed her body. 'Yes, doll, just let your leg relax and let me into those muscles.'" Sloane high-fived Savi as they both doubled over with laughter.

"I see," Ty muttered into his beer.

"Laugh all you want," I shrugged, "but that man knows how to use his hands. The oil, the pressure, the sweet words. Oh, my."

"Amen to that." Mia hit the table in a cheer.

"And the spa days have come to an end." Mark nodded at Ty.

"Same drink as usual?" Zack asked over the crowd, and I gave a friendly nod.

"Where were you through all this spa stuff, Quinn?" Mike turned the heat on him.

"I just kept my head down." Quinn shrugged. "I'm under orders to protect. I would never step one foot into any of those rooms other than to clear them."

Keith sat to one side of me, and though he was enjoying the fun, he was quiet. I decided to check on him.

"Hey," I pulled his attention to me, "have you spoken to Lexi?"

"Yeah, I did the other day." He cleared his throat. "We hashed out a lot of stuff over the phone. It's easier that way. Kind of makes a good buffer for our emotions." He shrugged.

"It's more common than you think." I validated his comment. "Emotions can be better controlled without the body language behind it."

"Makes sense." He sipped his beer. "I think there's a part of me that knows we're over. I just don't want to believe it. I mean, when you consider how much we went through to get here."

"Sometimes wanting love becomes more important than actually being in love."

"Mm," he nodded, "I can handle us not being us anymore, but her willingness to walk away from our kids is something I can't wrap my head around." He spun his phone on the table. "What, nothing to say to that?" He side-eyed me.

"Professionally? Or personally?" I huffed, and he turned to look at me.

"Both."

"Professionally speaking, and in fairness to Lexi and all women, we really have no idea how we'll react when we have children. I've had clients be over the moon excited for their baby, and when the baby came, they felt nothing. They were completely detached. Sometimes therapy helps, and other times it's doesn't. There are a few medications that can help, but that's a different side of things."

"Okay, and personally?"

"You sure you want to hear it?"

"I do."

"Personally, I'd never give up trying. A child deserves to be loved by its parents. It's a necessity to be brought up in a good, loving household. You don't need money or a huge house, but you need to know that at the end of the day, you're loved by your parents no matter what."

"Hm," he tapped his beer bottle while my words sank in, "you must have had some pretty amazing parents to have raised you right."

"I had a mom who loved me enough for two parents."

"No dad?"

"He's around, but he isn't overly loving." I caught Ty listening to us. "He left when I was fifteen and remarried a teacher at my high school. He didn't really care about us, so I went into the one profession that could fill the spot he sucked at. Helping people, caring for people."

"Well, if it counts, you're pretty damn great at your job."

"Thanks." I smiled. "Keep working on Lexi and communicate. If not for you, for your kids. They need to see you getting along, not fighting. When they hit their teens, they can make up their own minds."

"Okay," he let out a long breath, "I can do that."

"And in the meantime, you know where to find me."

He patted my arm and excused himself to use the restroom, and Cole gave me an impressed look.

"Nice job, Doc."

I felt Ty's eyes on me, so I turned to look at him.

"What?"

"You're incredibly smart, Dr. Knight." His eyes lit up. "You know that?"

"Thanks." I felt myself warm from the inside out.

"And incredibly gorgeous."

"Are you flirting with me, Beckett?"

"Yes, I am." The corners of his mouth tugged upward. His eyes held me captive, and I basked in the feeling.

"I like it."

"I do, too."

We ate, had drinks, laughed, and talked like one big, happy family, I guessed because we were. Behind all the love and laughter, everyone at the table knew it all could change in the blink of an eye, but not tonight. Tonight, we were meant to have a great time, and we were going to take advantage of every moment.

It was late as we stepped out onto the porch of the restaurant. John and Mike hurried off to get the trucks. Ty snagged my arm and then scanned above my head.

"What?" Instantly, I was on alert.

"Just making sure." He then stepped back, shrugged off his coat, and draped it around my shoulders. I wondered if he realized how thoughtful he was toward me, because everything just seemed natural with him. He tipped my chin, so I'd look at him again.

"I'm really glad you had fun today."

"I did. The girls are great." I pulled his coat tighter as I felt the chill of the rain around us.

"So, who the hell is this Victor guy?" he teased, and before I could respond, he leaned and kissed me as his fingers entwined with mine. "I'll kill him." I laughed a protest against his lips as he dove deeper, then he whirled and pulled me with him as we hurried to join the others.

TWENTY-THREE

ERIC

"Hey, boss?"

"Mm?" I flipped through the US news app on my phone as I tried to find anything that might have to do with the drop-off that day.

"You know what's weird?" Filippo muttered from the driver's seat. "I really don't know that much about you."

"Your point?"

"Like, do you have any family?"

"No."

"Everyone has family."

"I don't."

"You mean, like, you don't anymore?"

I lowered my phone, tired of his voice. "Do you have family, Filippo?"

"I do. Two sisters and three brothers."

"You want them to stay alive?" I caught his gaze when it shot to the rearview mirror.

"Yeah."

"Great, then shut the fuck up." I grabbed a water bottle from the cooler and downed a few pain pills in an effort to push my headache back. I held a hand over my eyes as I looked up at the sun. It tried hard to break through the tinted windows of the SUV. The time on my watch further pissed me off. The shipment was late by forty minutes. I pulled some cash from the payment stack. Every minute came with a cost.

"Ah, boss?" I forced back my urge to lash at him. "Chili is here."

What? He wasn't supposed to show up for another few days to get the girls from me. I was supposed to get them checked over and make sure they are in good health physically before they were sold off. I tossed my water, grabbed my sunglasses, and opened the door.

"Stay here," I ordered before I stepped out into the heat. I nodded at Alejandro, who drove a second truck in case something happened to the other. One could never be too cautious.

The window lowered on Chili's Escalade, and he gave me a nod to approach.

"Thought you might like to know your new driver made a few calls before you left." He spoke quietly.

The fuck. I was going to kill Filippo.

"Oh, really?"

"Seems he was looking for a buyer for two of the girls. Thought I'd pay you a visit personally to make sure we still had our deal in place."

"Hmm." I rubbed my jaw and tried to control my temper. "Of course, we do."

"Should I be concerned?" He half closed his eyes as he studied me, and I tried not to show my frustrations with Filippo trying to go over my head to make a deal.

"No, you *shouldn't* be." I licked my dry mouth. "I appreciate the heads up."

"Buyers talk." He studied me again. "I decided I'll transport these girls myself."

"Understood." I nodded. I wasn't about to mess shit up because my newbie decided to step around me. I'd deal with him later.

"Boss!" Alejandro called and pointed to the tunnel. "They're here." I nodded, and Chili and I watched the girls emerge from the darkness. Their faces were covered by cloth bags, arms bound with rope, with a foot-and-a-half-length of rope between their feet. I noticed right away they were still wearing their shoes and had water bottles hanging from their waists. Damn, these women must be top notch to get that kind of treatment.

"Should we inspect them?" Chili asked, but I shook my head.

"No, I was told to move them the second they arrived. I know whose head will roll if any of them are marked."

"Mr. Noah?" The head coyote stopped the girls in front of me. "Which truck?"

"This one." I patted the side of Chili's truck. The coyote motioned for the guys to load the girls. He kept a strong hold on the girl he escorted.

"This one goes with you."

"No, they're going with the buyer tonight." My voice was steel. I didn't like being questioned.

"No," he held up his phone, and I saw the call was connected to Castillo, "he wants a word."

The fuck. A cold prickle shot up my back as I lifted the phone to my ear.

"Noah," I offered as a hello.

"Eric, I heard your buyer got nervous and picked the girls up tonight."

"Yeah, something's got him spooked." I left out it was my man that spooked him.

"Fine. Get the money before he leaves. But you'll personally escort the one I indicated."

"What am I to do with her?"

"You'll take her back to your place. I'll be in touch."

"Understood." I hung up and handed the phone to the coyote, and he shoved the girl at me.

"I paid for four girls, not three, Eric." Chili called out.

"I know. I'll figure it out. You have my word. You know where to find me if I don't." I grabbed the girl's arm and pushed her toward the truck Alejandro was in. "Get out," I ordered, and he jumped out holding the door open for the girl. I helped her in, as the rope made it nearly impossible for her to lift her foot up to the step, then slammed the door.

"What's going on, boss?" Alejandro looked worried.

"I've no fucking idea." I rubbed my lips. I felt uneasy about the entire drop. "Meet me back at my place." He went to leave, but I snagged his shoulder. "Don't let Filippo out of your sight."

"Okay." He nodded and left. As I got into the truck, I glanced back at Chili, who was watching me. I was sure he was as jumpy as I was about the entire exchange. In this business, anything off the norm was cause for concern. Lives were cheap.

I better not be gettin' fucking played here.

We all left in different directions, and as we hit the road on the way to my place, I got a call.

"Noah."

"I have eyes on you." Castillo flooded my speakers. "Don't make any stops. Just head right to your place."

"That was the plan." I searched my mirrors and saw a brown car three lengths back.

"Making history means covering all the bases, Eric." I heard the Zippo light. "She'll stay in your pen until I say otherwise."

"Chili paid for four elite girls. He wasn't happy."

"He'll get his fourth. One comes in tomorrow. I'll have one of my men deal with her. You watch this one personally."

"Understood." I disconnected the call. I rubbed my chin and wondered if they'd bugged my truck. I knew it wasn't earlier, as I always checked. I decided to play it safe and figure it was.

I glared at the woman behind me. What the hell was going on? When the traffic slowed, I reached back and tried to grab the cloth bag off her head, but she screamed and tried to hit me.

"You want to see, or do you want to stay in the dark?" I shouted. The bag moved in and out of her mouth as she fought to breathe. "Move forward. I don't have much time before we start moving again." Slowly, she leaned forward, and I was able to tug the bag off. Her hair was wild around her face. She blinked and squinted to adjust to the light as she brushed her hair away awkwardly with her bound hands.

"You thirsty?" I tossed her back a bottle of water, but she chucked it back at me, her eyes full of fury. "Fine."

"You seriously don't know what you've done! You're in for a shit pile of trouble," she spat.

"Oh, yeah?" I kind of liked her spark. "And what did I just do?"

"You just kidnapped a Blackstone wife."

The End

ACKNOWLEDGMENTS

To my mother, my inspiration in life, my cheerleader, my
best friend.
My husband, who helped "see" my vision when I couldn't.
To Elizabeth Clark and Jamie Johnson, thank you for the
push in *that* direction, for spinning with me, and for
always being in my corner.
To my betas and proofers, Kim Kelchner, Kasey Griffin,
Veronica Nelson, Maggie Savarese, Rachel Womack,
Jamie Johnson, and Elizabeth Clark.
My editor Lori, thanks for always being there.
My street team, ARC team, my reader group, and my
fact-finding group, thanks for providing me a safe place to
go to hang out, ask questions, and laugh!
And of course, to my readers. I wouldn't be here if it
wasn't for all of you.

Thank you.

ERIC

"You're never gonna make it," she huffed from the back seat, and I stole a hasty glance at her pissy face in the rearview mirror. I needed to concentrate on the washed-out road in front of me and knew I didn't have much time. Normally, I'd be thrilled that the rain had returned to cool off this Godforsaken country, but the thought of who I had in the back had me in more of a sweat than I cared to think about. I needed to get behind the protected gates of my house. The wipers beat across the windshield, and I squinted at the quickly forming river ahead of me. My phone rang, and I chanced it and stuck it between my shoulder and my chin as I quickly put the car in reverse.

"Stick to the opposite shoulder, gun it, and get the fuck out of there," a voice screamed at me. One of Castillo's men, I assumed. I tossed the phone on the passenger seat, lined up my wheels on the shoulder, and gunned it.

Water started to seep around my boots as my passenger shrieked, and I could feel the pressure of her feet as she propped them up out of the water.

"You're crazy!" she yelped.

She had no idea.

I shifted into four-wheel drive. A plume of water flew out behind me as I plowed along the edge of the steadily rising water. Finally, all four wheels were clear, but I never slowed down until I hit the city limits. I took the turns hard as I wove up the hill and finally took a deep breath as I drove through the wrought iron gates to my house.

I reached for my phone as my men approached the car, but I hopped out and held up a hand to stop them.

"I got her." I opened the door. "How do you wanna do this?" I immediately saw fight flicker in her eyes as she took me in. "You're highly outnumbered, so we can get you inside, cleaned up, and settled, or you can make a scene. Believe me, lady, you'll be the one who'll end up gettin' hurt. Your ass'll be inside one way or another. It's up to you how." I watched her weigh the odds. If I'd learned anything over the years about the kind of woman Blackstone attracted, I knew it wasn't going to be easy. These women were a tough lot, and if I gave her an inch, I knew she'd take advantage of it. I had to set the ground rules now.

When she didn't move, I reached for her hand. She'd been waiting for that and tried to headbutt me. I wasn't stupid and was ready for her. She wouldn't be the first woman who'd tried that one on me. What I didn't expect was as she fell, she twisted hard and caught me with her shoulder. I stepped back quickly and let her fall to the ground hard. Her knees hit first and then her hands. She spat like a cat and screamed obscenities. I was impressed by her repertoire, but I was done with her, and I was pissed when I heard a snicker from one of my soldiers.

"Done yet?" She tried to kick out, but I carefully stepped out of the way. Her feet were still tied, so she could only do so much. Rain beat down on her as she looked up at me in fury. Her hair hung in strings over her face. I'd had enough, so I grabbed her and threw her over my shoulder and carried her kicking and screaming toward the house.

"Get your asses back inside," I yelled at the men as I went by them.

Alejandro gave a quick, low whistle as I entered the house, and I glanced at him. He moved his gaze to a few new men I hadn't met before. I wasn't a newbie in this business and immediately understood what I was up against. They sat at a table pretending not to notice me. Smoke from their cigarettes swirled thick above them as they played a card game.

I glared at them as I hauled the woman through the room and down the stairs. I used my fingerprint to open the door but made a note to remove the security device for later. Given who our new guest was, I needed all hands on deck at all times. I dumped her on the bed in the cage and held her still with my foot. Leo, one of my men, had left the needle on the small table, ready for me, and I grabbed it and gave it a flick.

"No, no!" She started to panic, but I grabbed her arm and injected the drug under her skin. Within seconds, she went limp, and I sat down beside her on the bed to catch my breath.

"Little wildcat." Leo chuckled. "Hope this cage holds up."

"Take off her shoes," I ordered as I ignored his comments about what she might look like underneath her clothes. "Socks too." I cut the ropes and examined the raw marks on her wrists and ankles. I rubbed cream into the red areas. Then, satisfied, I decided to give her a second shot that contained pain meds. I knew the journey wouldn't have been easy, and the bruises on her arms and cheek told me she she'd put up a fight.

I didn't know who grabbed these women from the streets, and I didn't need to know, but it pissed me off when they were marked up. Time was money, and it took time to get them ready for sale. This particular woman concerned me more than usual, and I sure as hell wasn't going to be blamed if she was scarred up.

"What about her shirt?" He grinned at me.

"No." I shook my head. When she woke, I didn't want her to find herself undressed and think I was some kind of creep who did shit to her while she was drugged.

"Whatever, I'll just watch the reruns." He chuckled, and as I shot him a questioning look, he pointed at a camera in the corner of the room. I didn't react but swept my eyes around the room. I could see a few cameras had been installed while I was away.

Fucking Castillo.

I stood, about to rip them out of the wall, but stopped myself. Who was to say there weren't any more? Maybe this was a test, and if there were cameras, maybe there were mics around too.

> Castillo: I need a proof of life.

> Eric: I said no cameras.

> Castillo: It's merely a precaution.

> Eric: Bullshit.

I thought for a moment then took out my switchblade and carved an oval on the wall then cut in my recently designed signature tag. I stepped back and snapped a quick photo of her with my mark in the background.

"Why'd you do that?" Leo came up behind me.

"Proof of life, amigo, and I feel like playin' the game this time."

"The game?" He looked puzzled.

"Who made the biggest score, who made the loudest noise. You know, like in the media. This," I snapped a few photos, making sure the light was perfect, "is for braggin' rights. You never heard of a tag? When he shook his head, I pointed to the oval with my initials inside. "Shows she's held by me." I rubbed my finger over the engraving. "Eric Noah's possession. Braggin' rights."

"Kinda like a signature on artwork without sharing your name."

"Precisely, and if she isn't art in our world, I don't know what is." I laughed and sent the photo off to Castillo and a few others then flipped on the TV to an American news channel.

"Impressive." He grinned and went to slap me on the back but thought better of it and backed off.

I dragged over a plastic tub and set it next to her bed. I pulled out some clothes, a water bottle, and a pair of flip flops.

"A tracksuit?" He looked at the black pants and over-sized hoodie with a raised eyebrow.

"Do you ever shut the fuck up?" I'd kept enough women here to know they were more comfortable in sweats. Something warm that didn't show their woman shape. It was too tempting for the men around them, and I didn't need the hassle. My part of the operation was to keep them as clean and safe as possible until they were sold off to Chili, who could do whatever the hell he did with them.

"I'm just sayin' maybe something silky would be better." He reached out and fingered her shirt.

"Know your place," I warned him and batted his hand away. I wasn't sure I could trust him with a caged woman in the place. "You touch her, and I'll break your fingers, individually, with a hammer."

"Sure, sure, I hear you." He put his hands in the air. "I'm just sayin'."

"Well, don't." I pointed at the door, and he left with a quick glance back at her. My gut told me he shouldn't be allowed down there at all, not even with someone else. I had a reputation to uphold, and I wasn't about to let some punk kid ruin it for me.

The woman stirred just as I stepped out and locked the cage using a five-digit code. I didn't trust she couldn't pick a lock, and at least she couldn't see when I entered in the numbers. Only a few would know the code. One could never be too careful.

Her eyes fluttered open, and she shot straight up, then heaved over and gagged. I knew after the drugs she'd had she might get sick. I could have warned her to take it slow, but I knew it would be pointless. Her feet hit the floor, and she tried to stand then fell forward on her hands and knees with a moan. She put a hand to her head and sat up.

"If you sit still and take small sips of water, it'll help with the side effects," I said calmly.

Her head whipped over to me, and her hair fell over one eye as she blinked her anger at me.

"Or maybe you don't drug me at all." She lowered her head and tried to fight it.

"Okay, look." I eased onto the table and felt a weariness come over me. This part of the process exhausted me. "Let's look at this from my point of view. You're here in a cage, and I'm here outside the cage. Clearly, I've done this before. I'm very good at it, by the way. I know what I'm talking about. So, if you just sit back and drink some water, maybe you'll see I'm just trying to make this easier on you."

"Screw you." She huffed and managed to stand for a moment then allowed herself to sink to the bed as the room spun.

"Fine," I sighed deeply, "clean clothes are there, water is there, and there's food on the table." I pointed. "If you're done trying to prove to me how tough you are, I'll leave you be. In the meantime," I stood, "smile for the cameras."

I waved over my head, and as I walked out, I eyed the cameras to see how they were being used.

"Wait," she called. I almost kept going but thought about it and turned around, then as I walked toward the cage, I nudged a paintbrush forward a bit on the floor with the toe of my boot. "Can I get some sugar?"

"Sugar?" I pretended to entertain her odd request so I could take a moment to move the bucket that stood against the wall a bit closer to the cage. "Why would you want sugar?"

"I have low sugars, and I faint easily." I could see the lie but used it to my advantage as I pretended to think about it. I scuffed a mark in the dust with my heel.

"I'll see what I have." She nodded, and I headed back toward the stairs.

Pedro, one of Castillo's higher-ranked soldiers, watched me as I came toward him. He put his cards down on the table. I grabbed him by the hair and yanked his head back. With the other hand, I snatched the cigarette from his mouth and put in out on the side of his neck. He bucked straight up, but I used my weight to slam him back in the chair.

"Have some fucking respect in someone's home," I hissed and tossed him backward in his chair. He toppled onto his back then leapt to his feet, where he was met with my gun in his face. "You're here to watch over this place, so fucking do it!"

I pulled out my phone and called Castillo.

"How's she settling in?" Castillo mused from wherever he was.

"If you insist on your dogs being here, they stay outside," I seethed inches from Pedro's face. "This is my house, and you hire me to do my job. Now I have to have your pets and your cameras invading my space?" I shouted and knew I hovered the line of disrespect, but I didn't care. "We had a deal, and you broke it."

He went quiet, and I half expected him to walk through my front door with guns blazing.

"Eric," his tone changed to a quieter one, "the cameras are for us."

"I don't seem to have a link to the feed."

"I'm sending it now." A moment later, my phone vibrated, and I saw a link had been shared with me. "I know things are different with this one, but you must understand, Eric, one can never be too careful. She is, after all, a Blackstone bitch."

"Yeah, thanks for the heads up on that one, by the way." While I talked, I motioned with my gun to Alejandro, and he stepped forward and began to herd Pedro and his buddies outside. I gave him a nod as I moved to my office. "The bitch told me on our drive here."

"Interesting." He seemed amused. "Was she feisty?"

"A bit." I knew I'd better feed him the truth on that. I still wasn't sure just what he could see and hear. I also knew he liked his women a bit wild, and I didn't want to stimulate his imagination. I used my fingerprint to open my Mac and clicked on the link. It brought me to the basement cameras.

"Hang on, I have a call coming through," he rasped, and I rolled my eyes as I was placed on hold. While I waited, I grabbed a pencil and sketched out the basement room in my notebook. Then I quickly made notes of all the blind spots that the cameras couldn't see. Only half the bucket could be seen, the paintbrush was in full view, but the line next to the cage where my chair was tucked in the far back corner was completely hidden. Whoever installed the cameras didn't put much thought into where they were pointed. I turned up the volume, and it crackled a bit then cleared, and I could only hear some white noise. All of that told me it wasn't hardwired. The fact that it was more than likely Wi-Fi connected worked in my favor. The phone in my ear went live as Castillo clicked back on.

"I have some guests arriving soon. I have to go."

"Wait, what's her name? Which Blackstone is her husband? How can I sell her with no information?"

"You're not selling her." He chuckled. "We'll pump her for information then dispose of the bitch."

United States:

Human Trafficking Hotline

1 (800) 373-7888

SMS: 233733 (Text HELP or INFO)

Humantraffickinghotline.org

J.L. Drake, born and raised in Nova Scotia, Canada, later moving to Southern California. Though she loves the weather in Cali, she would sell her left kidney for a good rainstorm. Jodi's love of the seasons back home in Canada definitely appear in her books.

When she's not writing, you can often find her sitting somewhere along the coast of Huntington Beach, reading, or at home curled up on a couch with her two children and husband, binge watching a good movie.

AUTHORJLDRAKE.COM

FOLLOW ME ON SOCIAL MEDIA

facebook.com/JLDrakeauthor

x.com/jodildrake_j

instagram.com/j.l.drake

tiktok.com/@authorjldrake

bookbub.com/profile/j-l-drake

<u>**BROKEN TRILOGY**</u>

Broken

Shattered

Mended

<u>**BLACKSTONE SERIES**</u>

Honor

Escape

Freedom

Courage

<u>**DEVIL'S REACH TRILOGY**</u>

Trigger

Demons

Unleashed

<u>**QUIET MAFIA SERIES**</u>

Quiet Wealth

Quiet Secrets

Quiet Power

Quiet Empire

<u>**DARK WATER SERIES**</u>

Shadows

Whiskey

Alpha

Tango

HAVOC OF SINS

Grim

Havoc

Sins

DARKNESS SERIES

Darkness Lurks

Darkness Follows

Darkness Falls

STANDALONE BOOKS

Behind My Words

Christmas At The Cabin

Omerta

For the suggested reading order, please scan the QR code: